This book is dedicated to the people of Canada, who, as a nation, always seem to come through in a pinch, and never seek adulation.

FORWARD

While backpacking through Europe during the summer of 1988, I stumbled upon the World War I memorial at Vimy Ridge. I had no idea I was standing on hallowed ground. In fact, at the time, I had no knowledge that I was standing on Canadian soil. Poised at the base of the memorial, I appeared confused enough that a French visitor, considerably much older than I, offered some information. Tentatively, he asked if I knew what had happened here, 71 years earlier. I shook my head.

The gentleman was dressed simply, in a light blue windbreaker and pressed beige pants. I had been flopping from hostel to hostel for a month, and was not so nicely turned out.

He gazed up at the two great monoliths, craning his head back very far. I just stared at the thousands of names etched into the limestone. Then he looked out at the green grass and well-defined pathways, and waved his hand across the entire valley and hillside. "This was nothing but mud," he said. "Not just mud ... but twisted metal, barbed wire, tattered cloth and bones; rotting carcasses everywhere. There were many bones—of men and horses." He looked very serious and sad. "Of course, I wasn't here, in the war," he told me. "I was just a boy... but I knew some who fought here."

He said he had come here many times, that it wasn't too far for him to travel. He told me he had come with his parents to see all the Canadians at the memorial's dedication ceremony. He told me a lot of what he knew of the battle. "We French had tried for over a year to take the heights from the Germans," he said, "but lost more than a hundred thousand men." A disgusted look appeared on the old fellow's face. "It became a revolving suicide mission. They just couldn't do it." The old man pointed a bent index finger at me. "The Canadians ... they figured it out."

After over an hour, I offered to buy him lunch, but he declined. He had to go, he told me, and then finally introduced himself. When I told him my name was Denis, but that most people called me Dee, he asked, "Your family name?" I looked back at the wall of names, reached out and tapped a name on the cold limestone: *Dauphinee*.

Over the last quarter century, I have forgotten the gentleman's name and cannot find it in my journals. It is another name lost to history—if only my own. But other names from that day have stayed etched in my memory, as they are in the cold stone at Vimy Ridge. Who were these boys who died so far from home? What were they like? What were they facing in 1917?

Many years later, I started a search for a nineteen-year-old named Stanley from Nova Scotia who turned out to be a distant relative.

A simple inquiry became an epic journey of discovery and learning. It became an odyssey, one that helped me understand a gallant moment in history—a moment that defined an army, and helped shape a nation's sense of self.

—D. Dauphinee

PREFACE

The following are two letters written at the onset of the Great War that offer differing points of view about the conflict. The first letter speaks to the zeitgeist felt by so many young people during 1914-1916. The second, written by a prophetic, astute officer from the Labatt Brewing Company family, issues warnings heeded by few people at the time. The spellings are as originally written.

Letter from Private Robert Davis to his mother in Ontario, Canada:

29 December 1916
Dear Mother,
Just a few lines to let you know I am doing fine. Mother and Dad don't forget me I have been a bad boy. I know but forgive me. This time Dear Mother & Dad you must be glad that you have a son in the army. It is a great thing to have a son serving King and country. You must understand there are lots of young fellows who have not got the pluck to enlist but they will have to come forward you mark my word. It is a hard thing to do, but someone has to help the country out.
Please forgive me. Love to you both and please give my love to the boys and to Lil.
Yours Truly
From your loving Son
Bob

Letter from Lt. John Labatt Scatcherd, age 22 to his cousin John in Toronto, age 19.

August 10, 1914
My Dear John,

For the life of me, I cannot see why you wish to join a regiment at the present time. You cannot possibly have weighed this matter in the manner in which you should or you would never want to get into this fracas.

You cannot appreciate what this war means. It is one of absolute extermination, and is far different from anything that any Canadian or Englishman, or in fact, anyone ever dreamt of, as is daylight from darkness. Men will be mowed down without seeing each other, and the loss of life is going to be appalling.

There are thousands of men who are looking for a fight, hundreds of thousands of them, and are going into this thinking they are going into a frolic, but I am afraid they are going to be sadly fooled.

The Canadian troops that are going abroad will after a little while be shoved to the front; this was the case in Africa, and it is simply done because the blood that is in these men is the blood of a young nation, not the worn-out product of Europe, and you will find that in every instance they be shoved right into the very heart of all the trouble.

You say in your telegram that many of your friends are joining; that is undoubtedly so, because your friends are young, if they were not young, they would not join until an absolute requirement takes place.

Very sincerely yours,
R.C.S.

Pte. Robert Davis was killed by a shell explosion while sheltering in a small hole on the 2nd of September, 1918.

The next day Lt. John Labatt Scatcherd died from bullet wounds to his hand, both legs, and his chest. He was awarded the Military Cross.

Highlanders
Without Kilts

PART 1

THE CALL

———⋄⋙⋘⋄———

Stanley, careful not to move his head, gazed across the field to find his cousin. He could not make him out in the faces of over a thousand men. Standing at attention, he tried to train his eyes to the left, hoping to see Lady Borden present the colours. He must have moved ever so slightly. "Boutilier!" Sergeant McDougal whispered his name, like a hoarse ventriloquist, "Eyes front!"

Stanley knew that his parents and his siblings—all ten of them—were somewhere behind him in the audience. His mind started to stray. His thoughts had wandered more than usual since he'd enlisted in the army. He thought of fishing in the bay at Hackett's Cove, and rowing the skiff along the shore on warm, sunny summer mornings, and how sometimes he would just drift, hanging his head over the gunwale and staring down at the floor of the bay watching for mackerel, lobsters, and crabs. He thought of school, and he thought of Lily and wondered what she thought of him now. Suddenly, a deep melancholy enveloped him as he realized that this might be one of his last days in the province.

It was overcast and raining softly on the common at Aldershot, the young men who would be soldiers standing stiff and straight in their drab, brown uniforms, the plainness offset by their rosy cheeks and bright eyes so full of pride and dreaming. The city streets and dirt roads of the provinces were silent of the bells that hung from the recruitment cars as they drove from town to town. The cars stopped for water and for fuel, and for anyone who flagged them down. The young men filed up to the vehicles, their minds filled with fields of glory that would not keep, and the boys ran to the cars to see the officers in their uniforms, and the girls hurried to the porches and doorways to see which boys approached the cars, and the mothers, hating the cars, stared out the kitchen windows over the top of the recruiters and into the blue, rolling hills beyond, the weight of worry and sadness obvious in their eyes.

The common was quieted now by the solemnity of the occasion, a quiet made softer by the haunting silence that always follows after the bagpipes stop, when one feels that prideful, lonely, warm feeling in their gut.

It was September 26th, 1916. The flag of the 85th Battalion of the Nova Scotia Highlanders, along with those of the other battalions of the regiment, were consecrated by chaplains of the brigade, and the Prime Minister's wife, Lady Borden, presented the King's and Regimental colours to the colour bearers of the various battalions. The flags were beautiful. On the 85th's was embroidered in gold on a maroon field, the battalion's official Gaelic motto: "*Siol na Fear Fearail—Breed of Manly Men.*"

Dedicated trains had been sent to Aldershot, paid for by the government for the special occasion, and they brought thousands of people from all over the province. It was a day long remembered by those who attended. In just a few months, the Nova Scotia Highlanders had joined the battalions that had become the pride of the province: the Pictou Highlanders, the Fighting 25th and others. For several days, tourists and holiday seekers had already been traveling to the military camp at Aldershot to watch the 85th Battalion at work.

For hundreds of the visitors on the drizzly September day, it would be the last time to visit and speak with their sons.

∞

June 28, 1914, was a sunny, warm morning in Sarajevo, deep in the heart of the Austro-Hungarian Empire. When nineteen-year-old Gavrilo Princip stepped up to the car in which Archduke Franz Ferdinand of Austria and his wife Sophie, Duchess of Hohenberg, were riding and shot them both dead from five feet away, it is doubtful he or any of his five accomplices realized those shots would start the largest armed conflict the world had ever known. A conflict that would become a war which would rain destruction on much of Europe—a bloodletting and devastation beyond belief.

Europe was already a powder keg. Western Europe had experienced an unprecedented population growth since 1875. People there and in North America were living longer, and the infant mortality rate had been steadily decreasing because of advances in medicine, developments that were inevitably followed by an increase in the demand for food, goods and services. The Industrial Revolution of both continents answered those demands. French and German desires for economic outlets and opportunities were on a collision course with Russia's border suspicions. Britain's evolution from a country whose history was one of isolationism (combined, paradoxically, with imperialism) inched slowly toward the crash. The European empire-building efforts over the past three centuries yielded nations infringing upon many existing borders.

The traditional aristocracies of the German and Austro-Hungarian Empires over the last half of the nineteenth century were being threatened—if only subtly—by a rapidly increasing population of wealthy men in cities like Berlin, Venice, Zurich, Vienna, Budapest, Belgrade, and Sarajevo. These middle-class, non-royal, non-aristocratic men were able to build their wealth because of a new, evolving world trade system and the growing western industrialization. With their wealth and rise in the strata of society, the burgeoning middle and upper classes became more involved in urban civic affairs and national politics. The land-based gentry' class in much of Eastern Europe was being challenged by these "leftist liberals," who were often backed by industrialists, bankers and publishers. The monarchies were starting to weaken. By the start of the war, the treaties between countries and monarchies and the negotiated alliances amongst kings, emperors, barons, dukes, and archdukes were becoming less respected, yet still fervently defended. In the four decades that led up to the Great War, the convoluted, intricate system of alliances was confusing the masses so much that many people began to focus their passionate, disparate emotions on something they could grasp onto: their *nationalism*.

One can add to the medley of tensions the fact that more people in all classes of life were reading—and reading works not just by poets and novelists, but by men like German Karl Marx, who struggled to draw a line of distinction between the ruling classes of the states and the working classes. Marx felt the states were ruling with their own interests in mind while professing them to be the interests of all citizens. He believed that capitalism created tensions from within that would, in the end, destroy it and pave the way for socialism. Marx pined for a classless world.

Nationalism was a new and powerful doctrine taught

to the masses not by Marx, or aristocrats, nor professors but rather by the simple man's enthusiastic, inquiring mind and in the political writings of the day in newspapers, cartoons, pamphlets, even by word-of-mouth. A.E. Housman's poems— almost all of them—glorified the young lad's supreme sacrifice for his country... for his *nation*. Rudyard Kipling's poetry exalted the manly virtues. Nationalism became the sentiment of the day.

In 1914, when the bugle sounded and the British Empire called her sons once more to the line, there was no distinction between war with Great Britain and war with Canada. It was still seventeen years before the Statute of Westminster, and Canada's constitutional position within the Empire disallowed her from declaring war or making peace. Even her foreign policy making was limited.

When, on the 4th of August, England declared war on Germany, Canada was in the fight. She had not been asked or consulted. She had in no way contributed to the events and missteps in the diplomatic exchanges which had inexorably led to the hostilities. Yet, there was never a doubt of her commitment, nor that her contribution would be passionate, generous and whole-hearted. And generous it was; even though the population of the entire country was less than eight million souls, Canada contributed 620,000 men and women. That was almost eight percent of the country's citizens, compared to about four percent mobilized from the United States. Also, the Canadians were in the fray from the beginning. From the first days of sabre rattling, a surge of loyal demonstrations swept across Canada. As in many cities around the world, young and old poured into the streets waving flags, singing, driving through the streets in decorated automobiles, crying out for a quick end to the Boche. The young and old exuded pride—particularly the young.

Those thoughtful Canadians whose nature it was to measure their words steeled their minds and begged for calm. Some saw the grim possibilities of the realities of war, even though most were sure it would be a quick fight—a war concluded by the upcoming Christmas. (All the young Canadians who burned to take up arms were certain of that.) So, too, felt the British and the French. The Germans and the Austrians felt exactly the same. Those who feared the worst were those who had already been to war—any war. Those unlucky men who had seen combat and had spent so much time trying to forget it, or at least bury it in some seldom visited place in their minds, were the men who dreaded war most.

On August 4, a cable was sent to London from the Governor General:

> Great exhibition of genuine patriotism here. When inevitable fact transpires that considerable period of training will be necessary before Canadian troops will be fit for European war, this ardour is bound to be dampened somewhat. In order to minimize this, I would suggest that any proposal from you should be accompanied by the assurance that Canadian troops will go to the front as soon as they have reached the sufficient standard of training.

They did.

Canada had never been an overtly military nation. Still a Dominion State of the British Empire, the country had evolved somewhat differently from its neighbour to the south. She had no epic, defining war of independence, and her history was riper with tolerance than with genocide or slavery. One has to consider the early explorers throughout the hemisphere:

Pizarro who murdered tens of thousands, as did Cortes, Drake and (to a lesser degree) Frobisher, who exploited, cheated and killed indigenous people (for which the Inuit shot him in the arse with an arrow). Compare them to Champlain, for example, who was as much an anthropologist and a diplomat as a soldier. When he founded the city of Quebec, he not only desired to expand the French Empire in North America, but he genuinely hoped for a more refined, gentler dominion. Samuel de Champlain was a man of vision. While Canada's western expansion was not without troubles (mostly for its native-born), her history is not rife with murder.

Champlain was a man devoted to an ideal of tolerance and compromise, and he was just one of the building blocks in the foundation of an evolving country. Another leap forward for Canada's independence would come in the year 1917.

Prior to 1914, the actual strength of the active militia for all of Canada was about 43,000. As early as 1910, Canada had invited several inspections by knighted British military experts, whose chief concerns were increasing the militia's proposed numbers of ranks, roughly 60,000 men, and raising the standard of training, clothing, ammunition, and stocks of equipment. Money was allotted from the government, and the accepted plans were put into action, albeit slowly. The man chiefly responsible for seeing the increased military activities come to fruition was Colonel Sam Hughes (later, Honorary Lieutenant-General Sir Sam Hughes). After assuming command of the Ministry of Militia and Defence in 1911, he continually warned anyone who would listen of the grave threat of war with Germany. He twice convinced Parliament to increase the military budget by three and a half million dollars between 1911 and 1914. Always an outspoken champion of imperial defence, speaking in Vancouver two years prior to the outbreak of hostilities, he is reported as announcing: *"Germany has to be taught a lesson, and the lesson to be taught her is that Canada, South Africa, Australia and New Zealand are behind the Mother Country."* (Sam Hughes, after being knighted, would prove in the end to be no soldier at all, but rather a very effective politician and something of nepotist.) The Dominions *were* behind Britain and proved it at places like Ypres Salient, the Battle of St. Eloi, Mount Sorrel and the Battle of the Somme. It was in the autumn on 1916, at the Somme, when the Canadians confirmed their reputation as hard-hitting shock troops—at the cost of 24,029 casualties. Less than five months later, at a gently sloping upland called Vimy Ridge, the Canadian Corps confirmed their place in the world, firmly planting their feet in the arena of nations, and helped hasten the end of the unspeakable horror in the trenches of Europe.

☙

On the common at Aldershot, the men stood on parade as Lieut.-Col. Joseph Hayes addressed the regiment, Lady Borden, in her wide-brimmed hat with pheasant tail plumage standing beside and slightly behind him.

"Men, we are called to duty in this great endeavour. Already our sacrifices in this war in men and riches have been vast, and through them we will obtain victory. Before this conflict, our children have had little to inspire them which was truly Canadian. We have never been invaded and laid waste by enemy hordes, and although we have participated with great honour in wars as part of the British Empire, the issues were remote and so obscure that they did not have a national aspect, and could not inspire us beyond our sense of duty to King and Country.

Now, the very rights of mankind have been challenged, and it matters little where the battles are fought; the issues are clear.

We Canadians have thrown ourselves into this fight with body and soul. We will be victorious. We will defend the rights of all. And in victory, we will obtain something even more priceless than peace: the creation of tradition which will forever inspire Canadian manhood, and will lift our souls to a higher place.

Men, together we will make a Canadian history rife with glory. Godspeed, men, and know forever that your remembered deeds will never be in vain."

Stanley had told the love of his life that he joined the Expeditionary Force to "do my duty," but neglected to tell her when he learned that the fate of the 85th battalion was to become a "work battalion," not a "first on the line" combat battalion. He was ready to fight—they all were. His heart sunk when the rumours were confirmed that the battalion's first orders would be to construct roads and trenches in France, once they finally got there. Lily wouldn't care, as long as he returned to her safely.

Oswald Boutilier, on the other hand, wanted to know everything possible about his son's position. He was a serious, slightly controlling man, yet he never disciplined any of his eleven children. The children's discipline fell to his wife, Clara. When people first met him, he might have given the impression of a very hard man, too serious a man, perhaps. In reality, he was a strong, gentle man, tender at the core.

There had been quite a row when Stanley enlisted in the army. Oswald had gone to considerable trouble to make sure his son was accepted into school. Some people felt—but never said—that Stan was the favourite son. Within days of learning about his brother's enlistment, the next youngest son, George, lied about his age and signed up also.

On the 12th of May, 1916, when George enlisted in the Canadian Expeditionary Force, he was immediately placed in a different company from his brother, but it was close enough.

Somewhere in the audience, sitting in the temporary bleachers, were the entire family: Mother and Father, and all nine other siblings. George's "D" Company was on the far end of the parade ground. Stan knew the young ones would be excited—for the train ride, the parade of soldiers, the spectacle, and simply for being away from the drudgery of chores at home. Lieut.-Col. Hayes's speech was stirring; the men would have marched into battle right then and there. The oration moved the entire mass of people packed onto the common. There was British and Scottish pride in the air, to be sure, but the *Canadian* pride was profound.

When the ceremony was over, each company on parade marched either to the north or south end of the common, where the units were dismissed. In the middle of the field, the pipes continued to play "Cock 'o the North," and the men began mixing with their friends and families. Stan saw his cousin weaving through the crowd towards him, and he held up his hand. Hazen was obviously excited.

"Stan! Won't be long now! We ship out in three days... finally." Hazen slapped him on the back when he reached him.

"I know. Can't wait to start digging ditches."

"Oh," said Hazen, "they won't be able to keep us a work battalion for long; we've got too many good shots." He scanned the grounds. "Have you noticed all the pretty women here? Wait... I forget, you're a married man!"

"Very funny," Stanley replied. "I've only asked her to wait." (Lily had said only days before that she would.)

"Stan!" Belle ran into him hard and hugged him around the waist. "You look so handsome." Stan clutched her and picked her up. "Oh... you're getting too big. You mustn't grow at all 'til we get back."

"I won't—promise." Hazen tapped her on the left

shoulder and snuck to her right side, and she fell for it again, swinging her head both ways, and giggling. "Hello, Haze," she said.

"Hello, Cuz." Hazen was full of energy and lively. He was *always* lively.

Belle was the youngest of the eleven children, and was doted on by Stanley. They shared a closeness which everybody said was nice to see in siblings twelve years apart in age. Hazen Gibbons was a first cousin of the Boutiliers'. Born only a month apart, he and Stan were as much best friends as cousins.

Not far behind Belle came the rest of the family, along with Hazen's mother, Hattie. There were many hugs, slaps-on-the-backs, handshakes and a few tears as everybody congratulated the boys. Stanley stood dumbfounded for a moment as he saw Lily step out from behind the small crowd of sisters and brothers. He had not expected her. Her letter had said that her father had forbidden her to ride the train alone to Aldershot, and that they would have to say their goodbyes in two days when he, his brother George and their cousin came home for a day's leave before shipping out. Stunned at her appearance, Stan looked at his father. Oswald almost smiled. "It was your mother's idea." Stan stepped forward, giving Lily an awkward kiss on the cheek, his lips not actually touching her, and said, "I'm so glad you could come." She couldn't speak. She just bit her lip and nodded with a smile.

Lily looked beautiful; her wavy, dark brown hair lapped over her shoulders and contrasted sharply with the light pink in her cotton seersucker dress. The very thin lines swept inward and then out along the natural curves of her athletic body. Her brown eyes shone, devilish and full of life. As the group walked towards the concession tables, Stan's Aunt Hattie clasped his arm, drew him slightly away from Lily and whispered, "Your papa went over to Lil's place and personally talked to her father. He knew it was important to you that she could come."

That statement shocked Stanley more than Lily's appearance at the ceremony had. He glanced back at his father. He had lagged behind and was standing alone, arms held behind him, surveying the sea of young boys. He looked very serious.

While still standing motionless, Oswald Boutilier greeted younger son George, who had walked over from on the opposite side of the common. Stanley watched as the father and son met and shook hands. The relationship between the two had always been loving—though not particularly affectionate. But today, Oswald held his son's hand for quite a long moment, placed his left hand on George's right shoulder and spoke. Stan watched and thought, *this is the longest I've seen them talk, except when Father was giving him instructions.* It looked as though his father did not want to let go of his boy's shoulder. *I wonder what he's saying.*

When they broke, George smiled weakly at his father and then walked over to the rest of the family.

"Georgie!" Belle, Laura and Eleanor skipped towards him and almost tackled him.

"Well," he said, "they'll let most anybody into these things." The girls giggled.

"I saw Lady Borden, right up close," said Eleanor. "Her dress was lovely."

"I saw her too," said George, "She was a bit frumpy, don't you think?"

"George! She was not!" snapped the girls—and his mother—all at once. His mother and her sister, Hattie, looked worried that someone might've overheard George's joke. Stanley and Hazen shook hands with George, and Stanley mockingly did a headcount, pointing his finger at each sibling, and said, "Who's minding the store?"

"Uncle Leo," said Mother. "He said to tell you that he'll play the fiddle for you, day after tomorrow while you're home. He's so sad to see you and the boys go." Stanley, still standing nearby and still holding Lily's hand, smiled, hugged his mother and kissed her temple.

છ૭

Two days later, the ride home for George, Hazen and Stanley was quiet except for sporadic talk of girls, the Boche and fishing. They would be shipping out from Halifax in four days, but not a word was mentioned about it. For most of the two-hour drive to Hackett's Cove, Stanley simply stared out the window, thinking about home and the family and Lily. He had hoped for a two-day pass so there might be a chance for the three boys to fish once more before leaving. But they all received only one day to visit home.

When they arrived at The Cork & Pickle, Oswald and Clara's diner, general store and post office, the place looked different to George. The big front porch had been whitewashed. New curtains hung in all the windows except the two that served as the post office.

When the tiny bus pulled up to the front of the house, out poured the entire family. Guy, only nine, was first out of the house. He was wearing a mock Canadian infantry uniform which older sister, Hazel, had made for him. Skipping after Guy were seven other siblings. Ann, the eldest sister, arrived on the broad wooden porch with the boy's father and mother, still in her apron. Uncle Leo (whom the children called "Ace-e-o") stood by waiting patiently for the chance to shake the boys' hands.

Hazen said hellos to everybody and waited for enough of a lull in the conversations to announce, "Well, folks, I'm itching to get home to see Mother, so I'll be leaving."

"Nephew," Oswald said to Hazen, "we've got you a ride the rest of the way ... Leo's going to drive you and pick you up in time for the bus back to base." Uncle Leo waved his hand in the air and scooted around behind the diner to get the family's Russell. Once it finally started, he pulled around to the front porch and Hazen hopped in. Clara Boutilier called to her nephew, "Tell Sister, I'll see her Sunday!" Hazen waved, and the two were off up the dirt road, the Russell sputtering and coughing like a machine with consumption but never wavering.

The car had just gone out of sight when a 1914 Dodge Tourer careened around the corner; Oswald held up both arms for the driver. He stopped, stepped out of the Tourer, and reached into the back seat for an armload of equipment. "Right on time," said Oswald. He smiled at the man, who grinned and nodded.

Oswald turned to the rest of the family. "Now, before we have lunch, I hired Mr. Thompson here to take a family photo. I've wanted to do it for some time. Cyril will be moving to the city before George and Stan get back. It won't be a blink of an eye and more of you will be leaving the nest." He winked at Belle, the "baby," who smiled and tried to wink back, but blinked both eyes.

"We're all yours, Mr. Thompson." Now the girls understood why Mother had them all wear their Sunday clothes, keeping after them all morning to stay clean.

"Yes, sir," said the photographer. "If it would be alright, I think it would be best if we went to the south side of your building, where the light will be best. Perhaps if we could get some chairs." The children ran for some kitchen chairs and brought them to the south side of the house. The family had never been photographed together before, so there was quite a rigmarole getting everyone situated.

They were finally set. Oswald sat in a chair with Belle on his knee. His wife stood behind him. Guy, who was tiny, stood to the side of his father opposite from Belle, and the rest of the family found their places around the parents. George also sat in a chair (he was only five foot three-and-a-half inches) wearing a canvas bandoleer on his uniform. Stanley stood perfectly erect, as if at attention, looking handsome and smart. A few of the sisters were very nervous about getting their picture taken, though they didn't know why.

When Mr. Thompson was ready to expose the plate, he asked everybody to hold perfectly still and to look directly at the camera. Everyone did, except for Clara. Like millions of mothers everywhere, she was carrying too much of the burden of worry to focus on a camera. Her eyes were not on the lens. Her eyes were cast towards St. Margaret's Bay and beyond towards the Atlantic, that same cruel ocean that would in only hours take two of her sons away, and to where? Glory and honour may have meant something to Oswald and the boys, but to her they were fool's words. Tripe bandied about by aristocrats to stir the young working class into a patriotic frenzy, to get the lads to do their fighting for them. It was maddening for her, this war, though she knew to hold her tongue. The boys were going now; there was no stopping them. She thought of Hazen, her nephew, an only child, and his father gone. What would it do to her sister if her son didn't return? The boys were all here now and they were safe, yet her heart ached like never before.

After the photograph had been taken, Stanley walked up the trail behind the house that wound through the copse of trees behind the back yard, through the stacks of wood stock piled high behind Arthur Dauphinee's block shop, across the brook where the trout lived, uphill behind St. Peter's Anglican Church and into the big field behind Lily's farm. He only had an hour. What would he say to her? He had thought about that for weeks and now, less than a minute from seeing her, he had no idea. He hadn't yet told her he loved her, though he had since the age of ten. Behind the church was another small woods, a mixture of spruce and fir that darkened the path. As Stanley stepped into the clearing of the big field, he looked up and slowed almost to a stop. There stood Lily, bathed in bright sunlight at the edge of the field where the path disappeared—waiting.

Lily's dress played in the wind, the sun almost shining through it. She was smiling and biting her lip again, just as she had two days before. She always bit her lip when she was nervous. When she and Stanley were twelve, she cut her lip badly when *someone* dared her to try to ride the family cow. The cow jumped and ejected Lily, and that would have been alright if she hadn't already been nervously biting her lower lip. Stan felt bad about that for a long time.

Today, he was about to dare her again. He stiffened his pace the last few steps and held his arms out to her. She fell into them. He held her close, closer than ever before, and he could smell her hair and feel her belly, her legs, her breasts pressing into him. He loved her. He knew he loved her and at that moment—they hadn't even spoken yet—he felt his resolve for her.

"I will miss you so much," said Lily. She was crying just a little. Stan held her apart from his chest and looked into her eyes.

"We have only a few minutes…you know that." She nodded, and Stan wiped a tear from her cheek.

"You wrote in your letter that you would wait for me," he said, "but I wanted to ask you in person. I've got another year of school when I get back, but it is my hope—my dream—to be with you then." Lily nodded in affirmation.

"Lily, I've loved you ever since I can remember," he said. "I think you should know that."

"Stanley Oswald Boutilier, I've known that for years." She smiled at him. If she loved to do anything, she loved to tease Stan when he got serious. He kissed her hard on the lips... almost too hard.

"I'll write you every day and post the letters at every chance." He kissed her again and hugged her once more. He brushed her hair behind her ear and kissed her forehead.

"Bye, Honey," he said, and turned and walked down the path. Three steps and he turned back to her. She had just turned away. "Lil!" he called to her, and she spun back around. "I dare you to wait."

Through soft sobs she laughed out loud. "Oh great... now I *have* to." She waved him off and strode up the field, head down. She did not look back.

PART 2

OVER THERE

———⊶∞⊷———

On the 11th of October, 1916, the 85th Battalion marched down Cogswell Street to Pier 2 in Halifax Harbour, and on arrival embarked onto the HM Transport *Olympic* and could not get off again. Announcements had been circulated that the public would not be admitted to the pier, but that the different units, upon arrival in Halifax, would march to the common and there would be plenty of time to meet the troops and say goodbyes. This information was not communicated to the 85th, and consequently the battalion was marched directly to the boat. This change of route didn't affect Stanley, George, or Hazen, as neither the Boutiliers nor Mrs. Gibbons could make the trip to Halifax Harbour. Their goodbyes had all been said days earlier in Hackett's Cove.

From the common, the troops passed along the many old, wooden shops of the block makers, coopers, and cobblers. People lined the streets and cheered, and while some waved the Union Jack, more waved the St. Andrew's Cross. Down on steep Cogswell Street, policeman held up their hands as the men marched through the intersections of Gottingen and

Brunswick Streets. At Water Street, the column wheeled left and marched onward to the pier. The men, as they marched, could look to the north up the Narrows and see the big smoke stacks of the tall sugar refinery. Just before Pier 2, the battalion passed the workers in the busy coaling yard at the naval dockyard. The men and boys, some of whom seemed only ten or twelve years old, covered in coal dust, stopped shovelling for only a moment to wipe their brows with grimy neckerchiefs and wave to the soldiers. The pipers stopped playing and covered their chanters as they walked past the dusty yard.

During the Great War, Halifax Harbour was one of the busiest in the hemisphere, only an hour's sail to the Great Circle Route, a shipping lane connecting Europe and North America. Ships heading east would fill their holds with coal and wait to rendezvous with convoys and escorts. The threat from German submarines attacking merchant and troop transport ships both in the harbour and the ship convoys as they crossed the sea was *very* real. In fact, many people feared a German attack on the city itself; at night, two huge submarine nets were stretched across the Narrows.

It wasn't until just before dusk two days later that the *Olympic* weighed anchor and passed slowly down the harbour, along the notoriously dangerous Narrows that connected the largest part of the harbour, the deep, sheltered Bedford Basin and the part of the bay called the Northwest Arm that empties into the Atlantic. Bedford Basin could shelter hundreds of ships at a time. The harbour pilots on the huge ships passing down through the Narrows—a constricted passage which had seen its share of bumps and near misses—took their turns and saluted the huge *Olympic* as they passed her to starboard. All along the shore were people moving about, waving flags and handkerchiefs. They cheered, but the ship was too far out for them to be heard by the troops. As they passed the docks, the men gave a loud shout. They passed the huge building of the Halifax Sugar Refining Company, its ten-story tall smoke stack a familiar landmark for mariners. Many of the men on board had never before left their home province. Some had never ventured more than fifty miles from home. Now they were off on a grand adventure, on the largest ship afloat (since the *Titanic*) and into the grappling arms of the largest armed conflict in the history of the world. In less than thirty minutes, the men could feel the ocean swells under their feet.

The 85th Battalion was one of the first units to board, and Hazen and Stanley found quarters with berths together, amidships. George and the rest of "D" Company were bunked further aft. As all the other men settled in for the voyage, it became clear very quickly what a crowded and hot week it was going to be. Even in October, the heat of the lower decks made the air oppressive. The ship was loaded to the gunwales. In addition to the entire Nova Scotia Highland Brigade, the 166th Battalion was on board, along with a full complement of officers and other detachments.

As Hazen and Stan unpacked, they both looked over their embarkation packets. Each man had received a Troopship Booklet when boarding. They also received a "Billet Card," with aboard ship instructions and a post card courtesy of the Canadian Red Cross Society. The post cards were to be filled out on the first day at sea and handed in to each company's sergeant, who delivered them to a mail room. Upon arrival in Europe, the cards would be mailed home en masse to let the families know the ship had made it safely.

Hazen wrote:

Everything going fine Mother, no need to worry. We are well taken care of, and I'll post a letter when we get over there.

And Stanley:

Hello to all; the Olympic *seems like a good ship, in her prime. Conditions are fine. The entire battalion is eager to do its bit in this fight. Please someone let Lily know you've received this card—we were allowed only one. Love to all.*

The trip was relatively uneventful. On the third day out, the *Olympic* was met by an escort of three torpedo boat destroyers. A wireless bulletin was issued daily that allowed the ship's company to keep abreast of the leading events in the world, including the ongoing struggle at the Battle of the Somme.

By the fifth day at sea, the stench of perspiration hung heavily below decks and mixed offensively with the smell of diesel fuel and oil. In the evening, several of the men were crowded around a tiny writing table playing pinochle. Hazen was in his hammock over Stan's berth, staring into the grey sheet of metal eighteen inches in front of his face which formed the deck above him. He asked, "Stan … do you think we'll ever see home again?"

Stanley laid the postcard and a half-written letter on his chest and looked up at the bulging hammock. "Of course, Haze—but Blighty first, and not before we give Fritz a bloody nose." Stanley reached up above his head and twice patted the bulge where he figured Hazen's shoulder was. Hazen smiled ever so softly and closed his eyes. It was some time before Stan picked up the letter.

Late in the evening of October 18th, the sea was flat calm as the ship reached Liverpool Harbour. Onboard there was a collective sigh of relief. The ship lay overnight in the River Mersey, and squads of men took turns going topside to stretch their legs and to get their first look at the island—except for the lads in the company who had grown up in England or

Scotland. They had moved to Nova Scotia only a year before. The young soldiers stood along the rail. They could see in the waning light the long, solid piers of stone and granite-lined docks. They gazed at the towers, stevedores, cargo nets and cranes. The boys read the sign along one immensely long building: *Mersey Docks and Harbour Company.*

"Stan," said Hazen, slumping forward on the rail, his chin resting upon his forearms. "It's ugly."

"I know, Haze. I prefer the wooden docks of home."

"Me too," said Hazen. "But I don't know why."

"Because of the character," replied Stan. "The old wooden piers and docks, with their barnacles, the stains from the rusted cleats and seaweed hanging from the cracks gives them character."

"I suppose so," said Hazen. "And they are home. I'm going back below."

It was the first sign Stanley had seen that his cousin might become very homesick. It was almost welcome for Stan; Hazen's consistent appraisal that this endeavour was going to be nothing but a grand adventure worried him. It wasn't that Hazen didn't grasp the danger—he was top of their class in school. However, Stan was worried that his cousin's natural, upbeat attitude might crash too hard and too fast in the drudgery of the trenches. Stanley had told himself on several occasions, *We're only going to be a work battalion... it won't be like we're going to have to be sharp and battle-ready at every notice.*

In the morning, debarkation commenced. The brigade entrained for Witley Camp amongst the Surrey Hills of ancient England. By mid-afternoon, they reached Milford Station, and from there it was a three-mile march to South Witley.

Camp Witley was an ideal training centre for artillery and

engineers; it was surrounded by large tracts of rolling common land covered in gorse and heather. The soil was predominately sand, making it easy to excavate while practicing trench building and construction of gun emplacements.

The brigade's adjustment to being away from home was helped, slightly, by the fact that the lush countryside there formed one of the most attractive districts in England.

After a short speech by Colonel Andy McNaughton, the men fell out to their assigned barracks, with eighty men in each. Hazen was housed in a building adjacent to Stanley's. Once settled, Stan looked over his kit and sat down on his cot to write Lily a letter. It would be a proper letter this time, his first from overseas.

> *18 October 1916*
> *Dearest Lil,*
>
> *We have found Old England. The voyage was uneventful, unless you call seasickness an event. Hazen is doing well—adjusting better than I expected. The country here is quite beautiful; looks a bit like the Highlands of Cape Breton. There are lovely old world villages, and spots of historical interests lie within easy distance. Good roads run in every direction, and on each side there sweeps good agricultural land dotted with picturesque little cottages and barns ... so pleasing to the eye. The countryside, after such a smelly, boring journey, fills up my senses and makes me long for you even more than the usual.*
>
> *I swear, Lily, if I were home right now I would march through the woods, past St. Peter's, up from the field and ask your father for your hand!*
>
> *I hope you do wait for me, my dearest—have faith in me, and I will return to you—hopefully whole, and*

try to make you happy for the rest of your life.

That's all for now, Dear. I will write you as often as I can … they keep us very busy (I think mostly to keep the men from fighting and gambling).

All my love,

Yours,

Stan xxxxxxxxxxx

No sooner had he finished sealing the envelope when, off in the distance, there came a lilting drone of pipes bellows being filled with air. *He's striking in*, Stanley thought. He rose from his bunk and headed for the sound. Three of his barracks mates did the same, and as they walked along the front of the buildings, Hazen caught up with them, smiling. Others were walking along, and as they got to the end of the barracks row, they all stopped when they saw the lone piper, high on a knoll at the south end of camp. Backlit by the setting sun, he was playing the soft, mellow tune, "Deirdre's Lament."

The boys plunked themselves down on the old stone wall that lined the dirt road into camp. For the longest time, no one spoke. Finally, Hazen whispered to Stan (but so all could hear him), "What tune is that?"

"'Deirdre's Lament,'" said Stan. His eyes never left the piper.

"Can you play that one?" asked Hazen. Stanley just shook his head.

"Nice to hear the pipes when we're not marching," said Hazen, "and so close to Scotland."

"Aye," replied Stanley. "But it's an Irish tune … not Scottish."

"*Irish?*"

"In Irish mythology," said Stan. The pipes pulsed beautifully in a slow rhythm. Stanley paused for a moment before continuing. "A druid in the court of the King of Ulster prophesied that the king's storyteller's daughter would grow to become a very beautiful woman, and the king's lords would fight over her. There would be war and much bloodshed. Some men of the court urged the storyteller to kill the baby at birth, but the king, excited by the account of her beauty, decided to keep the child for himself. When she was of age, he would marry her. The king had her raised in seclusion by an old woman. Before the king could marry her, she fell in love and eloped with a hunter in the king's own court. The king had him killed, and married her anyway. She was so cold to him that he decided after a year to give her to her first husband's murderer. On her way to be delivered to him, she threw herself from the carriage and died. Then again, some say she died from a broken heart."

The piper was still playing. He shifted slightly, a bit to the north, then to the east, as though he wanted all the distant lands to hear. The soft, moving music seemed to roll down the dark green hill, filtered by the gorse.

All the men on the rock wall had listened to the story. All the men had loved ones left behind, and all the men now longed for the green, remembered hills of home.

৩৩

The camp was quite civilized; plenty of accommodations, large dining halls, showers, and lavatories. In no time, the men got down to some specialized training. Each battalion in the brigade went about learning their duties with diligence and enthusiasm.

On the 2nd of December, Lieut.-Col. Allison H. Borden (the Prime Minister's cousin) returned from spending more than two months in the trenches in France. He had left for the front lines before the *Olympic* sailed from Halifax. While there, he had been wounded in the thigh, which only elevated his already exalted status amongst the men. There were other officers of the 85th Battalion who were respected by the "other ranks," such as Lieut.-Cols. Hayes and Ralston, but Borden was considered the "father" of the 85th Battalion. Known as a man of character and energy, his thoroughness in all matters would be a contributing factor in the battlefield successes to come—successes which changed the outcome of the war and saved thousands of lives.

3 December 1916

Dearest Lily,
Glad to get your letter yesterday before leaving Witley. I am very excited that you've committed to becoming a teacher. I hope you like Halifax—I don't know anything about the Richmond School, but one of the boys in my platoon is from Dartmouth, and he said it's very close to an army barracks. So be careful! I know how you like a man in uniform. I'm sure you will be good. I miss you terribly and long for the day when I can hold you once again. I surely don't know when that is. We took a beating at the Somme, and it looks like it will last a while unless some battle turns the tide.

George, Hazen, Jack Fraser from Halifax and I went to town last evening. I bought you this shawl that I hope you will like; it's wool, but the thread is very fine so it doesn't feel coarse. It almost feels like cotton, it's so soft. I know at least you will like the colour. I can picture you wearing it over your jacket as you walk to and from school this winter. It will protect you from the cold, biting wind that blows off the harbour in Halifax, and in my dreams I'll be walking with you. I am always

walking with you.
 Well, I will close for now, my dear, but promise to write as soon as I can.
Yours always,
Stan xoxoxo

The parcel with the letter in it had only been en route for a few days, probably still in England, when Lily buttoned up her heavy coat in front of the tall mirror in her boarding house room. She thought of Stanley every day, and she was thinking of him then. It was cold outside and a winter storm was forecast. What a nice couple they would be, she thought, when he returned.

☙

The Nova Scotia Highland Brigade, the pride of the folks back home, stood well in the eyes of the British high command. The men were in great anticipation of the move to France. When a demand was made for an overseas draft, hundreds of men wanted to go, despite consternation about breaking up the battalion.

6 December 1916
Dear Father,
 Hope all is well with you and Mother, and all the siblings. Saw Jack Fraser a couple of days ago, and he was telling me of his orders; his unit is about a day's ride by train from here, so I don't think I will get to see him again before he ships out. I still wish he hadn't joined up. Not sure he has the temperament for war—if any of us do. He wouldn't even hunt with us at home, as you know. Even when we fished, he let most of them go,

trying not to hurt them. I will try to find him in France and check on him. Please say hello to his folks, his wife and three little ones if you get to Halifax.

The men have behaved marvellously; we have become an efficient unit, and are awaiting orders for overseas. There are rumours that certain units will be sent over early as reinforcements. Some of the men are itching to go, but there is some dissension in camp because no one wants the battalion to break apart. Whatever comes, I am sure we will all do our duty. I keep telling my pals, all things come to those who know how to wait.

Father, I hope you've forgiven me for enlisting. I know you worked hard to get me enrolled in school, but being a surveyor can wait just a year or two. Not wanting to let you down, I've continued my math lessons even now, when I'm not too tired from training. I think that will make you happy.

Could you please stop by and check on both Lily and her folks if you have the time?

Please give my love to all.

Your affectionate son,

Stanley

The brigade was indeed split up. Different battalions were sent from Witley Camp to be used as reinforcements in those ranks battered at the Somme. Jack Fraser was transferred to the 85th and joined his friends. In the end, the 85th Battalion stood alone at Witley. Even in France, until the very beginning of their first battle, the 85th Battalion would not be attached to any brigade. They would have no home, they would have no kilts. They were a misfit work battalion ... but they would have each other. They would have their pride.

Part 3

BAPTISM OF FIRE

———◇◆◇———

By early February 1917, the men were chafing to go to France. They had had plenty of advanced training in England. They were ready.

At last the announcement was made which every officer, non-commissioned officer and man had anticipated. The 85th Battalion was to proceed to France. When definite word came the time was short; at five o'clock on Friday afternoon, orders were received that the battalion was to move out from Witley Camp and march to Milford on Saturday night, February 10th. All the men's huts were scenes of enthusiasm. Everybody forgot about the rain and mud and slush through which he had been slopping for four months and felt that at last his time had come for a real soldier's life. France, the Mecca of each aggressive soul, seemed now moments away.

The first of the men to march for the train at Milford left at midnight on February 10th. The battalion band led the way, playing "The Cock 'o the North." After four months of being cold and covered in mud, the Highlanders wanted the villagers to know they were leaving. Platoon after platoon and company after company followed the pipers until the entire battalion was strung out along the winding macadam road between Witley Camp and Milford. George's company was in the middle of the line of men. Hazen should have been with them, but he was one of the 269 men with the mumps in the hospital in nearby Aldershot. Hazen was disappointed; he felt he had only traded Aldershot, Nova Scotia, for Aldershot, England. He wasn't very ill, but in quarantine all the same. As Stanley marched, he wished Hazen would get sicker and be sent home. He marched in the blackness of the night and thought of home. He felt anxious, yes, but he was happy to do his duty. He gave some thought to the fact that he did not feel the animosity towards the Boche that many of his comrades did. In fact, he spoke fairly good German. (Most of the men in his company had taken to calling the Germans "Boche," a habit picked up from the French.) German had been Stanley's great-grandfather's primary language. The Boutiliers and the Dauphinees from Lunenburg and St. Margaret's Bay had French ancestry, certainly, dating back to the 1400s or 1500s, when many ruling families were expelled from France. The families stayed together, scattered throughout Europe. The Boutiliers, with others, ended up in the principality of Montbeliard, along the Swiss border. Over time, some families spoke German, some spoke French, and some were bilingual.

In the mid-1700s, the British, worried about the Eastern Canadian provinces becoming overpopulated with enterprising French settlers, initiated a campaign to actively recruit non-French nationals to move to Nova Scotia. The British Parliament, through the Commissioners for Trade and Plantations, sent agents to Switzerland, Germany, and small duchies and principalities like Montbeliard to seek Protestants who might want to immigrate to Nova Scotia. They found many takers. Stanley's great-grandfather and his brother amongst them. As many as thirteen ships at a time were arriving in Halifax and other harbours. Many of the immigrants were allotted parcels of land along the South Shore, specifically around Lunenburg. For the King of England, the plan worked. For many of the immigrants, it did not—at least not at first. Men and women of all professions applied and made the trip across the Atlantic. Men who were cobblers, coopers, shopkeepers, and most of all farmers were quick to discover no arable land and no real town infrastructure. They would have to start from scratch. The farmers, many of them, would have to learn to build boats, to work the boats, and to fish if they were to survive. Many of them died at sea. Stanley and George's great-grandfather's brother was one of those who drowned, tossed overboard by a swell while hand-lining for cod in a dory he had just built. It had been his first attempt at boatbuilding.

The men of the 85th marched along, heads held high, in perfect rhythm. They were striding off towards the shining triumphs they were sure would be theirs, towards the unimagined devastation and horror that was to consume them, toward the masses of graves, marked and unmarked, where so many would ultimately rest. But this day they had pride bursting from their tunics, songs on their lips and smiles in their hearts that would not fade. Not for some time.

It was a rough crossing of the English Channel, and the battalion landed with 41 officers and 845 other ranks. When they arrived in Boulogne, no one knew what to do with them. It was an inauspicious beginning. They found their way to St. Martin's Camp outside of town. There the officers found the camp adjutant, an imperial officer who immediately set about supplying quarters, blankets, and food. He was overheard by some of the men to ask the 85th's second in command, "If they are Highlanders, why no kilts?" It was Major Ralston who said with some hesitation, "We are, unfortunately, detailed to be a work battalion."

"Ah... well," the adjutant replied, "we all have our parts to play in this tussle."

Once settled, Stanley sent off a letter to Lily:

12 February 1917
France
Dear Lily,

We've made landfall on mainland Europe, finally. Hazen is still in England in quarantine for the mumps. I'm sure it's hard on him being left behind. George's company left two days before us.

Some of the lads and I explored the town and countryside this morning. We got to meet some of the local French allies and did some shopping (for food, mostly). It was hard enough to understand the English as she is spoken in the Old Country, but now we have to try and communicate with the French. They are quite kind to we Canadians, and some of our officers had told us it would be so. They were right. We did well though. It's not so hard to communicate with people who can express so very much with just a shrug of the shoulders, a few expressions and waving of the hands. It was fun, actually. The novelty of the new customs in a new land adds interest to the surroundings—made better by the unfailing geniality of the locals. As you probably already guessed, I bought some chocolate.

We are camped for the time being just by the English Channel (can't say which town). Looming above the camp is a statue of the Emperor Napoleon, staring over the Channel, still coveting the English coast. When I and some of the lads walked up to it this morning, 1805 didn't seem like so long ago.

Anyway, I wanted to write another short note, as I believe we will move up the line very soon, and it may be a while before I can post another letter.

I lay awake last night thinking of you in your school. I want you to know that I'm very proud of you, and I can't wait to be with you again.

Write whenever you can.
All my love,
Stanley

On a cold, frozen February morning, the 85th boarded a long line of small box cars. Each one held eight horses and forty men. The sign above each sliding door read:

"8 Chevaux   40 Hommes."

The box cars were heatless, lightless and seat-less. If a soldier had to urinate, there was a bucket towards the back of the car near where the horses were tied. The men sat on the floor of the car on mildewed hay or, if they were lucky, on one of the pieces of canvas tenting that lay on the floor. And they waited. The first men to board had to wait for over 1000 more men and scores of horses to load. As the men sat, there was no bravado, no talk of killing the Hun, or even of teaching the Boche a lesson. It was a very solemn wait. It was to be a very solemn ride.

The train at last pulled out of Boulogne with the battalion on the last leg of its odyssey. The steam engine chugged along all day and into the night, the smoke from the coal pouring behind the train making the black, cold night blacker still. It was not, by all accounts, a pleasant trip.

En route to the train's terminus, there were stops in Marquise, Calais, Saint-Omer and Aire-sur-la-Lys, amongst others. At midnight the train arrived at the coal-mining town of Houdain. The entire battalion detrained quickly. Under the dark, starless sky, they started the eight-mile march toward their new camp to the east, in the tiny farming community of Gouy-Servins. There they bedded down, and most of the men finally slept, while some wrote home.

14 February 1917
Dearest Lil,

We are at the front now. It was a long walk from the train station to where we are now, through a freezing night. Though it was quite cold, our hearts were warmed by the pure excitement of the sight. As we climbed up the narrow valley from the station to this commune, a flickering like lightning was seen in the distance, on the horizon and over the hills. Soon there seemed to be some distant thunder. This became louder and, as we marched on and on, we all became aware that it was actually the flash and sound of the tireless cannon fire. We all warmed up in a hurry. Even though we knew this was our destination, and we had thought about the battlefield for many months, our shivering and even our hunger disappeared temporarily with this new thrill. It is real now. Some men even got emotional—nothing untoward, but you could see it in their eyes. I will admit to you now, my thoughts were of my father and his pleading with me not to enlist.

We are billeted in the remains of an old, ruined French mansion. I think it was once a very noble chateau. The whole battalion—almost 1000 men—is quartered in its old rooms, most of which leak. That should tell you how big this place once was. I would like to have seen it before the war. Now it is very dilapidated and the floors are mud. We all were lectured again as we set up camp about trying to keep our feet dry. At this point, I'm more worried about my feet than Fritz.

Once settled, we had a good breakfast of bread and butter, hot tea, bacon and beans. Once fed, we were in good cheer, despite the deep mud and falling-down rooms. Many of the walls have been pierced by shells, back when the fighting was closer.

Tomorrow we are to clean up this place, so goodnight for now, my sweet.

We'll take care of these Germans. You just keep studying! I am very proud of you, and I count the days when we will be together.

With great love and affection,
Your Stan oxxoxo

Life seemed surreal to the men of the 85th, this world of destruction and mayhem. They watched the farmers continuing their daily work in the fields, only six miles from the battle. Each night, the poor farmers would bring the horses and cattle in under the same roof where they lived.

Their new quarters were cleaned as well as possible, though the well from which the drinking water was drawn was next to an ancient manure pile and a stagnant pond. All the water was chlorinated, inoculated, and re-inoculated. No soldier in Lieut.-Col. Allison Borden's brigade contracted the dreaded typhus. As for the French, typhoid persisted throughout the year. Many of the young contracted it, and they either became immune or died.

Immediately parties were formed for trips of two or three days to the front-line trenches for "instructional purposes."

The instruction was to keep one's head down always, unless you were to "go over the top." The first to go to the trenches were the officers who had not seen action. It took the rest of the month for the balance of the men to receive their baptism of fire.

The route to the front lines wound through several obliterated towns, supply and ammunition dumps and trash heaps. Some of the towns had been fashionable resorts and summer getaways, with populations in the thousands. Now, the names on the maps were simply annotated: "In Ruins."

During the day, no one could advance beyond a sheltering hill, just beyond camp. There a soldier would enter the deep, winding trenches leading down the far side of the hill, across the Zouave Valley and uphill again to the front line on the lower third of the slope of Vimy Ridge. In this labyrinth, the enemy in some places were as close as thirty yards. From the crest of the hill, the Germans could survey the entire region. All the approaches were continually under harassing fire. The routes through the winding trenches to the front lines were, to say the least, unnerving. They wound past the advance dressing station of the field ambulance. New troops would often stop there to deliver supplies, and would become initiated to the grim ugliness of war: seeing laid out in the aid stations the ashen, lifeless faces of some poor chaps who had made the supreme sacrifice for the cause.

21 February 1917
Dear Mother and Father,

Got your package yesterday. Thanks so much—especially for the cookies. I shared them with my mates, and I can tell you they didn't last long. Also thanks for the socks … I am running some now, so they will help a lot. I don't want to run often, because if am good at it, they could pluck me from the battalion. I wish we had more carrier pigeons!

We are quite close to the action now, but don't worry... as I said, we are just a "work battalion." The trenches are not a good place to live. At first glance, they seem like those we constructed for training purposes in Witley, except there are splotches of blood on the walls, and damage from the shells. If you dawdle there for any time at all, you will see men limping out, or on stretchers, lying very still, and you realize quickly that it is a place of death and destruction.

We are sent there in small groups to "get used to trench life," but I doubt any one could ever get used to it. So don't worry, Mother... I won't dawdle while I'm up there! I will keep running supplies and messages back and forth until I am back home in school.

And thank you again for visiting Lil and helping out.

Love to all,
Your Stan

In February 1917, Vimy Ridge was well known to the reading public, written about in every major paper in the world. *Vimy* had already been on the lips of people in forty countries for two years. The ridge itself is an escarpment on the western edge of the Douai Plains. It is between 200 and 450 feet high and runs in a northwest direction from the town of Arras for almost seven miles. Strategically its importance lay in the broad view of the plains below for many miles. During the "Race to the Sea" in October of 1914, when the French and German armies tried to outflank each other for over a month, the ridge fell under German control. By the end of October, German forces had dug in on the summit of the ridge and into the slopes, occupying the valley to the east, or "behind" the hill. The French army that year, desperate to stop any further advances of the Germans, also dug in, building a complex trench system along the western slopes of the ridge. The French knew the German army intended to swing their advance eastward to gain control of the coast, proceeding south to march on Paris. If successful, France would be cut off from England. The frozen, battered French troops must have felt as though their backs were against Paris itself.

There was intense fighting throughout the 1914 winter with constant skirmishes. In the spring, the French 10th Army launched an all-out attack to try to take the ridge and break the German lines. Again in the autumn, the French hurled another savage attack, inflicting enormous casualties on the Germans, but they could not seize the high ground. However, French had gained enough ground that the defenders became somewhat "cramped," and the logistics of defending the fortifications changed dramatically.

The French attacks put the German defenders in such a position that it helped to make the success of a Canadian-led battle a possibility nineteen months later. Sadly, in the course of the year, the French suffered grievous losses: over 150,000 casualties, and a severely dented morale. Early in May 1915, the Moroccan Division under French command boldly attacked and took the summit of the ridge at its highest point, Hill 145. The bravery of the Moroccans was talked about amongst the Allies for years. Unfortunately, there were inadequate plans for reinforcements, and the Moroccans' precarious hold on the hilltop was overrun by German counterattacks.

France was committed to fighting all along the French and Belgian sections of the Western Front, including the terrific battles at Verdun, and after the devastating losses at Vimy, the Allied powers felt the 10th Army was in need of relief. The British Army assumed responsibility for Vimy Ridge in March 1916. Although there were many skirmishes, night raids and increased mining activity while the British Imperials held the line, there was no further attempt to capture the summit of the ridge until the Canadian assault in April 1917.

It is important to note that the German Army did not feel as though the ridge was easily defendable. Although some historians have called Vimy Ridge "nearly impregnable," the German defenders were well aware that several sections were geographically and tactically vulnerable to a determined attack. The Kaiser's forces had learned in previous battles the importance of depth of defence; several lines behind the front were critical to the overall defence of a ridge. A significant problem at Vimy was that the summit is narrow at some places. Near Hill 145, it is only 700 yards wide. There the defenders were forced to place some of their critical field guns further to the east of the ridge, too far behind the lines, rendering them nearly useless. In many spots the plateau was far too narrow to hold batteries of artillery, especially along the northern range, which had the highest elevations and were supported only by mortars and by the smallest howitzers. In these positions particularly, the Germans knew the defence of the ridge was all about reinforcements and the speed with which they could be delivered.

In November of 1916, the Canadian Corps started departing the Somme to take over the lines below the ridge.

At the Somme, the Canadian forces had proven to be superior troops, leading the way on several fronts. Several individuals had been awarded the Victoria Cross. From those experiences, several Canadian officers longed for the time when the Canadian Corps would fight as one unit. Although some Canadian Expeditionary Force officers felt the Dominion troops had been used "inefficiently," they did not complain. Even General Arthur Currie, a protégé of Sir

Julian Byng, Commander of the entire Canadian Corps, did not complain—at least not on paper. Though he did advocate for Canadian autonomy.

Arthur Currie lacked charisma. He possessed a great attention to detail, always wore his uniform impeccably, and was ever after his officers to dress sharply. He was tall, well fed, and could not help that he often looked a bit frumpy. Currie did not interact easily with the other ranks, yet he cared deeply for them all. He came from humble stock.

Julian Byng and Arthur Currie were raised in very different backgrounds. Currie (born "Curry") was born and raised in the small town of Napperton, Ontario. He attended local public schools and never graduated from university. Byng, on the other hand, was born into a well-to-do family in Hertfordshire, England, the youngest child of the Earl of Stratford, and entered Eaton but was an uninspired student. At age nineteen, Arthur Currie received a second-class teaching certificate after attending Strathroy District Collegiate Institute (he also attended University of Toronto for a short while). A gifted student, he intended to study medicine or law, but when his father died when Arthur was only sixteen, the financial burden was too great to continue his studies.

Julian Byng did everything he could to get out of a long academic career, so his father sent him at age seventeen into the militia with a commission as second lieutenant. Over the next thirty years, Byng rose through the ranks, graduating from the Staff College. Early in the Great War, he attained the rank of lieutenant-general. Because of his leadership and actions during the First Battle of Ypres, he was knighted. By June of 1916, he was commanding the Canadian Corps.

Arthur Currie's military career took a different route. After gaining his teaching certificate, he moved to British Columbia where he taught school for several years. At about age twenty-two, he changed the spelling of his name from Curry to Currie, and continued to reinvent himself by working his way into the world of finance. He did very well in real estate and insurance. At the same time, Arthur joined the Canadian militia. He took his militia commitment very seriously, rising to the rank of lieutenant-colonel. Shortly before the war in Europe broke out, the real estate market throughout much of western Canada stalled, and in British Columbia went bust, leaving Arthur in financial ruin. The bankrupt lieutenant-colonel attended the Militia Staff Course and, when war broke out, was given command of the 2nd Brigade of the 1st Division in the Canadian Expeditionary Force. There, he would make his mark.

In the Ypres Salient in April 1915 (the Second Battle of Ypres), Currie proved himself to be cool under fire and to have a knack for putting together extemporaneous battle plans. At Ypres, the Germans first effectively used poison gas. They had tried it several months earlier at the Battle of Balimov, but the gas had become liquefied by the cold air and rendered inert. At Ypres, it was employed again in an effort to dislodge the French and British troops from their trenches. The Germans carried ninety pound chlorine containers to the front line and opened the regulators on the containers, relying on the prevailing wind to carry the poison gas towards the enemy trenches.

Chlorine is heavier than air, causing it to settle into low spots in the terrain. The trenches that were filled with men were quickly filled with gas. When the vapour comes in contact with water, chlorine becomes hydrochloric acid. The moisture in the men's lungs and eyes boiled and burned with the chemical reaction. The victim's lungs would fill with frothy fluid, causing the poor man to foam at the mouth. The bronchial muscles would go into spasms, obstructing the airway. Many of the soldiers died within minutes. The first forces to experience the gas at Ypres were the French and their Moroccan allies, for on that day that was the direction the wind blew. There was chaos in the trenches. No one was prepared for the effects of the gas attack, including the Germans. The Frenchmen poured out of the trenches, fleeing for their lives, retching, coughing and holding their throats. Many were blinded and unknowingly ran across No Man's Land towards the enemy, only to be mowed down by withering machine gun fire. Hundreds of poisoned soldiers ran to the rear of the lines, ahead of the gas. One British Imperial officer in the rear lines, unaware of the what had happened, stood in front of the panicked hoard, his revolver levelled, calling them cowards. The first man to reach him was foaming at the mouth, his skin turning black. He fell at the officer's feet and died. Others started collapsing around him. The officer was mortified. In an instant, he knew the rules had changed. The world had changed.

In the chaos, Lieut.-Col. Arthur Currie shone. From his brigade headquarters (it had been gassed and was burning around him), and in a unique situation not before encountered, he remained calm and issued unconventional orders which proved invaluable in holding the lines vacated by the French. He rallied his men, re-established lines of communication with the front and with headquarters and demanded reinforcements that had earlier been denied. That stand was the first great contribution by the Canadians to the Allied cause. The Canadian stand may have saved Ypres. It may have saved the whole Franco-British cause in that sector, rendering impossible a German advance to Calais.

Noting Currie's instinct for tactics, his superiors promoted him to major-general, and he was given command of the Canadian 1st Division. In addition, he was invested as a Companion of the Order of Bath (KCB), Sir Arthur Currie.

Sir Julian Byng and Sir Arthur Currie did have one thing in common. Both men felt that the old-world, frontal assault tactics weren't working. In this new, stalemated war of attrition and modern weaponry, they were becoming quickly outdated. Both leaders were appalled at the numbers of men dying in every battle. Both men agreed new tactics were in order, with new techniques, and more detailed preparation.

General Byng ordered Currie to visit with the British and the French corps commanders and their staff to examine the mistakes and successes at the Battles of the Somme and Ypres. He also ordered each of the Canadian units to evaluate themselves in the same regard. It was painful, but Byng wanted written evaluations.

Currie worked tirelessly. While he was in reality uneducated, overweight, a bit pompous and overly conscious of his appearance, he possessed a genius for organization and administration. He was dedicated. He stayed up late working throughout the war, sleeping at most four hours a day. He took his evaluation assignment from Byng seriously. Currie studied the French ordeal at Verdun in February 1916 and at the Somme six months later, and analyzed all the information the international corps commanders had to offer. He tried to filter out the nationalistic bravado (there was at least some in all the reports) and evaluated the scores of battlefield decisions that had been made. He weighed his own interrogative analysis with both the known successes in each battle, and his with his own ideas. He knew that simple, full-frontal attacks, broadcast to the enemy with artillery barrages and whistles blowing to signal the men "going over the top," were worthless. "A senseless slaughter," he wrote in one private letter. The report he generated for General Byng would become a tool in the battle plan for Vimy Ridge, a nearly impregnable defensive position (or so the Allies thought), that had to be taken as part of the larger Allied offensive: the Second Battle of Arras.

Arthur Currie's report highlighted the lack of artillery support for attacking soldiers and the lack of imagination in battle preparations over the past two years. It also stressed the repeated lack of communications during battles. Byng shared these concerns with Field Marshals Allenby and Haig.

Autumn 1916 through February 1917 was an interesting time for the Canadian Expeditionary Force. All four divisions had made their way from the battlefields of the Somme and from England and had assembled at the foot of the German-held fortification of Vimy Ridge. They were bolstered by additional battalions of recruits which included the "work battalion" 85th of Nova Scotia. The order from Byng was for his Canadian Corps to capture the ridge while the British engaged the enemy along different fronts in the battle. It would not be easy. The Germans had occupied the ridge for two years and had constructed a state-of-the-art system of dugouts, tunnels and machine gun nests. They had fortified the natural defence of the long escarpment. By 1917, the only people who didn't think Vimy was impregnable were the Canadians and the Germans. Diary after diary illustrates the German commander's grave concerns of the ridge's defence.

Vulnerable or not, Vimy was considered a crucial conquest on the Western Front. The German-held land behind the ridge (and to the north, behind the trenches of Ypres) was a series of sloping plains stretching to the North Sea. This land held important seaports, coal mines and railroad lines, forming a barrier between the Allied land forces and the German submarine fleet at Bruges. If the Allies could take Vimy, they would not only wrest those resources from the Germans, but they could effectively outflank the Germans to the northeast and change the balance of the entire Western Front.

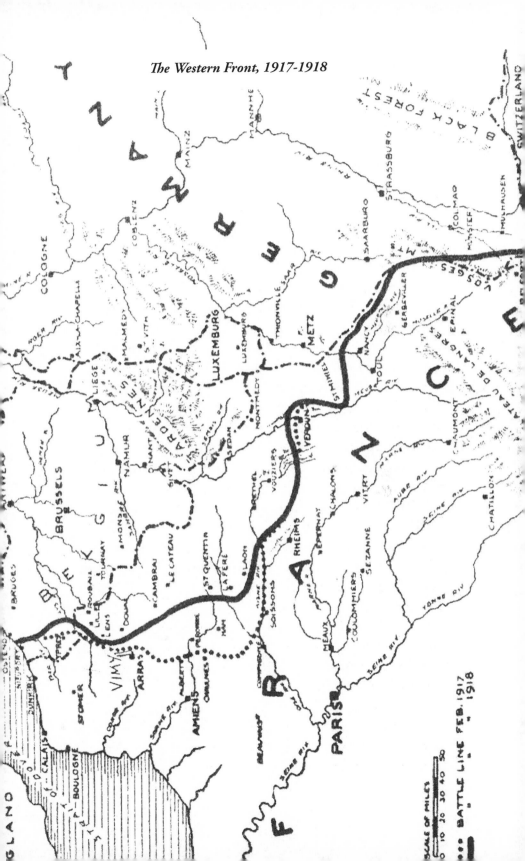

The Western Front, 1917-1918

After Ypres, a number of Canadian officers petitioned their superiors in the British Expeditionary Force for some battlefield autonomy and more involvement in the battle plans. At Vimy Ridge, they got their chance. It was General Currie who advocated for it and General Byng who made it so.

The assault on Vimy would be the first entirely Canadian effort in the war, and the first time that the Canadian Corps would fight together. There was a lot at stake. Not only would attainment of the ridge finally break the German lines on the Western Front, it could potentially demoralize at least one important Bavarian military leader.

Deep into January 1917, large scale preparations were underway. The Vimy offensive was slated for the spring. February and March would see all the battalions of all four divisions practicing the most elaborate battle plan of the war so far. While Byng and Currie were involved in the planning of the offensive under Field Marshals Haig and Allenby and the French High Command, they spent a great deal of the battle observing. Their greatest contribution to the Battle of Vimy Ridge had been the diligent preparation leading up to it. History would show their work had made all the difference.

Excitement built behind the lines, all around Arras, for civilian and soldier alike—none more than for the Canadians. Even the most battle-weary of the C.E.F. welcomed the chance to fight together under their own command.

Each battalion took turns holding the trenches. Squads from each company were selected to go on nighttime raids near or penetrating the German lines, seeking prisoners for interrogation and recording gun placements. The combatants had little time for leisure. Normally, when not on the line, men would bathe, rest, play baseball, box, compete in track and field games, or attend make-believe cabaret shows put on by other soldiers who tried to lighten the mood for the troops.

There would be time for all that once there were Canadian soldiers on top of Vimy Ridge.

Every battalion—a company at a time—took part in the practice assault in the fields around Arras. There were carefully selected pieces of land which were made to resemble the topography of Vimy. Every company knew exactly what their job was going to be and the location of the German machine gun nests, dugouts and tunnels. Each Canadian infantryman and medic understood, when the hour came, exactly how fast to walk across No Man's Land toward the enemy, the "creeping barrage" of their own artillery sailing over their heads, exploding the earth a few hundred yards before them. The advancing firepower aloft would hold the Germans in their dugouts and bunkers until the attackers were upon them. There would not be sufficient time for the Germans to emerge, shake off the effects of the bombardment and tend to their machine guns and mortars.

While all these practice sessions were taking place, the sappers and engineers were completing their mining operations and constructing new tunnels for the troops to approach the front lines from where they would go over the top. At the ends of the mines (hopefully directly under the German trenches), large amounts of TNT and various other explosives were stockpiled, ready for detonation at "Z hour." Those unfortunate men who were unwittingly over the mines would be blown sky-high or buried—or both. If a man were within 100 yards of the mine's detonation, he would be thrown like a rag doll, chunks of chalky earth and metal raining down on him. Occasionally he survived. The psychological impact of being near a mine explosion was devastating, and it could take some time for one to regain his wits completely, if ever. In an artillery bombardment, any man hit directly with a twelve-inch artillery shell would be blown to bits, so much so that he would be unidentifiable, as was the case in so many of the Great War's "lost in action" casualties. Too often, the men were just simply blown away in an instant, as if vaporized.

As the C.E.F. practiced its role in the orchestrated assault, the British, New Zealand, Newfoundland, Australian and South African troops honed their own assignments near the town of Arras.

The Germans had their own intelligence and knew something was afoot. The Bavarian Crown Prince Rupprecht commanded the German 6th Army at the outset of the war, but in the previous July he had been promoted to field marshal in command of Army Group Crown Prince Rupprecht which consisted of the 1st, 2nd, 6th and 7th Armies holding Vimy Ridge. He wrote in his diary for 26 March, 1917:

Sixth Army has written its weekly report for 24 March: The reinforcement of the enemy artillery, which has been observed since the end of February, has been confirmed further… The reason for the massing of enemy forces on either side of Arras is still not completely clear. Possibly the enemy fears an attack and, therefore, has only deployed some of the available divisions in the front line. Whatever the explanation, the development is not normal for a major offensive. Because the possession of Vimy Ridge would be of far greater significance than the gaining of ground around Arras, it would seem, despite the greater concentration of force near the latter, that an attack on Vimy Ridge is the more probable. Nevertheless, both possibilities must be borne in mind.

By the end of March, the Canadians had completed their build-up. Byng, Currie and the other Allied commanders had moved in over 1000 artillery pieces. Some were hidden from view, and some were set in place for the attack. There were six tanks (a relatively new weapon) allocated to the Canadians, hidden in the trees behind some large cannon near the southern end of the ridge. The new communication and access trenches were nearly finished. Every soldier in the Canadian Expeditionary Force knew what to do. It was up to them now.

Through intelligence gathered from captured Allied men and from one deserter, the Germans were methodically making any preparations they could and trying to steel themselves for the attack to come.

❧

The boys of the 85th Battalion participated in the same practice sessions and meetings, despite their status as a work battalion. They also took their turns in the trenches, though much of the time they were moving ammunition, transporting supplies, and building ladders or crib works in the trenches. On a few occasions, members of the 85th were selected to guard small groups of prisoners being transferred to and from battalion aid stations, or to internment "cages"—small courtyards built up with wire fencing. When they served on those details, the men felt as though they were contributing to the war effort. Stan had been on two guard details. He liked to listen to the banter of the Germans in the cages while not letting on that he spoke their language. Apparently, the P.O.W.s were happy to be out of the incessant artillery shelling. They all expressed surprise at the strength of the force assembling in Arras. They also loved the food they were getting from the British. *That* surprised Stanley.

On the ides of March, Stanley wrote two letters on the same day that painted very different pictures:

15 March 1917

Dearest Lil,

I was happy to get your letter, and happy to hear you're enjoying Halifax. Are your accommodations okay? I hope you are staying warm.

I have now had my turns in the trenches. Not to worry—they are more boring days than dangerous ones. Like everywhere else in the Army, in the trenches and dugouts there is some order to most day. About an hour before sunup, we have "stand to" when we are roused from sleep (hopefully we're able to sleep in the mud) by the sergeant or the C.O. We are ordered to fix bayonets and climb to the first step where we can carefully peek ever so slightly over the top. All this is to guard against a dawn raid by the enemy. Of course, there hasn't been an attack here for a year, and we can hear Fritz doing the same thing.

This is to keep us ready and wound up, I think, and it works. Once the sun is up, we perform the "morning hate," in which, to relieve the tension, we fire off some machine gun rounds and a few mortar shells in their general direction. I suppose it also helps ensure the Germans stay in their trenches.

After the morning hate, the stand-to is over, and we have to clean our rifles. Before long there is an inspection, after which we have breakfast. It's interesting that there seems to be a sort of unofficial truce during breakfast. Then we just do our daily chores: repairing trenches or filling sandbags, repairing duckboards, etc.

So as you can see, it's all pretty boring.

I don't think you have to worry about me, Dear. I haven't heard from your father in response to my letter. Whether he writes me or not, he now knows my intention to propose to you the moment I get home. I do hope for his blessing, though.

That's all for now, Sweetheart. I long for your touch, and think of you every waking moment, and dream about you every time I close my eyes, sleeping or not.

Your loving man,
Stan xoxoxox

꧁꧂

15 March 1917
Dear Father, (For your eyes only)
You wrote that you want to know what's going on here with our units, so I'll write what I can. I've had my turn in the trenches twice now, and it might be too difficult to describe, but I'll try. If this letter is one selected randomly by the sensors, you will not receive it at all… but you asked, so I will write down what I can—though I fear this letter will not tell the story.

The trenches vary in depth, most being about six feet. If you look even a little like a newcomer to the trenches, everyone you encounter reminds you to keep your head down on account of the very good snipers. As you can imagine, it shouldn't be a problem for me! If we ever do get called into action, I'm worried if I'll be able to get over the top with my short legs.

There are boardwalks made from planks to walk on (most new ones being built by the 85th, I think), and ladders stacked along the side facing the enemy everywhere. The trenches are always muddy. Cut into the sides here and there are dugouts where men can lounge and "rest." Unfortunately, there is no rest from the pests who seem delighted with the whole arrangement; there are rats everywhere. There must be millions of them. Black ones and brown ones—the brown ones seem to be feared the most, because they eat the remains of the poor men who have fallen in No Man's Land, whose corpses are carefully watched by snipers. When possible, bodies are retrieved by returning nighttime raiding parties and are made quite gruesome by the rats. The brown rats get as big as house cats. One "Old Timer" from the 25th told me when the rats disappeared from view, he would sneak into a dugout, because he was convinced the rats could sense when Fritz was about to hurl a mortar round into the trench.

The men who've been here a long time tell me that in the summer, the trenches and shell holes are filled with frogs, and that might not sound as bad, but the fellows say they are as annoying as the rats. For me, still being alive, the worst are the lice and the nits. We have our clothes washed and deloused every ten days or so, but the eggs stay hidden in the seams, so when you put the uniform back on, your body heat makes them hatch, and the horrible itching and scratching starts all over. The nits are bad enough that I and all my buddies shaved our heads yesterday.

Trench foot used to be the biggest problem (other than the snipers), but the Army has gotten much better at getting us dry socks, and they buy us better boots. The first year of the war, the men wondered what was going to cause more casualties, the enemy, or gangrene of the feet.

Father, I can tell you the most impressive thing for me on my first trip to the trenches—it was the smell. In the trenches is a world of cigarette smoke, overflowing latrines, cordite, stagnant muddy water, chloride, body odour and rotting corpses—of animals and of men.

Thousands of men lie dead in No Man's Land from the last two years of fighting, some in shallow graves, some not.

I can't help but paint such a dreadful picture, but you wanted to know the truth, as always. But don't worry about us; the 85th is in the rear of things 90 percent of the time, as we are still a work battalion.

That's all for now—I hope this letter answers your questions.

Please ask the girls to send more cookies ... the boys really enjoy them.

Your faithful and obedient son,
Stanley

Stan slogged through the mud, past the mess and the men on KP, and along the boardwalks next to the dirt road to the post tent to mail the letters. There was a queue, and he took his place in line

"You there!" Someone was yelling, and Stanley looked around but didn't know where it was coming from. He looked back the way he had come.

"Careful, now, son—don't want to be a casualty before you get a crack at the Hun, now do we?" It was a sergeant ... an old one, who winked and waved Stanley off the side of the road. As he did, an ancient looking ambulance came chugging around the corner of the muddy dirt track. The truck stopped, and the driver asked the sergeant if there was still room at the infirmary. Having cleared the road for the ambulance, he now stood facing the truck, his feet wide apart and his fists on his hips, like a prize-fighter posing for a photograph. There were a few beds empty, he told the driver and waved them through.

Stanley had stood watching the scene, and was amazed that the driver and the passenger in the front were women—and beautiful, at that. He could see their white and blue uniforms and the Stars and Stripes patch on their blouses. Each had a red cross on one sleeve. One was blonde—very blonde, almost white haired—and the other was a pretty brunette. The blonde driver smiled at him as she wrestled the ambulance into first gear and drove off around the corner. Most the men paid no attention to the commotion, and in fact seemed to be trudging around, paying attention to nothing at all. Stanley turned around to face the queue again. He missed Lily very much.

"Easy, fella, you're a married man!" Stan spun around. It was Hazen. "Or have you forgotten?"

"Haze!" Stanley almost dropped his letters in the mud. They hugged each other, hard.

Stanley slapped his cousin on the back. "How long were you in quarantine?"

"Too long... I was supposed to get here weeks ago, but there was a mix-up with the paperwork. Can you imagine that?" Hazen smiled. Stan pretended he was shocked. He was next in line to post his letters.

"Have you been up front yet?" asked Hazen.

"Twice," said Stanley.

"Is it as bad as they say?"

"Well," said Stan, "I'm five foot two." Hazen nodded. "You're five foot three." Hazen nodded again. "Cousin," he said, putting his hand on Hazen's shoulder, "I don't think either one of us are in trouble from snipers... those trenches are *deep*." Hazen chuckled.

After Stanley paid for the letters, they headed back to the camp, and as they did, he slapped Hazen on the back again and squeezed the back of his neck. "Did you bring extra socks?"

"No. Why, should I have?"

PART 4

"LISTEN FOR THE WHINE"

———◦◊◊◦———

Once Hazen had reported to his N.C.O., he was given permission to rejoin his old company, along with George and their friends: Colin MacKenzie—the tough one of the group—and Jack Fraser from Indian Point, who had been living in Halifax when he joined up. Jack was the same size as Hazen and Stanley. He always told anyone who would listen what he could do if given the chance to fight. Colin, on the other hand, stood over six feet tall and was all muscle. He never talked tough or big, but always looked out for his friends. His father had preached to him even as a young lad that he had been blessed with an athletic build and quick hands—it was his duty to protect the less fortunate kids at school from the bullies. It wasn't Colin's nature to fight, but he accepted his father's guidelines. More than once there was trouble in the young life of Colin Mackenzie as he carried out his ministrations.

Stanley, Jack and Colin saw Hazen coming up the dirt track, returning from the N.C.O.'s tent.

"That didn't take too long." said Stan.

"Nope." said Hazen, waving at each of the guys individually, while directing his words at Stanley. "They asked me if anyone in my old squad spoke German. I wasn't sure if you wanted them to know, so I said if they did, I hadn't heard it."

"I'm glad you didn't tell them," said Stan. "If they find out, they'll yank me from the platoon for sure. I'd end up following some paper-pushing captain around, helping interrogate prisoners day and night." It was getting late. There was a pause in the conversation.

The boys started a tiny fire to warm the draughty room they were billeted in. After a while, Hazen asked, "Have you guys seen anything really bad yet?"

"I met a guy from the 2nd Division," said Colin. "He told me he was at the Somme *and* at Ypres. He said it was murder, plain and simple, what he saw." The boys listened intently. They had not seen much in France except shovels and hammers.

"The guy said the battle lasted for months. He was at Beaumont-Hamel, with the Newfies," said Colin. "His unit was supposed to be there for artillery support, but on the very first day they were sent on an assault across some open land." Colin paused and stared into the little fire. "The artillery barrage had done nothing… not a goddamned thing. The Boche opened up with rifles and those fast machine guns. Two-thirds of the battalion mowed down in forty minutes… almost 700 casualties. Over 300 were dead." Colin stopped at that.

The men didn't speak. Finally, Hazen said, "There was a fellow in hospital in Surry a week ago who was there. He told me he had heard there were a million casualties at the Somme. A *million*. He was a nice fellow from Doncaster. He lost his foot, and seemed happy about it."

In the morning as the sun was coming up, someone threw open the tent flaps. "Morning, ladies!" George was squatting in the doorway.

Hazen snapped, "Hey, George!"

George nodded. "Haze, is this all you guys do in this company? Sleep?"

"I take it this is your bro," said Jack. George waved.

Stan said, "And this is Colin MacKenzie from Sydney." Colin squinted and acknowledged George.

"I had a few minutes on my way to Lens," said George. "Thought I'd stop by. Haven't had breakfast yet." Stan and Hazen were already putting on their boots. George stared at the boys' feet for a moment and said, "Have you guys seen trench foot yet?" The boys all shook their heads. "It's disgusting...the feet just rot off. Doesn't seem like it could ever happen, but it does. Well, let's get some chow!" The boys just stared at Stanley, who was smiling with Hazen.

On the way to the mess, Stanley grilled his brother, who was now permanently in "D" Company, which was being used as an ammunition column. "What have you heard, anything?"

"Probably nothin' more than you...but I think it's going to be soon. We've drilled so much we know every inch of the ridge, even though my company is just going to be running ammo," said George.

"We're supposed to be in reserve of the reserves," said Stanley, "and you know what that means. We're going to be digging more trenches. We've nearly completed the new subways. Hell, we're so close to the Boche below Hill 145 we can smell the sauerkraut when they eat lunch." George laughed and looked mockingly at Stan. "It smells pretty good, actually." George slapped his brother on the shoulder.

"All I know is," said George, "my sergeant says we've moved well over a million artillery shells. Everything from mortar rounds to the shells from those big naval guns that take two men to lift. They've taken the cannon off battleships and they're mounted on boxcars, and we had to lay new railroad tracks to position them. I believe the sergeant. We've been lugging ammunition for four straight months."

Once the boys had some oatmeal and biscuits, they found some dry ground and sat. "Have you guys learned the sound of the shells yet?" asked George.

Stan nodded, and Hazen said, "I haven't been up yet."

"You've got to get used to the whine of the shells going overhead," said George. "And you've got to learn which are ours and which are theirs." The guys looked incredulous.

"I'm serious," said George. "There are guys so good at it, they can tell which kind of shell, and from which direction. When you're new—Hazen, you think every incoming round is going to hit you in the head. But with practice you'll know when to duck and when not to worry. Mortar shells, for instance; the guys who have spent a lot of time in the front line kinda subconsciously know when to ignore the whine of the shell. They can eliminate the non-dangerous ones." George paused and then continued, "Those high-velocity ones though, they say if you hear them at all, you're safe. You won't hear the one that hits you."

"You are really full of good news today, aren't you?" said Stanley. George shrugged and ate his biscuit.

Before George left to rejoin his company, the boys took a long look at the ridge from a spot where they could see through the trees. They were near the town of Arras, along the southern end of the slope, very close to where the Imperials were camped. When the day finally came, the Brits would be attacking German positions outside of Arras, to the south and east, while the Canadians would attack the ridge itself. As they looked at the gently sloping mound of mud, all pockmarked with craters big and small, they contemplated Vimy Ridge. They all knew its history. They all knew the massive amount of blood spent on the battered slopes by the heroic French Zouaves, the Moroccans, the French regulars, the British *and* the Germans. The ridge was right in front of them, staring them in the face.

The four main tunnels that led to the German lines, Tottenham, International, Vincent and Cavalier, had been enlarged and improved upon. Tottenham Cave could hold 1000 men and was only 500 yards from the German line. In March, the raids into enemy lines became more frequent. Some were large raiding parties, and they were often carried out at night. The men could cross open ground in No Man's Land much more safely under the cover of darkness.

On March 20th, word was passed through the sergeants that Company "C" would fall out in the morning to receive orders. Stanley, Colin and Jack knew this meant another tour in the front line trenches. It would be Hazen's first.

At 0600 the men fell out in the courtyard of the ruined chateau. The officers and the sergeants were already at attention. Lieutenant Manning addressed the company.

"At ease men," He waited a few seconds. "Alright lads," he said. "We all get a day off from training today. Tonight, we have a turn in the mix. It's just for the night… first, second and fifth platoon will prepare for a raid. The objective is to note any new trench works and to welcome any of the poor Hun buggers who want to give up and escort them back to our lines. If none of them do, our job is to persuade a few." The men laughed.

"I know you'll all do splendidly. Fall in by platoon. Some combat veterans from the 25th will give the instructions."

The men were dismissed, and the boys fell in as the sergeants waved the troops this way or that. Second Platoon's first sergeant, MacLellan, yelled, "Big Deuce! On me!" The entire platoon hustled forward. "Take a knee." Hazen's chest was pounding.

Sergeant MacLellan turned the platoon over to Sergeant Dunbar of the 25th. Dunbar was twenty-one years old, but looked forty.

"Okay mates," he said. He pointed to the west. "The route you're going to take is the Souchez Road west out of camp to where it meets the Arras-Bethune Road. That's called the Souchez Corner, which you've no doubt heard of. It's about five miles from here. From there you'll have to negotiate some small paths that will peter out into No Man's Land. Before going into the paths, each platoon will have a sapper or a pathfinder guide to show the way. Each sergeant," he nodded at MacLellan, "will have a map and you have all day today to study it."

"Now listen up," Sergeant Dunbar said, "I know you're a "work battalion," (the men stiffened) and you haven't seen combat. But you'll do fine. It's in-and-out, grab a few of the bastards and head for home." Colin and Jack were still bristling from the work battalion comment. It wasn't their choice to be digging ditches and running errands … they were just trying to do their jobs as best they could. They would rather be fighting. That's what they signed up for. They were excited for this opportunity.

"One other thing," said Sergeant Dunbar, "Fritz has a habit of sending up flares periodically. They always seem to do it when a large party is caught in the open ground. If that happens, you have only one option if you want to live; freeze and stand perfectly still. If you're very still, they can't distinguish you from a branch, or a mound of dirt or some twisted metal … if you move at all, they'll see you. Learn this, mates. If you get caught in a flare, staying still and not running for cover or diving to the ground can be very ... *trying*. I'll leave the details up to each company's sergeants." He turned away, but his head was down as he swung back facing the group of excited youngsters. Still looking at the ground, he said, "One last thing." Then he looked the men right in the eyes.

"Where you lucky men are going tonight is a highly contested place. There is a spur of slightly higher ground that juts out from the ridge which *they* hold," he gestured with his head over his shoulder towards the enemy lines. "It juts out into the valley which *we* hold. It is said that two years ago 80,000 men lost their lives battling for that position." He thought for a minute. "I'm not saying this to try and scare you, or as some sort of pep talk, it's just that I want you to be prepared for what you will see on your way in. When that battle in 1915 was over, the two armies' front lines were only a few hundred yards apart, and there was such bitterness after the fighting that neither side allowed the other to bury their dead. Those poor soldiers have been there ever since, the bones bleached by the sun over the past two summers. Thousands of 'em."

He looked at Sergeant MacLellan. "I'll leave you to it, then." Sergeant Dunbar looked at the men one last time and smiled slightly. "Just didn't want you to be shocked and get distracted, is all. Good luck then, men." He turned and left.

After being dismissed by Sergeant Dunbar, Sergeant MacLellan called the troops once again to attention. "The following men front and centre! Mackenzie—C., Frazier, Lane, Boutilier, Hill, Ross, McDonald, Borden, Dee, Mackenzie—A, Mines, McDougall, Kuhn and Carron. I will be team leader." All were from Company "B." The men stepped forward on the quick.

Sergeant MacLellan spoke almost lyrically. "You men are the lucky ones for tonight's raid. Briefing will be in an hour next to the battalion aid station. Get something to eat, drink some water and write home if you want to ... move out."

The other men, including Hazen, stepped forward to congratulate the raiding party with handshakes and slaps on the back. Soon the company left for their billets.

Outside his tent, Stan penned two quick letters—one for Lily and one for his parents. They were short and rather incomplete, but were only meant to be mailed in the event he didn't return from the raid. Stanley explained that to Hazen when he entrusted him with the letters, but couldn't help feeling he was being a little melodramatic. He drank some water and filled his canteen to the brim, then walked to the aid station. Along the way, he met up with several of the others in the raiding party. They were quiet as they walked, and instinctively fell into a march along the muddy, moonlit dirt road.

Sergeant MacLellan was already there and waiting. He told each man to take a knee under the skeleton of a huge, battered ash tree.

"Well, men," he said. "This is the first chance for anyone in the company to possibly see some action, and to do something other than dig ditches and build duckboards." The men nodded and smiled approvingly.

He went on, "This raid will be all about stealth." The sergeant shook a cigar box which rattled and handed it to the closest kneeling man. "This is burnt cork. Use it just before we rendezvous to blacken your faces, the backs of your hands and necks. Wrap your canteen in a neckerchief so it won't clang on something hard. We're taking pistols and hand-to-hand weapons. You can choose your weapon. McDougall, I imagine you could come up with some brass knuckles." The men laughed at the Irishman, who had never met a man he didn't want to fight. "Bayonets are good, though we need at least a couple of entrenching tools. Each man will be given three Mills bombs—remember—they have a seven-second fuse, so plan your throw if you have to use them, which will only be in an emergency. Got that?" The men answered, "Yes, Sergeant," in unison.

"Now boys, we've all practiced this hundreds of times." MacLellan sounded almost fatherly. "If we can get into their lines undetected, we'll be alright. Remember our training. I'll go over a few things one more time." He paused and went over in his mind the rehearsed speech.

"The objective is prisoners. We'll follow the guide quietly and get as close as we can. We'll have to cover about 400 yards. We'll use craters for cover, moving from one to another. If we can get less than thirty yards from their trenches, we'll watch for the sentries… look for the glow of cigarettes, and listen for conversations. We'll pick a sentry nearest to a sharp corner in the trench line. We'll cover the thirty yards quietly and quickly as we can—two men first, the rest a few seconds behind. Kill the sentry fast, and we'll board the trench." The men listened intently, to say the least.

He went on, "Each man will carry a notepad. Remember a pencil. In addition to prisoners, we want you to take notes of the positions of any dugouts, communication trenches and MG08s. If we find any machine guns, we'll destroy them with entrenching tools. Grab any documents you see—especially maps—and shove them into your tunics. Try to grab officers for interrogation. If we get one or two officers, kill any others that come out of the dugouts. We have to do all this and get out before any reinforcements make their way along the trenches. The pistols and Mills bombs are only for an emergency. I will remind you "Princes of New Scotland," an emergency is *not* a single German!" The men all laughed. "No, Sergeant!"

"If we find the trenches are filled with the Boche and we're outnumbered, we'll simply observe and make good notes, and fight another day."

"Lastly," he said, "the password for the raid tonight is *Dartmouth*. If you forget that, our own sentries will shoot you on the way back here."

Sergeant MacLellan added, "It's a four-mile walk to Bouvigny Wood. You all know the maps, and you know that we'll be below the Pimple. We'll meet the guide there and depart from that spot, so get there early and we'll rest up in the trench. We'll leave at 0100."

The men walked back to their billets to gather their weapons and to prepare. It was 6:00 p.m. At first all the men were silent, until Colin finally spoke. "Well, this is our chance, boys." The young men all replied with what sounded like reserved enthusiasm. Somebody said, "Damned right." These men had thought about this chance for months while they toiled at menial jobs. They had talked about it. They had dreamt about a shot at glory—or at least a chance to prove themselves. The whole battalion had. Instead they had been subjected to barbs from other battalions about being highlanders without kilts. It was bad enough to not have a battalion feather in their balmorals signifying they had seen combat, but an absence of kilts for a highland battalion in any brigade was tough to take. But perhaps that was the problem. The 85th had arrived in France still unattached to a brigade. In the middle of the largest war ever fought, with hundreds of units bustling all around them only yards from the enemy, it was almost as if they were soldiers of fortune, a thousand men plunked down in the middle of all that mayhem, alone. That is how most of them felt. At least they had each other. The officers wanted a chance to prove to the other battalions what they were capable of.

The 85th and other battalions had been recruited in Nova Scotia because the British Army needed manpower. It was thought in the Canadian Expeditionary Force that a 5th Division was needed. Later, it was decided that four strong divisions would be better than five divisions potentially left without reinforcements. In the end, it proved to be the right decision, but for now, it left the 85th battalion unattached to any division.

Hazen clung close to Stanley, Jack and Colin as they blackened their faces and hands and laid out what equipment they were to take with them. As they got ready, their speech was quicker. Stanley, who usually spoke less than the others, chattered as he worked.

꩜

When the squad met up with their pathfinder guide, a Sergeant John Clarke from Baddeck, in Cape Breton, it was almost 6:00 in the morning in Halifax. Stanley lay back in the cold dirt at the end of the path. The men had walked along the duck boards that led from the new communication trench. Once out of the shallow trench, they were in No Man's Land. Lily, he thought, would be just about ready to wake up to get ready for her new assignment at the Richmond School. *What a great teacher she will be.* He wondered what she would wear. He couldn't help but think of how beautiful she was ... what her legs looked like. He imagined her hair, her waist, her breasts and her eyes. Stan stopped himself. Once in a while—in a great while—he wondered if he had done the right thing by enlisting. This was one of those times. Had he not signed up, he would be finishing school in three months. He and Lil would have married then. He would have been able to support her while she was in school. They could have gone home to Hackett's Cove for the weekends and holidays, and had great meals at each other's homes, and teased his younger siblings. It would have been wonderful. But he had known he had to join. He could not have lived the rest of his life with the thought that people wondered why he hadn't joined up. He was no coward. So here he was.

With all these thoughts racing through his mind, Stan stared up at the night sky. The *French* night sky. It was beautiful. It was cold, and black, with millions of stars blinking. Some were shining so brightly, as if something—or someone—were trying to push their light through the night. As he stared into those stars, the blackness gave way to colour. Was it colour? Dark blue, maybe? Was there a lighter blue along the edges of what he could see, far along the horizon? It reminded him of the copy of a painting he saw in Halifax by Van Gogh. That painting was a bit different, he thought, but Stan remembered that he had loved it. He had stood and looked at it for over an hour. It had made him late for an appointment. It had been painted only twenty-eight years earlier. He thought of the article that had been posted below the copy. Van Gogh had painted it at some lunatic asylum in France, but he couldn't remember where. *Maybe it was painted very near this place,* he mused. He stared hard at the stars again. He wished he would see them like Vincent could.

Stanley felt a tap on his thigh. It was the guide, Sergeant Clarke. "Time to go," he whispered. "Pass it on."

The squad got up quietly and formed a line behind Sergeant Clarke spaced about ten yards apart. There were hand signals only now, with soft whispers when necessary. They carefully made their way through barbed wire and tangled, twisted metal. The men tried to stay low along the edges of craters, one slightly to the left, then off to the right. By the time they got 100 yards, the men noticed the ground around them. Stanley had forgotten about the graveyard they were walking through. He had forgotten about the bodies. The carcasses were everywhere. They were only bones. He could see in the moonlight that some of the skeletons appeared just as they lain dying two years before—sprawled sideways or prone, on their backs, balled up in foetal positions—every position imaginable. The bones of many of the dead soldiers had been strewn about. The jaw bones of the intact ones had fallen open, gaping as if trying to take one last breath, and the eyes sockets gaping wide, staring into the night sky, or into what had been the faces of their fallen comrades. Some skulls seemed to gawk at the men walking past, as though shocked to see them there. The skeletons that had not been disturbed had rotting uniforms draped over them. All the dead were small now, little piles of bones as though melting into the earth, the cloth of the uniforms eroding into the topsoil... becoming part of the ridge.

Stanley and the rest of the squad were careful not to step on the bones; the crack of an ulna or a tibia underfoot would alert the Germans for sure.

The men crept slowly up the frozen slope. Several times, Clarke would hold out his hand and the group would freeze in their tracks. The third "halt" revealed faint sounds which they could not make out. Stanley was no longer cold. They inched closer. All fifteen men slowly lowered themselves into a large bomb crater, about eight feet deep and thirty feet across. Clarke put up his hand again. The sounds were closer, German voices having a conversation. The pathfinder signalled the squad to stay put, and he pulled himself up to the edge of the crater and peered over the side and into the night. In less than ten seconds he lowered himself down into the crater again. He held up three fingers. They were thirty yards from the German trench. Stanley swallowed hard. They were in it now. The men looked to Clarke for instructions. He motioned for them to huddle together and when they did, using tiny whispers and hand motions, he decided to move the squad even closer to the end of the crater to better observe the enemy trench. From there they would attack once they ascertained the location of the sentries.

Each man pressed his belly against the dirt along the crater's edge. Carefully, they all tried to peer over the top and into the enemy trench. Stanley swallowed again. They were only feet from the Germans. He felt his pulse quicken. It was thirty-eight degrees out, almost freezing, yet Stan felt hot. Every man in the squad saw the same thing; they saw many soldiers and *two* MG08s. All Allied soldiers hated the machine guns. The MG08 could fire over 500 rounds per minute, and could fire downrange well over 2000 yards. It was deadly. The raiding party was clearly outnumbered at least four-to-one. They were clearly outgunned. They were not happy.

Sergeant Clarke crawled next to Sergeant MacLellan. They huddled together at the bottom of the crater and pulled a jacket over their heads in hopes no one but they would hear the whispered conversation. They were disappointed that the raid would be a failure—the first chance for the battalion to *do* something. As the two sergeants decided what to do, the Germans made their way through the trench, even closer to the raiders. They were not whispering. The Canadians could hear the enemy clearly now. Stanley could make out every word.

At some point in the parley, Sergeant MacLellan told Clarke that Private Boutilier spoke "pretty good German." That was good news; if he could take back some translated information, well, that would be better than nothing in his report. So that was it for the raid. Clarke had the men settle down into the crater. Jack Frazer found a place to sit and sat on something uncomfortable. He leaned over to move the rock or stick under his ass and pulled from the dirt a human hand, still held together by ligaments. The other men just stared at it—it was very close to Jack's face. His eyes got big, and he tossed it away as quietly as he could in disgust. The men looked at Jack, who was trying to not look rattled. "It had a wedding band," he whispered.

Sergeant Clarke held up his hand for him to be quiet. He then cupped his hands over Stanley's right ear. "You write down everything they say for the next hour, then we're gonna vamoose." Stan was disappointed that the sergeant knew he was bilingual. Clarke gave him a second notepad and pencil. He took a third pencil from McDougall and made sure it had good lead before handing over to Stan. Stan had his orders. He lay down, half on his back, half on his side in the dirt, and trained his ears towards the trench only a few feet away.

German soldiers came and went for the next ninety minutes. They all talked. Some were officers, some were other ranks. Some were cold, some were hungry. They were all tired. Stan wrote everything he heard the entire time. He tried to use circled numbers, as in Soldier #1, 2, 3, etc. to later piece together the conversations. He could tell a few times when an officer spoke and he put an "O" next to the number. A few times, the soldiers quieted down, and there were long pauses when nobody spoke. Stanley could smell pipe tobacco, and it reminded him of home. For a moment his mind wandered and he thought of his father, but then caught himself and listened intently.

After the first thirty minutes, Stanley settled in and was simply transcribing. He was no longer scared. It was a simple task, nothing more. The rest of the squad, however, did not rest easy. They were all nervous as hell.

At 0300, Sergeant Clarke tapped each man again. He used sign language to let them know they were heading back. He made sure they were all focused, and each crawled to the back of the crater and slid on his stomach out onto the slope below.

Back safely behind their own lines, the men in the party were treated to a few hours' sleep in a large dugout in the Tottenham Tunnel. They were given a ride in the rear of a big truck (a real luxury) back to the aid station. Before dismissing the squad, Sergeant Clarke looked at Stanley's notepad. He could not make sense of it. Some of the writing was English, some words in German. Also, there were circled numbers here and there. He handed it back to Stanley. "Well, Private, you'll have to read this to the lieutenant and Captain Millar. Let's go then."

It was late morning by the time they arrived at the officers' quarters. They only had to wait two minutes before being led inside. They were very tired, and they looked it, but they managed to snap to attention as the sergeant announced their names and ranks. The two soldiers' faces were still partially blackened.

Officers were sitting around a small, square card table littered with trays, two bottles of wine and one of cognac, some glasses, maps, papers, a compass, and some lead weights. There were two captains and a lieutenant. The captain was a handsome man with wavy black hair and a neatly trimmed pencil-thin moustache who looked to be well bred. The officers turned in their chairs towards Sergeant Clarke and Stanley, and returned their salute. They looked tired also, but they were clean. John Clarke handed his report to the captain, who spoke as he started to read it.

"Well done, lads. I trust you all made it back alright?"

"Yes, sir. No casualties, Captain," said Clarke. Stanley stood as tall as his five-foot-three-inch frame would allow, his hands wrapped tightly behind him. The captain placed the report on the table.

"No attack, then," he said.

"No, sir. We were vastly outnumbered."

"Your report states sergeant that you have some translated dialogue?"

"Yes, Sir. Private Boutilier speaks German, and he recorded the conversations for over an hour. I thought that might possibly make the trip worthwhile." Clarke handed the notebook to the captain.

"Yes. That was good thinking, Sergeant," said the captain. He took the notebook and handed it to the lieutenant across from him, who looked at it briefly. The lieutenant looked up at Stanley. "Also, Obergefreiter... Sie sprechen Duetsch, oder?" Stanley thought the lieutenant might be trying to trick him, or at least test him. He had a rather smug look on his face. He might be simply trying to show off to the captain. What the lieutenant spoke to him was in terrible diction—as far as Stanley could tell, as one might speak German if learnt strictly from a textbook. Stan replied quickly, with perfect diction, as taught to him by his grandfather and father in the fluid, sometimes pretty way the German language can sound. "Ja, Lieutenant, das tue ich, wenn auch manchmal kämpfe ich mit den Dialekten des Nordens. Ich bin nicht sicher, warum." *Yes, Lieutenant, I do, although sometimes I struggle with the dialects of the north. I'm not sure why.*

The Lieutenant looked uncomfortable in his chair. He nodded at Stanley and said, "Ja." Then he looked at the captain and said, "Well I can't make it out, even the English. The handwriting..."

The captain took the book from him. "Yes, well, Lieutenant, I'm sure it was cold, and the private had to write in total darkness, I assume," he said. The captain's eyes shifted from the lieutenant who had been showing off back to Stanley, and he said approvingly, "Being that you were so close to the enemy, Private..."

"Boutilier, Sir. About twenty minutes in, several of the

men moved along their trench towards us and settled in at one of the MGO8s. At that point, fourteen feet, sir."

"And how is it you speak German so well?"

"From my grandfather, sir. We came over to Lunenburg with the Foreign Protestant settlements in the mid-1700s. My ancestors were recruited from a principality on the Swiss border. They spoke French also, sir, but I believe their primary language was Swiss German."

"Do you speak French also, Private?" asked the Captain. *Here it is*, Stan thought, *they're going to yank me from my mates and make me their translator.*

"Only as much as any Canadian who belongs to the Anglican Church, sir."

All three officers smiled. The captain said, "Perhaps you should read the notes to us, Private. We'll write down anything we think might be helpful." The Captain glanced at the lieutenant at the table who hadn't spoken yet. He picked up a pencil and a large notebook.

Stanley took the book back and opened it. "I started listening in the middle of a conversation," he said, "and there were some long pauses when nobody talked. I could see them quite well. They just sat for many minutes and stared at nothing, looking into the night." The captain nodded.

Soldier #1: "Heinrich?"

Soldier #2: "Ya, Ernst … was nun?" *What now?*

#1: "Did you bring anything to eat?"

#2: "Just some stale crackers. They're crumbled. You can have them if you want."

#1: "Do you think they would raid here, on Hill 119?"

"I think that's what they call the Pimple," added Stanley. The lieutenant did not write that down. Stan was nervous. He knew what was in his own notebook. He didn't think much of it would be useful to the officers, and he was worried that they might think the squad was a failure.

The captain said, "Read it as you have it written, Private, but translate as you go please." The captain looked at the lieutenant who had tried to speak German before.

"Yes, sir," Stanley proceeded.

Soldier #2: "Ich glaube nicht." *I don't think so.* "Zu viele Maschinengewehre hier. Plus, konnen wir alles von der Lorette sehen." *Plus, we can see everything from the Lorette.* " Now the second lieutenant was writing in his big notebook.

Stanley stopped and looked nervously at the captain. He pointed into his notebook and said, "This is where I started writing only in English, sir." The captain motioned for him to go on, and shifted in his chair.

#1: "Well, I don't like how quiet it is."

#2: You're not happy no matter if it's quiet or not. It could be worse... we could be to the south. Don't you hear the shelling there?"

#1: "I hear it. The British are starting to shell us a lot more every day and night."

#2: "Lieutenant Allgower told me he heard the captain say a big attack is coming. Don't worry, Ernst, we'll get plenty of reinforcements in a couple of weeks."

#1: "I'm just sick of it. The whole thing... this stupid war."

#2: (Agrees)

#1: "I'm nineteen, Heinrich, I haven't been home for two years. *You've* been wounded twice!"

#2: "I know, I know, Ernst, but we are here, and aren't we told it's for a good cause?" (Laughter from both soldiers.)

#1: "Yesterday, the sergeant and I were looking at the letters and newspapers from the captured British. They think *we* started this thing! They think *we* were the aggressors. How can they think that?"

#2: "It's just from propaganda, Ernst. Don't let it upset you so much. Just do your job and try not to get killed."

#1: "I just want it over. I'm tired of the shelling. I haven't written Mother in weeks. I have a girlfriend, you know. Anja…she's beautiful. Have I shown you her picture?"

#2: "About 100 times."

Stanley stopped and looked at the officers and said, "It's here that many more soldiers came up the trench. I couldn't keep track of who was speaking, so it's just conversational sentences. The captain nodded approval and poured himself some coffee.

(Many speaking): "What a night! The stars are beautiful."

- "What's wrong with Ernst?"

- "He's homesick."

- "Has anybody talked to him?"

- "I tried to. He's gone to try to sleep. I think he's worried about the attack, also."

- "I wish they would get on with it. I'm tired of waiting."

- "You think we're ready, Peter?"

- "Has anybody seen my journal?"

- "Did you hear Sergeant Fassbender got it yesterday? Just south of 119. A mortar shell hit in the absolute centre of the trench. There was a lot of rifle fire. We thought they were coming."

- "Killed?"

- "Yes. But not at first. He was hit in the head with shrapnel. He collapsed into the corner of the trench, in a crouching position with his head against the wall. There was no medic—we had to watch the line. Willy made sounds— like snoring—at longer and longer intervals. The death rattle was terrible. At the end he twitched and passed water."

- "Jesus."

- "Poor Wilhelm. His son will never know him."

- "I wish we could all just go home. I've lost track of what this"—Stan paused and looked at the captain—"ficken war is about anyway."

"Sorry, Captain," said Stanley.

Both lieutenants and the captain were staring at their glasses from the night before on the little table.

"These were all the things I could understand, sir," said Stanley.

"Well done, Boutilier... and Sergeant," said the captain.

Both soldiers replied, "Thank you, sir." Stanley thought, *Great, he remembered my name.*

"You're dismissed, men," said the captain. The two saluted and wheeled left and out the door. Stan thought about the scene that had just unfolded. The lieutenant who tried to show off that he spoke some German had seemed pretty gung-ho and excited to be in France in the war. The captain seemed to relate to the simple banter written in the notebook. The night before, lying only feet from the enemy, Stan had the odd feeling that he had spent the evening with the Boche, in their own trench. Eavesdropping can make one feel strange. Maybe the Captain understood the German soldier's concerns about the reasons for the war. *I'm probably imagining it,* thought Stan. Anyhow, he was glad they didn't order a transfer from his unit to become a translator.

On the way back to their quarters, Sergeant MacLellan told Stanley he had done a good job. "You're pretty smart," he said. "You better keep your head down and keep quiet, or somebody's going to promote you." Stan laughed the comment off.

Suddenly there was a loud sound and an explosion. Stan and MacLellan hit the ground. They were shaken but quickly sprang to their feet. A German artillery shell had struck behind one of the makeshift stables. Horses screamed and men ran towards the direction of the blast. The two men had not yet seen any combat. They had only heard the explosions of random shelling along the Allied lines but always in the distance. As the dust settled, Stanley and Robert were still standing in the same spot—unsure of what to do. They looked around. They weren't under direct attack. The men around them were not hurried or the least bit anxious. The shell landing in the midst of the quarters and stables seemed almost businesslike. It was all so orderly. It was as though this happened all the time—so much so that it was a manageable fact of life. Stan and the sergeant weren't used to it. Not yet, anyway. The shelling occurred mostly at night, when larger ration parties and supply columns were moving about. The Boche spent the daylight hours observing movements.

The sergeant lit a cigarette as they walked behind some buildings. As he put his brass trench lighter away, he pointed at Stan with the two fingers that held the cigarette. "And I bet you speak French better that you let on in there."

Stan smiled slightly and said, "Non, pas vraiment."

PART 5

THE WEEK OF SUFFERING

———◇◇◇◇◇———

While the Canadian divisions had been camped below
Vimy Ridge, they wrote fewer and fewer letters home.
By the first of April 1917, the men were simply working
too hard. They were constantly preparing for the offensive,
training for special operations and learning all the logistical
aspects of the pending attack. The 85th Battalion was tasked
with finishing two new trenches to access the German front
lines, branching out from the large "subways." The men
were repairing other earthworks and building duckboards.
What Stanley had told George was correct; the 85th was to
be a reserve unit for reserve units, an unattached battalion in
the 4th Division. They understood that what they were doing
was important. Somebody had to dig the trenches and move
supplies. Still, while they showed enthusiasm and dedication,
they were not pleased about having no kilts and being called
a work battalion. They were a disconnected battalion of
strapping, loyal young men, ready and willing to fight for the
empire. They yearned to make Canada proud.

At home in Hackett's Cove, it had been an unseasonably

warm March. Across the road from the Cork & Pickle, the little spring had been clear of ice for over a month. From the spring pond every winter, the boys would cut ice for the ice house. Next summer, the Boutiliers would certainly be short. Oswald knew he'd be buying ice in Tantallon by August.

Lily was still in school in Halifax for another two months. She loved the work, she loved what she was learning, and she loved the children. She found she was enjoying the city more than she'd anticipated. She hadn't received a letter from Stanley for weeks. He had warned her that he might not be able to write for some time. Lily was very happy and surprised to get a letter from George in late March. It was a simple letter, offering greetings and mentioning that Stan was doing well. He wrote that he was tired of digging ditches. She never thought she would get a letter from him, but was happy to get any word from France. The newspapers only depressed her. She refused to read the articles about the war.

Lily had made a few friends in Halifax, where she often felt rather cosmopolitan compared to her life on the farm. She was very fond of her mentor, Mrs. Page, with whom she had a somewhat professional relationship—never calling her Jane, always Mrs. Page, or ma'am. Mrs. Page was a fine teacher and was kind to Lily and to the children.

In Nova Scotia, as in all of Canada—in much of the world—the prime concern was the war effort. But in Nova Scotia, one could argue that things were different. Halifax was one of the best deep water harbours in the world. And it happened to be situated at the western terminus of the Great Circle Route.

Halifax in 1917 was a very busy place. The harbour, especially Bedford Basin, could hold a hundred ships and outfit them as well. Injured soldiers by the thousands made their way back from England, through Halifax on their way to homes throughout Canada. Lily was there as well, learning, experiencing and maturing in the centre of all the bustling wartime activity.

❧

Late March 1917, in the Zouave Valley in Northeast France, brought showers of hot metal and destruction raining down on the German troops unlike any ever imagined. The Allied bombardments of the enemy were occurring in quick succession to both punish him and keep him guessing about what was coming next from the Allies. Once the new access trenches to the front line were completed, Stanley, Hazen, Colin and Jack were all assigned to a work detail to help move equipment. There were no manoeuvres or training for the assault now. Every man in the four divisions—and the Imperial forces to the south and east—had learned every inch of the ridge and of the enemy positions. They knew the plan well.

Every morning, the boys noticed heavy artillery that had arrived overnight. Each piece had to be jockeyed into predetermined positions behind the lines. Some of the cannon required teams of sixteen heavy draught horses. Stanley and Colin hated the work; the ground everywhere in this part of France was muddy. It was quite a chore to move the equipment. George, for one, didn't seem to mind. As long as he was working with the horses, he was happy. Stan and Hazen had seen George only a few times in the past few weeks. Stan's "C" Company was often on very different details from George's "D" Company. When Stanley did see his brother, he seemed happy, as if in a lighter mood than usual. Since arriving in France, George, who had always been quiet yet jovial, seemed to be coming out of his shell. *He'll be a different man when we get home*, thought Stanley.

On March 26th, the first operation orders were given to each division regarding the upcoming attack. The 85th Battalion was assigned to the 11th Brigade. The attack was to be the entire length of the ridge. The 11th Brigade was to "attack Hill 145 along the eastern slope of Vimy Ridge." They were to "organize and maintain a continuous line of defence" at the summit and the upper reaches of the Lorette Spur. Stanley, Colin, and Jack remembered the Lorette Spur well from the raid—at least they felt they did, although it was unlikely they could've have found it without the guide. The 85th's orders were not very glamorous. Unfortunately, the 85th was, in the Operation Orders, assigned to "be in reserve and on specific tasks as under." The "tasks as under" listed digging dugouts, cleaning out and keeping up communication trenches, carrying ammunition, and looking after ammo dumps. This meant (again) that they would be a working unit, in reserve in case of an emergency. But the boys were there, in the great adventure, doing their part.

By April 1st, the 1200 artillery pieces were in place along ten miles below Vimy Ridge. Some were trained on the front lines in hopes of devastating the enemy trenches and clearing out barbed wire and other obstacles. Other cannon were aimed at the summit. Still more, especially the long-range naval guns, were set to lay down a withering bombardment *behind* the German lines in an effort to disrupt any reinforcements from climbing the ridge on the far side.

On April 2nd, the green 4th Divisional patches were given out. The battalion had performed their tasks extremely well and the men felt good about it. Stanley especially had come to terms with their assignment as a work battalion. He had been one of the fortunate ones to have had the opportunity of a mission, though he knew he was still untested.

In the damp, cold days and nights that led up to Easter,

the Allied artillery grew in intensity. In addition, the aerial activity picked up. Dogfights blazed across the skies. The photographs from the planes provided invaluable information to Generals Byng, Currie, Victor Odlum and the rest of the staff.

There hadn't been time to write home. For the last month, no letters had been posted on the off chance a soldier might have leaked some details about the planned attack—or of their specific training. The men throughout the C.E.F. and the B.E.F. practiced remarkable self-censorship for the entire war.

The commanders of the 85th, in their wisdom, were not content to let their well-trained, disciplined men to be simply carpenters and labourers. Lieut.-Col. Allison H. Borden, Adjunct Major J.L. Ralston and other commanding staff members continued the specialized training. Behind the Allied lines (very near to the British sectors of the Battle for Arras), was the Chateau de la Haie. It was there the entire battalion was taken to study the battle plan. At the chateau was a model of the entire German lines, including known machine gun locations.

On the eve of the battle, regardless of the fact that the 85th had been given menial tasks to perform, Maj. Ralston and Lieut. A.T. Croft made sure the men went forward equipped for frontline action—just in case. It was a very exciting, extremely nervous moment in time.

On April 8th, the battalion was camped in the destroyed village of Bouvigny Wood, about two miles southeast of the town of Gouy-Servins, which was just below the Lorette Spur. Unlike Arras or Gouy-Servins, the village of Bouvigny Wood was empty of civilians.

Hazen was the first to wake in the basement of one of the intact chateaus. It was barely light outside.

"Psst," Hazen whispered, "Stan, you awake?"

Stan did not open his eyes. "Why are you whispering, Hazen? Or don't you hear the constant artillery firing anymore?"

"I heard it all night," replied Hazen, "and every hour for the last week."

"Why don't you guys rest another hour?" asked Jack. Colin was sleeping soundly.

"How does he do that?" asked Hazen. No one answered. Hazen was nervous but tried not to show it.

"Do you think today's the day?" he asked.

"Maybe, so try to sleep a few more minutes. It'll be alright," said Stanley.

When the hour came for the company to form up before breakfast, the boys were already dressed and in the field next to the road, awaiting the sergeants and the lieutenant. Stanley looked up at the Lorette Spur and tried to imagine the route next to it he had snuck up in the dark a month ago. He tried to see the crater where he had lain under those lovely stars and eavesdropped on Ernst, Heinrich, and Peter chatting about girlfriends and wanting to go home.

Stanley turned around to the west and south, behind the Allied lines and towards the fields that were safely out of range of the German artillery. He could smell the recently upturned furrows of the fields. Just out of reach of the Boche's guns, the farmers over the past few days had been hard at work. Stan and Hazen had spent a lunch break watching one man driving two sturdy Belgians across the open field not 250 yards from where German shells were raising a pink cloud of brick dust.

Now as he looked at the neatly ploughed field, its furrows paralleling the gentle contours of the land where it sloped down to a tiny brook, he longed for home more than any time before. He longed for Lily, and he longed for his mother.

The Allied bombardment had lasted for days. Suddenly,

the sounds of the distant artillery and the explosions on the ridge were accompanied by another sound. Church bells throughout the villages were ringing out. It was Easter Sunday. For the first time since the previous autumn, the sun held a touch of warmth, though patches of snow remained in the shady spots of ground. The fence posts and furrows glistened beneath the wide, blue sky. It was a beautiful day. Only miles away bombs were still falling by the dozens. Tears began to well up in Stan's eyes.

"Boutilier!" yelled a sergeant from the road. Stan wiped his eyes and swung around. "Moving out," said the sergeant.

Behind the front of the battle, men, machines and horses were moving everywhere. There was more traffic than in downtown New York City. All the preparation and planning were winding up. The men had been extremely busy for over a month, but now it was different. Men and machines moved in concert. For miles along the road below the ridge, there were huge camps and stores. Nothing was lacking; not artillery nor small arms ammunition, not water or food. There was an endless tide of mules in long trains carrying supplies.

As Company "C" marched along the road to mess and then to the Easter Service, ambulances were driving in the opposite direction. The men could see the nurses in them. Jack, Colin and Hazen waved to them, and when the young women waved back, it made the boys' hearts leap.

Along the way in the fields by the roadside, men were lying on dry spots of ground to rest. They passed camps of cleaned and shaven men who were eating. They passed by men sitting on boxes between stacks of rifles writing home, smoking pipes or cigarettes; but the tide of men kept marching, flowing towards the edge of the front lines.

The Second Battle of Arras actually started nearly three weeks before Easter Monday, 1917. The terrific bombardment of the heights had been carefully thought out by Generals Byng, Currie, Odlum, and many other officers. Not only were the slopes and the summit of the Vimy Ridge being pounded by artillery, but so were the slopes on the far side of the ridge. Machine gunners also raked the German's front line and communication trenches. The intention was not just to punish him or to wear him down, but to keep him guessing. In the final week before the assault, the artillery corps would put down a rolling barrage in front of the enemy lines and every five minutes extend the range fifty yards farther, while simultaneously laying down suppressive fire on the enemy trenches. The shifting artillery range confused the Germans. It is clear in their diaries. For the first dozen times this method was employed, the Boche were certain the attack was coming. They expected the British (the Canadians—still the Germans made no distinction between dominion troops—they were all "British") would come over the top at the end of the barrage. But the "British" didn't come. Another reason for the rolling barrage carried out over and over was for practice. The Canadian Corps was zeroing in to employ the tactic of a carrying barrage. The infantry would approach the enemy trenches in an orderly fashion, well protected by the advancing curtain of friendly shells ahead of them. If it worked, the enemy would hopefully still be hunkering in their dugouts and tunnels as the Canadians reached their trenches. Timing was everything. The tactic had been tried before—even by the Germans—but it had not been practiced and disciplined.

The constant, burning rain of exploding shells deteriorated the Germans' morale. The Bavarian units of the Sixth Army, whose job it was to hold Vimy's defences at all costs, were taking the brunt of the artillery and air assault. Major Anton

Maier's 3rd and 1st Bavarian Reserve Divisions had been tasked with defending the German left flank, in the all-important Thelus-Farbus region. They had been shelled mercilessly for a month, camped in the path of the Canadian 1st Division.

On the 3rd of April, Major Maier sent the following report to his Brigade Commander, Generalmajor Lamprecht:

> *The enemy artillery fire and its effects have increased day after day. In none of the First, the Third, the Stop Lines or the Zwischenstellung (Intermediate Position) is it possible to speak of continuous lines of defence. For the most part the trench lines have been flattened to such an extent they are simply crater fields. The same is true of the approach routes. Due to crushing and burying of the dugouts, there has been an extraordinary reduction in the ability to provide protected accommodation for the troops.*
>
> *Enemy activity in the entire garrison is on edge. Raids, both large and small, keep coming; sometimes with artillery preparation, sometimes without; sometimes here, sometimes there. The usual artillery and mortar fire is often interrupted by repeated, violent and sudden concentrations, often in the strength of drum fire and lasting up to twenty minutes at a time. These concentrations appear to be lifted (by day) when white flares are fired.*
>
> *Deploying the battalions on the positions for eight days continuously, as has been the case up to now, cannot be continued in the present circumstances. But a rotation of two days in the front and two days in support means that the reserve battalion can have a rest period of only two days at a time. This routine cannot be maintained for more than a few weeks. The allocation of*

a fourth battalion for each sector, as already requested, is urgently sought.

One can read the angst in his lines. It's not hard to imagine the major in his dugout, dimly lit by kerosene lamps, the dirt falling on his dispatch as he tried to write it. He was again asking for reserve battalions—men who would mobilize too late, and who would not have the benefit of artillery support because the ground on the German side of Vimy Ridge was too pockmarked with bomb craters to move the cannon close enough.

Less than forty-eight hours later, Major Maier, possibly suffering from shell shock himself, sent another report to Generalmajor Lamprecht:

Following on from my report of 6 April, 5:30 p.m., I regard it as my duty to forward the enclosed report by the regimental medical officer concerning the current state of health, which he prepared for me on his own initiative. The trigger for this was my request for an explanation as to why thirty-one men from 12th Company reported sick simultaneously, and to make clear to him that all men, except the most pressing medical cases, were to be directed back to their companies.

"... The companies in support have already sent several sections to the forward companies because the front lines are under strength."

"...As a result, each company spends ten days on the (front line) positions, under constant fire and without a break. When this is coupled with the need to counter the daily enemy raids, both large and small, by day and by night, it amounts to a commitment which

leaves anything on the Somme or at Verdun in the shade; not, perhaps in terms of casualties, but certainly in the demands it makes on the battle worthiness of the troops."

In a subsequent report by the regimental physician, Dr. Schwesinger:

"The Medical Officers of 1st and 2nd Battalions reported yesterday in their weekly summaries:
    Increasing numbers of cases of exhaustion are appearing. The following ailments have been treated: foot conditions, coughs and colds, a noticeably large number of skin complaints and many cases of nervous exhaustion.

Softening up the enemy indeed.

The Germans felt that an unholy rain was upon them. The Sixth Army reported on 7 April that "Fire has been observed coming from 679 positions." Apparently, they could only observe about fifty-four percent of the Allied artillery placements.

Generalmajor Ritter von Möhl, commander of the 16th Bavarian Infantry Division, reported in his war diary that *"The bombardment, in combination with the weather conditions, has greatly reduced the defensive value of the position... The heavy bombardment, the ceaseless high state of alert in a severely shot-up position, protected by only fragments of an obstacle, coupled with the endless work each night on positions which are generally destroyed again the following day, has naturally had a negative effect on the morale of the troops and had led to some isolated incidents... My oral report yesterday was somewhat limited, because I had just been informed of examples of gross insubordination within a regiment in whose fighting ability I had previously had the highest trust."*

When the final hour arrived, the defenders would be fatigued and stressed, either pounded into mental submission, or wound up beyond belief. For generations to come, there were Germans who called the first week of April, 1917, *"Die Woche des Leidens"*—the "Week of Suffering." For those Bavarian men who were there, frozen to the slopes of Vimy Ridge, the suffering went on for a very, very long time.

PART 6

THE SHOW

————⊂∞∞⊃————

It was true that the 85th Battalion was a work unit and had
not been issued kilts, but these men were no misfits. They
never were. The 85th had two regimental bands, the Pipe
Band, and the Silver Band, both arguably the best in the 4th
Division. The men of both bands had to work the trenches
just like every other man. In the nights leading up to the final
assault on Vimy, the battalion was in the line taking part in
the immense preparations. Despite the largest artillery barrage
in history over a three week period, the Germans managed
to counter with artillery of their own. The 85th sustained
thirty-four casualties. On the morning of the 9th of April, the
battalion was not going into the fight unbloodied.

The 9th day of April, 1917, the fateful day had arrived.
By dawn, the Allied planes were buzzing the skies over all the
villages surrounding the city of Arras—or what was left of it.
They flew over the ridge itself and engaged the German planes
over the valley behind the enemy lines. Three of the British
planes were outfitted with new two-way radios which worked
only occasionally. The officers on the ground, including General

Victor Odlum, a veteran of the Boer War and a Vancouver newspaperman, relied on battlefield "runners" and pigeons. The runners, known to be carrying important communiqués, were shot on sight by both sides. So were the pigeons, if at all possible. At least two German battalions carried several 16 gauge shotguns loaded with bird shot explicitly to shoot down carrier pigeons.

Generals Currie and Byng's vision had reached fruition. The Allied lines were a miracle of supplies. The tunnels and trench network along the front were immense. The combined tunnels extended nearly ten miles. The twelve access tunnels, called "subways," led to jumping-off points for the attacking troops. Some subways were short, while others were a kilometre or longer. Some subways were outfitted with a special narrow-gauge rail system, hospitals, and bomb shelters. They were wired for electricity and were outfitted with fresh air pumps powered by generators. Two days earlier, on April 7th, the final operation order for the 85th was issued. The battalion was to move the next day through Tottenham Tunnel to Music Hall Line, a small communication trench that had originally been dug by the French two years before. A complete directive was included in the orders: "*The route will be via Gouy-Servins, Chateau de la Haie, Villers-au-Bois, and just after this town turn to the left over the open country along Cabernet (duck walk), thence to Berthonval Wood Dump where tools would be picked up, thence along Wortley Avenue (communication trench) to Music Hall Line.*"

By Easter Sunday, the anticipation was palpable. There wasn't excessive talking, but men were up and about getting armed and equipped to march to the battle line. Letters home had been written, and affairs were in order. After church services, the squads were paraded out by the battalion's Silver Band.

At 9:00 a.m., Jack, Stanley and Colin were sitting on ammo boxes writing letters when they heard a voice nearby.

"Hello, ladies!" It was George.

"Hey!" they all said at once, and jumped up to greet him. They hadn't seen him for a week.

"Where has "D" Company been," asked Jack?

"On the south side of Arras," said George. "The Yorkshire Rifles came up late from the Somme. We've been loading and unloading trucks and wagons for a week to get them set up and quartered."

Stanley shook his brother's hand and massaged his shoulder. "It's good to see you, brother." George had a cigarette hanging from his mouth. Stanley leaned back and scowled at him, "When did that start?"

George flicked the butt away and shook his head slightly. "I dunno. Some time ago. We got pounded from the German big guns on the other side of Arras for about three days, and after that the fags seemed to calm me. That shelling kinda shook me up for a while. Where are you guys tomorrow?"

Stanley spoke first. "We're building and filling the supply dumps along Music Hall. And you?"

"We're digging a new communication trench to the Basso Line," said George. "They want to be able to get some men and ammo to the Lewis guns in case the Boche counter on our left flank. Where's Hazen?"

"He went to fill the canteens," said Stanley. "He can't seem to stop volunteering for things."

"Well, he'll grow out of that," said George. Stan and Jack chuckled and nodded.

"I really stopped to say that I signed up for a boxing match against the 1st Division in three weeks. I signed up a while back—not sure when it'll be after all this," George said, waving his arm towards the ridge.

"What weight," asked Colin?

"Bantam. I tried to make lightweight but can't seem to 'cause they're working us so hard every day." George patted Stan on the chest. "Well boys, I gotta head back. Good luck, all of you, and somebody tell Hazen I said hello—and tell him to stop volunteering for things."

George trotted off, and only moments later, Sergeant MacLellan walked through the mass of men who were scattered about. "Platoon, on me!" The men gathered near him, some standing, and some taking a knee.

"Listen up, men; service in forty minutes at the "Y." You *Catholics* (most of the men chuckled) have a sacrament and mass in the courtyard of the chateau, also in forty. Directly after that, dress and full kit for the march to Gouy-Servins. We'll fall in by company and platoon along this road. Any questions?"

"No, Sergeant!"

"Alright," said MacLellan. "Don't forget, canteens full, and remember your rubber blankets and mess kits. Look sharp."

"Boutilier!" said the sergeant, and waved to Stanley to come to him.

Stan jumped up and stood in front of the sergeant. "Yes, sir."

"Don't call me sir, Boutilier, how many times do I have to say that?"

"Not sure, sir." Everyone laughed.

The sergeant mocked a laugh and went on, "I have an order here for you from 4th Division H.Q." Stanley gulped inaudibly. *What's this?* he wondered.

You're to report to Captain Millar in Tottenham Tunnel the day after tomorrow—that's 10 April—in the dugout at Exit 10. Just follow the signs from anywhere for Exit 10." Sergeant

MacLellan gave Stanley his written orders. "0700... don't be late," he told Stan. "Your sergeants and Lieutenant Manning already know."

"Do you know what this is about?" asked Stanley (though he had a good idea).

The sergeant, smiling, held up his hands chest-high as he turned to leave, and said, "Didn't know you could speak German, mate."

Stanley's heart sank. It was over for him now. He'd have one more day and a night with his friends, and then he would be some officer's flunky. If there was no interpreting to do, he would be getting coffee, filing dispatches, and running errands. Maybe that would be better than digging ditches and filling ammo and supply dumps, but he had trained with his friends for a long time. He had signed up with them. He was not happy. He decided not to tell the guys—especially Hazen—until after the big battle was over. He would go on as though everything were normal.

❦

Before departure from the camp, three of the lieutenants addressed each company individually. The always reliable Lieut. Manning gave a pep talk to Company "B."

"This battle is important, men," said the lieutenant, *"because on this battle line, it is the highest ground between these rolling hills of western France and the open plain of Artois and Flanders. This is a chance to turn the enemy's right flank. This is an opportunity to change this war from one where we live in stinking trenches to one of movement. More than two hundred thousand men have tried to take this ground since September 1915. Tomorrow is our chance. Tomorrow is a Canadian chance to do the job.*

You have all participated in the preparations. You are all aware of the ordinance we've cheerfully delivered to the Boche in the last three weeks. When the hour comes, there will be an artillery barrage upon the ridge unlike anything any human has yet experienced. Do not be overwhelmed by this. Stay calm. Remember your assignments. We will all of us do our jobs! Remember, men, we are Byng's Boys. He and General Currie have done everything possible to help us succeed. And we will succeed."

The men sent up a cheer, helmets waving overhead, even as German artillery shells landed a quarter mile away.

The advance platoon, led by Lieut.-Col. Earl Phinney from Halifax, left camp for the front at 1:00 p.m. Stanley and Hazen's No. 6 Platoon "B" Company led by Lieut. King didn't leave the camp until just before 6:30 p.m. For the first part of the march, which was along the dry, flat road to the flattened village of Villers-au-Bois, Stanley thought of how he would tell his cousin about his transfer. As the platoon in the dark of night turned onto the duckboards towards Wortley Avenue (a path in the mud that followed a gully), and on towards Music Hall Line, Stanley's concerns about the transfer melted away.

All the men were quiet now, as instructed, but they were at once sombre and excited. Any thoughts of sleep were soon dashed. The Music Hall trench was filled with waist-deep water, and it was *cold.* The men were already exhausted after carrying their full kit and shovels and pickaxes. At the Berthonval (ammo) Dump they had picked up everything they needed—their rifles, 30 rounds of ammunition, rubber ponchos, helmets, canteens, and construction tools. There was a dugout accommodation at Music Hall which held only about sixteen men. The rest would have to try to sleep in the watery trench, waiting patiently until "zero hour," less than six hours away.

Every man, whether he was in a work battalion or an

assault battalion, synchronized his watch. Easter Monday at 0530 would be forever etched in the memories of thousands of men, defining the futures of many.

Standing in water, shivering, the boys in Stanley's platoon waited patiently. They looked at their watches; 5:22, 5:25, 26, 27, 28 ... 5:30. Four or five seconds ticked by, and Stan felt uncomfortable in the odd calmness. Seconds seemed like minutes. Some of the men looked to each other for reassurance. Then the show began. First there were little waves in the water in the trench. No man was moving—it came from the ground below. There was movement in the earth around them. Stan put his hand on the side of the trench, as dirt started falling in from the sides. The men looked at each other, unsure of what was happening. Then, a few hundred yards in front of them, the mines under the German trenches blew. All along the German front lines, earth and masonry—and bodies—flew hundreds of feet into the air. Surely nothing near the explosions could remain alive. The walls of the subways beneath Arras from which troops were pouring to the assault shook and trembled. Before the dirt, debris, and body parts fell to earth, there was a deafening artillery barrage. It was as though the magnificent campaign from the Allied cannon over the past week had been only practice. The sounds of the mines and the barrage from the cannon could be heard in far off England. In London, 170 miles away, windows rattled.

In only one hour and forty minutes, five tons of artillery shells were hurled onto the enemy positions, at a pace of eighty shells per second. Added to that unprecedented artillery fusillade, machine guns opened up along the front lines. Hazen could see one of the Lewis guns firing only yards away. Its gunner was opening it up—over 500 rounds per minute. The gun was pulsating with every shot fired, but Hazen thought it odd that he could not hear it. There was enormous noise all around him, yet he could not hear the Lewis nor the support men next to the gunner who were yelling to each other for more "pans" of ammunition.

Immediately after the mines were blown, German rockets shot up, discharging green, white, red, and orange coloured stars, telling the forces in the rear that the battle had finally begun, and signalling—begging for support. The German artillery pieces in the rear that were still intact answered the call, but they were woefully inadequate. Many had been knocked out by the three-week Allied barrage. So too were the communication trenches and the few "roads" that switched back to the east side of Vimy Ridge behind German lines. It would be nearly impossible for the Bavarians to get reinforcements or supplies to the summit. Then it started to snow.

German Reserve Lieutenant Bittkau recorded the event:

> *"Gradually the first streaks of dawn began to light up the darkness. Light squalls of snow blew across the cratered landscape. There was a striking stillness. Suddenly between Arras and Lens came great flashes and streaks of light in the sky. Signal flares? Mine explosions? All of a sudden, as though at a single word of command, down came drum fire from thousands of large and small calibre muzzles. Shell fire rose to crazy heights. It was impossible to distinguish the firing signatures from the shell bursts. It was just one mass of fire amidst an extraordinary racket."*

In the Music Hall Line, the 85th stood in the water and waited. Every man was affected by the intensity of the artillery bombardment. Clearly, nothing was going to be able to fire back at them during such a barrage, and the men shifted their weight and changed their footing in the water. By standing erect, they could see the ridge from the shallow trench. Colin, Jack and Stanley could see the summit line and the earth flying in every direction. The dirt looked red with fire—or was it blood? The flying earth mixed with the colours of the German rockets. While they couldn't even hear the man beside them, watching the murderous show, they could imagine the screams of those on the ridge. No one spoke, until finally Colin said, as if only he himself was meant to hear, "Jesus Christ."

"I doubt it," answered Stanley, staring at the ridge.

Early in the artillery shelling, gas canisters had been fired onto the third and fourth German trench lines near the summit. Now there was not only snow driving into the faces of the enemy, but also chlorine, its deadly fingers of vapour trying to creep with the breeze, down into every trench, crevice and trachea as it moved across the German lines.

In spite of the historic bombardment, the German soldiers that were left alive in the second and third lines of defence fought like hell, though some, shell-shocked and bleeding—especially on the southern end of the ridge closer to Arras—surrendered quickly. The 4th Canadian Division—Stanley and Hazen's—was farthest north on the ridge, and there were still multiple intact Boche machine guns on that sector's high points, the Pimple and Hill 145. The other companies of the 4th Division piled out of the trenches and started across No Man's Land, their rifles slung on their shoulders and carrying shovels. They walked at first, slowly and calmly behind the "carrying barrage" of howitzers and field pieces. They sprang on the offensive once they got to the German front lines. As they made it farther up the slope, very effective sniping and withering fire from the machine guns on Hill 145 mowed down the Canadians. Below the hill, General Victor Odlum's 4th Division was stopped. The 102nd Battalion from Northern British Columbia, "Warden's Warriors," had secured their objectives but were being shot to pieces from the heights. The 54th "Kootenay Battalion" was supposed to pass the Warriors and take Hill 145, but they were repulsed. Not only were they taking fire from the hill to their left, but there was a small salient to their right where the Germans had set up three machine guns in shallow craters. By 6:45 a.m., the highly respected Warriors had already taken the 1st, 2nd, and 3rd German lines. By midday, they were being decimated. The Warriors stopped and tried to dig in, but they never stopped fighting.

The 102nd Battalion called themselves "Warden's Warriors" after their C.O., Lieut.-Col. John Weightman Warden, a broker from Vancouver. Warden was a veteran of the Boer War and had been wounded at the 2nd Battle of Ypres. The 102nd had made their way more than halfway up the ridge. In the process, every officer had either been killed or wounded. Front line command of the Warriors' "C" Company fell to a Sergeant-Major Russell, while Sergeant D.S. Georgeson held a platoon together in a huge mine crater and defended the ground the company had taken so far. Both men were quickly shot in the leg. Georgeson was also hit in his dominant hand.

The 102nd had done their job. They had taken their assigned objectives, but now could move neither forward nor to the rear. A company from the 54th Battalion was supposed to leapfrog past the Warriors' dug-in positions and advance along the base of Hill 145 towards the summit ridge. They also were stopped and took up defensive positions along with the 102nd's "D" Company. Both companies were pinned down. Generals Currie and Byng's "set piece" plan of attack, with each company and platoon having certain objectives instead of simply sending thousands of men rushing at the enemy, had worked remarkably well, all along the ridge. But the heights of Hill

145 and the neighbouring Pimple were proving strategically too difficult. Also, one of the few German trenches left intact from the massive Allied bombardment was near Hill 145's summit. Through that trench, the Germans were reinforcing the hill. The thought of a German counterattack on the Allied left flank loomed in every Canadian commander's mind.

Still the men of the 85th waited. By late morning, things were getting confusing. Communication was breaking down. The officers in the tunnels and above ground relied on runners to convey vital information, but the runners were dying by the score. Most of those who were still alive had been wounded and put out of commission. The few that did make it back from the front lines were offering conflicting accounts. The messengers could only report what little they saw—hand-to-hand fighting with platoons taking cover and getting shot to pieces.

A few of the 85th Battalion were called to help as stretcher-bearers. Colin got to go, and Jack. They ran with folded up stretchers into No Man's Land, following the medics towards the German lines. The freezing sleet was blowing harder. The woods around Hill 145 to the north had been reduced to splinters. The barbed wire entanglements had been torn to shreds. The thin covering of chalky soil on which they walked had been churned up and blended with the bones of long-dead Frenchmen. Nowhere was progress possible in a straight line, so broken was the earth with shell holes. The mine craters were filled nearly to the brim with muddy water deep enough to drown a man.

By noon, rumours were pulsing through the trenches and tunnels: the attack was being held up at Hill 145. The success of the whole operation was now in jeopardy. Every man in the Allied lines knew that at that very spot on the ridge, over 100,000 men had died in the past two years, and today two battalions had already been smashed underneath the fortified pillboxes. Death spewed from the MG08/15 machine guns.

General Victor Odlum knew it as well as anyone. Nearly all the other goals of the attack had already been realized, but if the Germans could maintain the hill long enough to mobilize massive reinforcements to Hill 145, they might then be able to turn the Allied left flank. It simply could not happen. Odlum knew there were men in trouble under the hill and under the Pimple. As the few reports came in, he began to realize he had lost many of his officers. The hill had to be taken, and it had to be taken *today*.

By mid-afternoon, General Victor Odlum, still in Tottenham Tunnel, was running out of solutions *and* options. He had to find some troops to attack Hill 145, and he had to find them in a hurry.

The 85th battalion had been in and out of the Music Hall Line trench since 10:00 a.m., trying to help any way they could. Men had volunteered to carry wounded and escort prisoners—some of whom had straggled to the Canadian lines on their own. They volunteered to run messages and carry ammunition. By three o'clock in the afternoon, the 85th Battalion's Companies "C" and "D" were the *only* troops available in the entire 4th Division.

Colin, Stan and Jack had just gotten back from transporting some wounded when a message was passed down the line for Sergeant McDougall. Colin had known the sergeant when they were youngsters. He instinctively swung around when the message got to him. "Alex!" The sergeant spun toward to Colin. "Lieutenant Manning wants you, on the double." The sergeant knew the trench was jammed with troops, so he jumped over the side, got his feet under him and sprinted to the rear of the trench. There, at the entrance of the Tottenham Tunnel, were the lieutenant and several other sergeants and officers. They were staring at some maps. "Sir!" said Alex, "Sergeant McDougall, 'C' Company."

Twenty minutes later, Sergeant Alex McDougal was running back along the Music Hall Line. He jumped into the trench and called for three platoons to assemble.

"Okay boys," he said to the tightly crowded men. "This is it. You wanted to get in the fight—now's your chance." The men stiffened with excitement.

"At dusk, we're to take bloody Hill 145. Captains Anderson and Crowell are in charge, so let's show them why they believe in us so much. We will proceed back through Music to Tottenham, where we'll move on to jumping off trenches. We dug those trenches…you should be familiar with them!" Some of the men chuckled.

"We're going over at six o'clock."

When the company reached the tunnel entrance, they were given two Mills bombs each and another forty rounds of rifle ammo.

"There's the spirit, boys!" said one of the N.C.O.s

"Give 'em hell, men!" said another. There were N.C.O.s standing on each side of the trench just at the Tottenham entrance, patting the men on their backs and helmets, offering whatever encouragement they could. The men smiled and nodded, though it was a sombre scene. But they were ready.

Hazen stood directly in front of Stanley, who tapped him on the helmet. It was meant to reassure his cousin. When Hazen turned back and looked at Stan, he had a grave expression on his face, as if to say, *Don't bug me right now.* Stan just smiled and nodded to his best friend. There was nothing he could do to help Hazen prepare now. It was fight or fail.

Captain Percy Anderson came strutting by, confident and jovial. He exuded professionalism. This, he knew, was a defining moment—in his life, in the men's lives and in history.

One of the superior officers said, "Well, Anderson, they have had to send you to take Vimy Ridge."

"We will take it or never come back," Anderson replied. He was very calm and determined.

At the other end of Tottenham, Captain Percy Anderson assembled his men at the edge of No Man's Land. The small communication trenches were wet and sloppy from men coming and going all day. Jack, Colin, Stan, and Hazen were lined up on the left of Company "D," standing ready to jump up and attack. There was supposed to be a short concerted artillery barrage just before "zero hour." As the moments ticked closer, with the men sweating in the cold, snowy evening, there was no artillery. Captain Crowell with "C" Company could not see Captain Anderson, as the troops were strung out along the edge of No Man's Land. They waited. The men, tense and nervous, knew the hour had arrived.

What they didn't know was that a communication had arrived at headquarters moments earlier questioning the possibility of the artillery obliterating some troops of the 54th Battalion who were dug in near the foot of Hill 145. The barrage had been called off. The 85th had no idea. All they knew was that 6:00 p.m. had arrived.

Crowell did not hesitate. Perhaps, in his single-minded commitment, he did not even notice. When "zero hour" arrived, with a wave of his arm, he *went*. Company "C" piled over the top, and upon seeing that, so did Company "D."

The 85th came out of the trenches firing. In the desperation of the moment, both companies had been given extra Lewis guns. Usually, there were two per company; now, both "C" and "D" Companies employed six. Each Lewis machine gun crew had six men assigned to carry ammunition and tools to unjam the gun if need be. The Lewis gunners were also firing from the hip—something not typically done. The men didn't walk forward as many of the previous battalions had done; they did not have an artillery "carrying barrage" falling ahead of them. This was a full-on frontal assault on a dug-in enemy which was holding the high ground. This attack would have to be brutal, athletic, and ugly. It was also beautiful and inspiring.

As soon as the 85th left the trenches, German machine guns started firing. Some unlucky men fell at the edge of the trench. After months of training, they never even got over the top. They simply collapsed, dead, and slid back down into the trench.

The first two hundred yards was fairly flat ground, except for the shell holes. As they approached the upward sloping foot of Hill 145, both companies attacked with what looked like fearless courage. They ran ahead, standing tall, firing their weapons as they advanced. Soon they were running past men of the 54th and 102nd Battalions who were dug in. Those men, who had been shot up and sniped for hours, rose up and waved to the men of the 85th imploring them to "Get down! Stay low!" They did not. On they went up the slopes with a deliberate audacity.

Stanley tripped on some debris as the company scrambled up the hill. He landed on his right shoulder in the mud, and as he did, he noticed the mud in front of his face moving. *Those are bullets*, he thought. He jumped to his feet and pressed on. He took three or four more steps and reached a Canadian soldier from the 54th. Stanley saw that the fallen man's face, no older than his own, was pale and his eyes were distant. He had been lying there all afternoon. Instinctively, Stan started to step toward him to see if he was alright. A few more yards and then, just as quickly, he saw another man lying on the ground, covered with mud. Stan turned back up the hill. He remembered Col. Borden's orders back in the tunnel: *"Keep moving. Men will be coming behind to attend to the wounded. If we don't take the hill, we won't be able to help them."*

Stanley suddenly got very scared—for only a moment. He looked to his right, then to his left. He couldn't see Hazen anywhere, or Jack. He didn't see anyone he knew well. Stan also hadn't heard anything except his own breathing for the first few seconds across No Man's Land. He wondered where George was; Company "D" was off to his left, he knew that. *God*, he thought about his little brother as he ran, *he lied about his age... he's not even eighteen.* There was a loud thud only yards away followed by a huge *bang*. The left side of his body was splattered with mud. German artillery was finding its way to their side of Hill 145. It almost knocked Stanley down, but he caught his stride and kept going. At that moment he could hear everything. Men screaming and moaning, men yelling as they ran, explosions like the artillery round that had just missed him. Oddly, amidst all the chaos and loud sounds, he could hear the sharp snap of bullets flying near him. *What a curious sound*, he thought.

Jack and Colin had stayed close together in the trench and were running beside each other on the way up the slope. Hazen was about seventy yards to Stanley's left. Mortar rounds were falling everywhere now. Each boy could see men falling around them. Some made all manner of sounds as they fell— wheezing, curses, a cough, a thud. Some made no sound at all. They just fell instantly in mid-step.

Stanley kept running up the slope toward the German trenches. He could see the muzzle flashes from the machine gunners near the top of the hill. He hadn't yet fired his gun. He could hear others firing around him. Stan ran past another fallen man, then another. They looked dead. A third was clearly gone. He tried to feel the safety switch on his rifle. On the Lee Enfield, the safety is on the left side near the back of the bolt. Running hard, he couldn't tell if he had switched it on or off. He stopped for a millisecond and looked at the safety. It was in the "off" position. He broke into a run again. This time, as he ran up the hill, he fired from his hip at the spot where he could see the German gunners. The cacophony all around him disappeared again; he could hear only his own breathing and the sound of his soggy boots hitting the ground. He no longer heard the bullets *snap* as they went by. He could not hear the screaming of the wounded or the dying.

Stanley fired once, and had to slow down to chamber another round. He fired again and stumbled. Again he put a new round in the chamber, but this time he shouldered the Enfield. He squeezed off a third round. As he did, he felt as though he had been punched in the stomach. *How odd*, he thought. He rose up and started to run again. He took two, three steps, but his feet felt like lead. He took a fourth step, and his legs went out from under him. Stan dropped onto his left side, his face driving into the mud. He let go of the rifle. He felt pain in his back. It made no sense.

Stanley tried to get up but couldn't. He felt his abdomen and saw the blood on his hands. He still couldn't hear the massive sounds around him. Rolling onto his back, he could see down the line of the German trench—their last line of defence on Hill 145—as though he were watching a silent movie. He saw Captain Anderson, running very fast with men falling all around him, jump into the enemy trench. Several Germans turned to fight him. Stan watched as the captain shot dead the first officer he came to and squared off on the others. He could see him throwing another to the ground. He had the man by his belt and was shaking him like a ragdoll. Within seconds, other men from "C" Company were piling into the trench.

Stan looked up at the sky. All he could see was the early blue of the evening sky, with occasional colours in the periphery from the unanswered German distress flares. He watched the sky and wondered how bad his wound was. He wondered where Hazen was. He thought about his mother. He thought about Lily. He noticed there wasn't an enormous amount of pain. Suddenly his view of the sky became obstructed. It was Jack Fraser's head. His friend was peering down at him.

"Stan!" he cried out to Stanley. "Stan!" Stanley saw Jack looking around and back towards the Canadian lines. "Medic!"

"Stan—you're okay. You're okay. There're coming. I can see them with stretchers." Stan tried to smile, and patted Jack on the forearm to reassure him.

"Medic!" Jack yelled again.

Jack grabbed Stanley's Enfield and stuck the bayonet in the ground next to Stan. He put his hand on Stan's forehead and wiped off the mud. "I'm gonna get a medic. You hold tight. I'll be right back." Jack left and Stan felt reassured. He closed his eyes. He tried to relax, but as he waited, he started to get frightened. Could this be it? No—he wouldn't allow it. He had seen men much worse at the battalion aid stations that came through it alright. On the other hand, he knew of men who had caught colds in the trenches and died. He resolved to stay calm. That's what everybody said; if you get hit, stay calm. Only now it was getting dark. What if they came for him and couldn't find him? He looked to his right and checked to see if the rifle was still protruding from the ground where Jack had stuck it. It was. Surely they would see it. He was getting very cold.

As the moments ticked by, Stanley became more aware of the sounds going on all around him. He kept his eyes shut. There was still shouting, and machine gun fire, and he could hear Mills bombs going off. Suddenly, he was rattled as someone shook him. It was George.

"Stan!" George was shaking him.

"George, I've been hit, I'm afraid." Stan lifted his head

to look at his belly. He tilted up his hands—they were covered with dark, dried blood mixed with newer, bright red blood—and clasped them both back over the wound. "I don't know … " said Stanley.

"I'm taking you back." George started to grab Stan to lift him up.

"Jack's gone to get a stretcher, George."

"We're not waiting. The medics are everywhere. I can't see any one of them that aren't already helping someone." George was still lifting him up. The pain in Stanley's back was much worse when George moved him. He wrestled his brother onto one shoulder, and while down on one knee he finally got Stan on his back. George's helmet fell off, and he left it and both rifles on the spot. He started carrying Stan back to the tunnel, half piggyback, half thrown over his shoulder like a sack of potatoes. George's knees buckled under his brother's 115 pounds. He didn't notice.

George fell three times on his way back to the tunnel, a distance of 400 yards. There were men at the entrance who offered to help him, but he did not slow down. Down into the Tottenham Tunnel he went, his limp, ashen burden draped over his shoulders. Two hundred more yards was an aid station in a very large dugout. Both boys had noticed it on the way to the attack, and had marvelled at the size of it. There were orderlies and doctors crammed between dozens of litters, and there was an awful, mournful din of the moans of men.

"Over here," snapped a doctor, who pointed at one of the empty, blood-stained litters. He and another man helped George lower Stanley down. They both went to work unbuttoning his tunic and performing a cursory exam. Stan said, "I'm quite thirsty."

"Can't give you anything just yet, son," the doctor said.

"Thank you, Private," the doc said to George, excusing him.

"He's my brother," said George. The doctor and the orderly looked sharply at George.

The doctor spoke, "Now, you better go on back to your unit, son. We'll take good care of him. This is a field ambulance—a triage area. Your brother will be taken to a Casualty Clearing Station."

George was holding his brother's hand. "Yes, sir." Before he went, he gently squeezed Stan's hand. "You be strong, Stan. You fight. You're going to be well taken care of now." Stanley tried to smile, but he was much weaker than only moments before, and he was in a lot more pain. "Stan?" Stanley tried to look at him. "You should know, brother, we've taken the hill." Stan tried to nod his head, but in truth he could care less now. He knew he was in a bad way.

George had considerable confidence in the doctors. As he reached the main part of the tunnel, he turned and looked back at his older brother. The doctor was cutting his shirt off, and the orderly pulled Stan's belt through the belt loops of his trousers. The two men were working very matter-of-factly. They were not panicky. Seeing that made George feel like perhaps everything would be alright.

George made his way back to the battlefield to find his platoon. Picking his way along the base of Hill 145, it was late at night before he found any of his scattered company. Along the way, he saw Jack.

"I found him," said George.

"I tried to find a medic, but they were used up. Is he okay?" asked Jack.

"He was talking when I left him. They made me leave. I think he'll need surgery. I think maybe it's bad."

❦

In the dugout field ambulance in Tottenham tunnel, Stanley heard the doctor tell several orderlies to "take him out, he's got to go now for the CCS." There was a manila tag pinned to his blanket, over his chest. Two men from the Royal Army Medical Corps grabbed Stan's stretcher and hurried out of the dugout and down the long tunnel. Stan was completely helpless. He tried to lie still, but the tunnel was full of men hurrying in both directions. When they exited the tunnel, he was placed on a wooden cart about eight feet long set on railroad wheels. Four other men were crammed on with him. It was pulled by a draught horse with a soldier riding it bareback. Stan was in agony, as his back was hurting worse now. *Thank God,* Stan thought when they stopped a half mile down the track. When they unloaded the men, two soldiers— one of them a German prisoner—took the stretcher, and carried Stanley to a large tent near some railroad tracks and put him down. The big horse was unclipped and led around to the opposite end of the cart, where he was hooked to it again and started clopping back towards the front lines. Other men stopped and looked at the tag on his chest, but not at him. Not at his face. There were hundreds of men lying in and outside of the tent. Stan was feeling worse and thought that was odd, because his pain was waning.

One man came to check the tag and told Stan that the train was coming, but he would send someone over to talk with him. Moments later, a Catholic priest bent over Stanley and then sat next to him on an empty ammo crate.

"I'm Father Gillis, son. I'm going to stay with you until the train arrives."

Stanley lifted his hand and Capt. Gillis took it and held it. "It will be alright," said the priest. "Are you Catholic, son?"

Stanley winced, "No Father, Anglican."

Father Gillis smiled into Stan's constricted pupils. "That's close enough, lad. The good Lord doesn't care this day. Were you baptized?" Stan nodded. "What is your Christian name?"

"Stanley, Father."

"Let us pray, my son." Stanley closed his eyes. Father Gillis leant forward, and spoke in a very calm, sober voice. It was very comforting to Stanley.

"Stanley, do you resign yourself to the will of God in your recovery?"

"Yes."

Father Gillis held his hand and closed his eyes, and with his beautiful, low voice spoke so that only Stanley and God could hear; "*Per istam sanctum unctionem et suam piissimam misericordiam, indulgeat tibi Dominus quidquid per.*" He then made the sign of the cross and blessed Stanley.

"Thank you Father." Stan felt fine, but very tired—and thirsty.

"Is there anyone you would like to write a letter to? You can dictate it to me, and while you are convalescing I can mail it for you."

"Yes Father, I would appreciate it. Would it be too much to write two short ones?" The priest smiled and nodded. He took out a small tablet and pencil.

"These can both go to Oswald Boutilier, Hackett's Cove, Nova Scotia. Stan paused, the first one is to my girl, and it can be to Lily Durand (personal), care of Oswald Boutilier." Stanley gathered his thoughts. The chaplain put pen to paper, and Stanley spoke with measured words.

When Stan nodded, Father Gillis folded the tablet and put away the pencil.

"Thank you, Father," said Stanley.

"You're most welcome, son. I think I hear the train coming."

Stanley and Father Gillis talked for a few minutes more about Hackett's Cove, and Stan told him about all his siblings, and about Lily.

"Father?" Stan asked.

"Yes, Stanley?"

"Could you please tell me what the tag on my chest says?" The good priest lifted the tag and looked at it. "GSW Abdomen—Laparotomy."

Stanley just kept his eyes closed. He was tired of talking now. "Father, can you stay with me another minute? I'll probably sleep."

"Certainly, son," said Father Gillis.

The priest looked at Stanley's handsome face; his straight nose, perfect cheekbones and his close-cropped brown hair. *My Lord, he thought, what a waste.* Stanley did fall asleep, still holding the priest's hand. He was pale as a ghost. Stan's breathing became shallower and shallower, and fewer in between. Father Gillis put down the tablet and put his hand on Stan's chest. "Just a boy," he whispered. He kept his hand on Stanley and closed his eyes and prayed again. He could feel the slow, shallow breaths as Stan's body automatically hungered for oxygen: one breath, two, then another—and then, none. Stanley died just before 9:00 p.m., about three hours after a German 7.92x57mm bullet ripped into his abdomen, tore through his intestines, blew apart his inferior mesenteric artery, and lodged in a spinal vertebra.

Father Gillis finished praying again for the young boy's soul. He then performed the rest of his duties and collected Stan's possessions from his body. He labelled them, put them in a canvas bag and placed the bag in a box with hundreds of others.

PART 7

PRIDE AND ONWARD

———— ⌗⌗⌗ ————

The last resistance from the Bavarian defenders at Vimy Ridge, apart from occasional shelling from the plains to the east, was at the top of the Pimple, just northwest of Hill 145. It took a total of four days to mop up the ridge.

Early in the attack, before the charge of the 85th Battalion on the first evening, the rest of Vimy Ridge fell either on schedule or ahead of it. On April 9th, as the 1st and 2nd Divisions took their objectives straightaway, the Canadians overran enemy artillery positions, spun the cannon around, and fired the German's own 7.7 cm field pieces on the retreating infantry. Much of the German artillery was left behind because most of the horses needed to move them had died in the gas attack first thing in the morning.

Though Vimy would be secure in four days, the Second Battle of Arras would officially be over on the 16th of May and would be considered a stalemate, like so many battles on the Western Front. While huge tracts of territory had not been won, Vimy Ridge had been taken. The Germans had been pushed back several kilometres. New tactics had been conceived, tried and proved successful. The Germans east of Vimy *had* ceded important tracts of land, considering the tactical advantage from the summit looking east and north. Many objectives of the battle plan were met. The Canadians had gained the high ground above the Douai Plain, kickstarting the Western Front into a "war of movement." The Allies had drawn the German army into the open east of Vimy Ridge, putting it on the defensive. These were significant accomplishments. The victory at Vimy Ridge might have failed if the 85th, the last battalion left in the 4th Division, had failed to take Hill 145. The four Canadian divisions won the day.

Crown Prince Rupprecht of Bavaria had a lot to say about the Second Battle of Arras in his personal and war diaries, but perhaps most telling are two sentences specifically about the Allied artillery barrage of Vimy Ridge, dated 9 April: *"It is questionable if we can hold on in the face of artillery fire of this increasing intensity. This prompts the further question: in these circumstances, is there any point in continuing to prosecute the war?"*

In all wars—in all battles—conjecture is dangerous, and it is often best to lean on facts and learn lessons from them.

The German garrisons on the slopes of Vimy Ridge were for the most part long, deep tunnels pierced through the hill. There were hundreds of ditches in the Volker Tunnel, and hundreds more in Prinz Arnault Tunnel, but even with these fortifications, when the Canadians poured onto them with wave after wave of bayonets, the Boche either fought and died, were wounded or simply came out with their hands up. From Vimy Ridge proper, there were over 4,000 Germans captured. Canadian casualties were 3,598 dead, 7004 wounded. Casualty numbers for the German defenders of the ridge are unknown. No one knows. Not even the Germans.

Praise of the Canadian forces was written in Allied

dispatches and, later, in the newspapers. Their heroism was even mentioned in letters home by German P.O.W.s.

Friend and foe felt a thrill of admiration for the achievement of the Canadian troops, including some Americans who were there. Though they were fighting as part of the Canadian ranks, having joined out of a sense of duty, or less likely a sense of adventure, they felt no little pride for what they saw and participated in. There were tens of thousands of boys and men who came from the United States to fight with their "Canadian brothers."

William Clancy from Boston and late of Texas had taken the night train to Toronto and joined the 97th Battalion there. More than half that battalion were Americans supporting Canada and her fight for human liberty. (There were other battalions in the C.E.F. made up of Americans.) The 97th Battalion was in the 3rd Division, and was in the first wave of attack on Vimy. Before going over the top, Clancy pulled out a small American flag and fastened it to his bayonet. In the brutal fighting in the attack on the village of Thelus behind German lines, he was "shot through the body." He lived. In his first letter home after the Battle of Arras, he wrote:

"There are some awful sights. One young fellow got hit with a piece of shell. He asked me to remember him to all his people in New Jersey. The last words he said were, 'Bill Clancy, I am glad I gave my life for the freedom of the world.' He died in my arms. So I let him lie, but just before he died, he kissed my flag. Poor chap, I didn't see him any more, for when I went forward under heavy fire I met my accident. Old Fritz sent a shell over and it struck near me, blowing up some of the ammunition. Of course, I can only remember now that I was being dug out from a trench where I was buried. Now I am

*in England and have about recovered from the effects.
I am waiting to be transferred to the American army,
though I have reservations about leaving my brave
Canadian friends."*

Many nationalities—including millions of Americans—
criticized the late commitment of troops by President Wilson,
but the Canadian soldiers that fought side by side with the
35,000 Americans who joined the C.E.F. did not complain.
While there may have been some difficulties in the courtship
when the Yanks first signed up, they dissolved once the men
had been through combat together. They were suited to be
brothers in arms.

☙

Five days after the attack on Vimy Ridge had begun, the 85th
Battalion was marched back to their home base at Bouvigny
Huts. They were dead tired after the worst of experiences.
George was terribly worried about Stanley—all the boys who
knew him were. He wasn't sure how to tell Hazen. He hadn't
been able to find his cousin since the start of the battle, but
he was on no casualty list. George and Jack had asked several
N.C.O.s, but nobody had any news. There were just too
many casualties. Hazen was going to struggle with the news
of Stanley's death.

The Y.M.C.A. had set up a tent at the edge of camp,
and each man was given a mug of tea and a big square of
gingerbread. George, Jack and Colin found each other and sat
under a huge elm. They hadn't seen a tree with intact branches
or leaves on it for five days. The gingerbread was splendid.
The men were heartened by the human touch in such an
inhumane place.

During two days of rest in camp at Bouvigny Huts, the entire C.E.F. reflected on their accomplishment. On the way to breakfast on the 16th of April, a sergeant and a lieutenant who looked no older than George stopped Colin, Jack and George on the road.

"Private Boutilier?" asked the sergeant.

"That's me," George saluted.

The youngster spoke, "I'm Lieutenant Holland, and this is Sergeant Waddin. We've been looking for you." During his time in the army, George had so far kept to himself and stayed out of trouble. Quite suddenly he realized this might be about Stanley.

"Let's take a knee," said the lieutenant, who motioned for them to step off the road. They did.

"I'm afraid it's about your brother," said Holland. George's stomach flipped.

"I'm sorry to report, Private, that your brother didn't survive his wound." The Lieutenant waited for a moment for George to compose himself. George was sniffing softly. Jack and Colin put their arms around him. "He's buried already, I'm afraid, in Pas de Calais, just outside of CCS 'B'—if you'd like to go and pay your respects."

George collected himself and thanked the lieutenant. He knew the young officer didn't have to notify him personally, and he appreciated it. The three started back towards the barracks. No one was hungry now. Colin said, "Wait"—and caught the lieutenant as he and his sergeant were walking away.

"Sir?" Colin asked.

"Yes, Private?"

"Is there a list posted? We're missing a mate, Private Hazen Gibbons, 'C' Company." The Lieutenant looked seriously at his sergeant.

"There's no list yet, Private." The young officer paused for a minute. "But I can tell you he also was killed in action." George felt his knees buckle. *Jesus, not Hazen too.*

"I know, because I was with him," said the lieutenant. The three boys were visibly shaken but composed themselves. "We were down by the Pimple on the second day. Our companies were all mixed together. He was helping me with what was left of my platoon. He got hit along with two of my men and died instantly." The boys looked at each other, each face showing profound pain. "I can tell you—he didn't feel a thing." That didn't help. It only confused Colin and Jack. George was too numb to feel anything but enormous loss. Loss that could never be fully assuaged. Colin thanked the officer again, but before they left he asked, "And Private Gibbons... do you know where he's buried?"

The lieutenant measured his words but found no way to communicate an answer. So he just told them, as gently and as adroitly as he could, "He isn't, I'm afraid. It was artillery." (The pause in the answer was uncomfortably long.) "There was nothing."

The boys could only stare at the bearer of such bad news. Then the young lieutenant, this time without measuring his words, said the one thing he could have that might someday help them all deal with such a painful loss. "Private Gibbons died a hero, and he will stay buried in the damned slopes of Vimy Ridge with hundreds of other brave men, from both sides." The lieutenant glared in the direction of the ridge. "Forever, I suppose."

The men walked back to the barracks.

Back at camp, George asked the boys if he could be alone. Colin and Jack left and said they'd be back in an hour. George lay on his cot, his forearm over his eyes. No one bothered him, but soldiers were coming and going, so he left. As he walked along the road to Bethune, the sun was high, and it was warm. It seemed more like spring than only a week ago. *Jesus*, he thought. *Poor Stan—and Hazen! What now? What will Mother do when she finds out?* He would have to write the folks, but what to say? What about Lily? Everything had changed, he knew, Hackett's Cove will be changed—everything was different. He felt numb. *It was supposed to be me*, he thought.

There were farmers working, still harrowing fields, once he was far from camp. Some of the farmers were taking a break. The men were lying in the warm spring sun along the first ploughed row. The horses were hobbled nearby. George stood and walked over to the Belgians. He still had tears in his eyes, and his throat was sore. The horses let George stroke their heads and pat their sides. The farmers watched and ate their cheese and baguettes. They did not care. They were used to soldiers walking the fields and petting the horses. The armies were full of farm boys longing for home—hoping to forget their place in the world, if only for a few minutes. Occasionally, a soldier on leave would ask if he could help card a horse, or go for a short ride. George didn't ride very often, but he found comfort around horses. He always had. He whispered to the Belgian. "My brother's gone, old boy, and my cousin too. I've got my mates, but now I'm all alone." The big horse liked George. He nudged him with his nose and almost pushed the tiny soldier down.

For the next two weeks, George asked nothing of anyone, but questioned everything. *What the hell were we thinking?* What would home be like for him now... for anybody? Stan had been the favourite son; nobody would say such a thing, but it was obvious. George wondered of his own fate; what would he do after the war—if he lived through it? Could he even go home? What the hell was this war even *for*? The few German prisoners he had met seemed like nice guys, actually, and they asked the same questions. They didn't know either. What a screwed-up mess. His head was swimming. Every night in his dreams, he carried Stan on his back towards Tottenham tunnel. He could see himself laying his brother, wincing with pain, onto the stretcher in the triage dugout. He was holding his hand, squeezing it, but not too tight. Night after night, he awoke with tears in his eyes. In the few moments when he wasn't thinking about Stanley, he thought of poor Hazen. It all was becoming more than he could bear. Increasingly each day, George withdrew inside himself.

In the days after the battle, there were many toasts, celebrations and speeches. Even those who had lost close friends seemed elated because of the victory, but not George. There were baseball games, track and field events, and plays put on by men of the signal corps dressed up as women. George, who in his unassuming fashion had always participated, found no joy in the games. Being around his mates made things worse. He felt very disconnected.

A week after the battle, it rained. The boys were sitting around the barracks shooting the shit. Jack was playing cards with two fellows from "A" Company. George was pacing, slowly. He would walk to the open door and watch the raindrops fall into the puddle at the foot of the steps, and then wheel around and walk to the back of the building and stand next to the little coal stove. He checked to see if it needed stoking and then repeated the process. No one noticed.

"Did you guys hear about Anderson?" asked one of the poker players, as he inspected his cards.

"Anderson from "C" Company?" asked Jack.

"No, Cap'n Anderson," said the man. "He's from Baddeck."

"Hear about it? I saw it," said one of the "A" Company boys. "He was a beast on 145."

"Captain Percy Anderson?" asked Jack. George paced by them, and then came back.

"I was on the left flank," said Jack. "I never saw him."

"Yeah," said the second man. "We could see you "C" Company boys the whole time. There was Anderson, walking around, cool as a cucumber, giving orders with bullets whizzing around everywhere. He jumped into what was left of the Boche trench, shot an officer dead and kept firing until his pistol was out of bullets. Two Germans rushed him, and he beat the shit out of them with his fists." All the men were listening now, with obvious pride.

The man went on; "We saw one of your guys get ripped through the hip and couldn't get up. Anderson could see him, and had his own men around him, but the MG08s were working pretty hard, spitting up rocks and dirt all around the wounded guy. So Anderson ran to the guy himself, and carried him to a safe spot where the medics got him."

George was feeling low. He was wholly sick with sorrow. He walked past the card table again, pacing quicker now. "Jesus Christ!" George yelled at the poker player. "Everyone was there! You gonna tell the Goddamned stories the rest of your life?" George stormed out into the rain, right through the big puddle at the foot of the steps, and walked off down the road.

The man looked across the table at Jack.

"We lost a couple of mates on the 9th," explained Jack. "One was his cousin, the other was his brother."

The man looked down at his cards. "Christ," was all he said.

Several weeks after the battle, The Maple Leaf Concert Band played a concert for the men at the Y.M.C.A. hut at Bouvigny Huts. All were urged to attend. The tunes were lively and fun and lyrical. They were meant to cheer up the boys who, in their thinned ranks, were missing their chums. George did not go. George was focusing on one thing now—not to cry in public. That would be the end of him. He knew that, but he struggled with the natural wave of emotions that swept over him day and night.

It wasn't only Stan and Hazen being killed; it was the whole goddamned thing. It was the war. George, like so many boys in every country involved, had lied about his age to enlist. He had never cursed before, but now he was asking anyone who wanted to talk about the battle, "What the fuck is it all for?" Before France, he had never had a drink, but now he never passed up a snort of hooch when it was offered. He had never tried a cigarette, but now he smoked regularly. It wasn't long until he didn't speak at all unless spoken to.

Rather than going to hear the Maple Leaf Concert Band, George instead sought out Capt. H. B. Cooke, a company chaplain. George knew that Captain Cooke was Anglican, and he had seen how the officer could help out and handle a mule train, so he respected him. George found him billeted in a small chapel near the village of Lievin. He had to wait for almost an hour, but he finally got to visit with the chaplain. They both sat on empty ammunition crates.

"How can I help, son?"

George sat uneasily. "I, ah, don't know exactly, Reverend." The skin at the corner of his right eye twitched uncontrollably. Captain Cooke noticed it as he waited patiently for George to express himself. The nearly eighteen-year-old soldier just sat on the crate, with both arms folded tight across his chest.

"I, um, suppose I'm a bit tired, sir," said George. The reverend smiled and nodded.

"My ... my brother was killed on the 9th, and my cousin too. We're from Hackett's Cove. I haven't gone a day without hearing shells drop for three months." The captain sat patiently, letting him speak.

"I'm afraid, Reverend, that I'm not myself anymore. I can't sleep, and then I'm tired all day." There was a long pause. "I was with my brother near the end, but I didn't know it then." George didn't even realize that there were tears in his eyes. He mustn't let anyone see that. He'd seen some sad fellows with shell shock and he knew what people said about them—what everybody said about them. "Cowards ... " or "he can't take it." And "yellow."

The captain looked into George's eyes. "How old are you, son?"

"Seventeen, sir. I'll be eighteen in a month." George looked at the floor.

"Did you lie about your age?" asked Captain Cooke.

"Yes, sir," replied George.

"Well, son, let's you and me chat for a while." Captain Reverend Cooke sat back and lit a pipe. "Do you want to talk about your brother? Or your cousin?" he asked.

"I dunno, sir."

"Then why not try and tell me what you're feeling. Is it physical?" asked the Reverend.

George had to think about that; most of what he was feeling was in his head, he figured. He did feel sick to his stomach a lot and he wasn't sleeping. "I don't know," was all he could reply.

"All I can tell you is that since Vimy, I've been in a dark place," George continued. "Mornings are the worst. For the past couple of weeks, I would feel melancholy and tell myself tomorrow will be better, but in the morning it would be worse. Sometimes my face will twitch, and I worry it won't go away. Other times, I feel like my skin is burning, like it's on fire. Of course, it's not. It makes no sense." George looked from the Captain's face to the floor again. "Sometimes I'm terrified that I won't be able to urinate."

"Son," said the Reverend, "This is a terrible, terrible war. I'm sure you've been a good soldier. You just have to get through this, now."

"Well, sir—there's a reason I came to speak to you, instead of going to hospital," said George.

"What is that reason, Private?"

"I feel… I've lost my faith." The captain sat back in his chair, and took the pipe from his mouth. George went on, "I feel I've lost my way. I feel so alone, for every minute."

The reverend leaned forward and put his hand on George's shoulder. "What you're feeling, lad, is no strange thing. Oh, sure, it's strange in that we don't yet know much about melancholy, but it's been around since Adam. Have you read the Old Testament?" George nodded, and gave the Reverend a look as though to say, *Don't ask me to quote much of it.*

Captain Reverend Cooke said, "Much was taken from Job, if you recall." George nodded. The captain went on; "Job said, '*Why is the light given to those in misery, and life to the bitter of soul, to those who long for death that does not come, who search for it more than for hidden treasure, who are filled with gladness and rejoice when they reach the grave?*' Job didn't seek death, George, or lie down in misery, even though everything he held dear had been taken from him. He lived his life for the Lord and was rewarded with a full life and ten more children."

The Reverend, still holding George's shoulder, squeezed it and said, "I've often wondered—with ten more children, perhaps there was misery piled on misery." For the first time in over a month, George almost smiled.

George walked back to his billet. The moon and stars were out, shining brightly, and it was very cold. Occasionally, an artillery round would explode off in the distance, and no matter how far off it was, George flinched terribly. His gait had a slight limp, and he had no idea why.

That very day, over 3000 miles away in Hackett's Cove, Oswald Boutilier was sorting the mail bins in the little post office that was part of the Cork & Pickle, the Boutiliers' general store and home. The two oldest daughters were in the kitchen, helping their mother clean up after breakfast. Oswald prepared the mail just as he had done a thousand times before. He poured the small bag of envelopes and packages onto the wide sorting table next the mail boxes. He flattened out the pile, and started sorting; the Dauphinees' letters in their little box, the Slauenwhites', in theirs, the Richters' and so on.

Oswald could hear two of the girls arguing in the adjacent great room of the store and diner. They were filling napkin holders at the lunch counter. Oswald peered through the sliding window that separated the store from the little post office room. "Girls!" he snapped. "Quiet down now. I'm trying to concentrate."

Both sisters stopped their teasing. Oswald froze over the sorting table. He hadn't seen it before. Staring him right in the face from the top of the pile was a letter addressed to him and to Clara. It looked official. It was from the government. It looked ominous and it looked hideous.

Oswald picked it up. He plunked himself down into the old wooden swivel chair. The girls in the next room were arguing again, but he did not hear them now. He stared at the ugly, manila envelope with the Canadian Expeditionary Force stamp on it. *It's bad*, he thought. *It has to be bad.* Oswald glanced over his shoulder to see if anyone was watching him. No one was. The girls had left the great room. He could hear Clara and their oldest daughter in the kitchen. He slid the post office window shut. He was shaking.

Oswald turned in the chair with his back to the window. No one could see him from inside the store. He was alone in the little post office, and he *felt* alone. Again, he stared at the small envelope. *Was it Stanley? George? Was one of them gone, God forbid, or only wounded?* He picked up his ivory letter opener, pointed it into the envelope and ripped it along the seam. His hands shook even more. He took out four pieces of paper, closed his eyes and took a deep, trembling breath. He looked at the first page and read it. It was a form.

Army Form C. 104-82
No. 18929
Infantry Record Office
Arras Station
21-4-1917

Dear Sir,

It is my painful duty to inform you that a report has this day been received from the war office notifying the death of (No.) *222154* (Rank) *Private*
(Name) *Stanley Oswald Boutilier* (Regiment) *85ᵗʰ Battalion*

Which occurred at *Vimy Ridge* on the *9ᵗʰ* of *April*, and I am to express to you the sympathy and regret of the Army Council at your loss.

The cause of death was *Killed in Action*.

If any articles of private property left by the deceased are found, they will be forwarded to you from this office. Be aware some time will probably elapse before their receipt, and when received they cannot be disposed of until authority is received from the War Office.

Application regarding the disposal of any such personal effects, or of any amount that may eventually be found to be due to the late soldier's estate, should be addressed to "The Secretary, War Office, London, S.W., and marked outside "Effects."

I am,

Sir,

Your Obedient Servant,

Capt. RM Larsen,

Officer in charge of Records

All Oswald could do was to stare at the cold, sparse form and blink his eyes. His heart sank. His heart raced and then slowed. *My boy!* Tears welled up in his eyes, and at once he coughed and spat and began to cry. He glanced over his shoulder at the store room, and toward the kitchen. No one had ever seen him cry, not even Clara. He was still alone in his grief in the little post office. He put his head in his hands. He had never felt such pain. He started to vomit, but held it back. He looked over his shoulder again. Still the store and diner were empty.

Oswald, the strong, capable man to whom many people looked for common sense and wisdom, had no idea what to do. He opened the door between the Cork & Pickle and the attached post office. "Girls!" he yelled.

Eleanor, twelve years old, one of the "middle girls," came skipping into the store.

"Yes, PaPa?" she asked.

"Elle, go get Cyril," said Oswald. She hadn't noticed that her father could hardly stand. She hadn't noticed the tremble in his voice.

"Yes, PaPa." Eleanor spun around and ran up the stairs at the back of the store that led to the living area of the building. Oswald slid the window closed again and eased himself back into the chair. He could hear his eldest son running down the stairs. Eleanor waited by the kitchen door, watching the post office. She had never seen her father look scared and it confused her.

"Yes, Father?" Cyril was at the door.

"Come in, Son," said Oswald. "Shut the door."

Oswald was holding the letter in his lap. Cyril could see the redness in his father's worried face. He saw his father's eyes. Cyril was the businessman in the family. Astute and serious, he lived in Halifax with his young wife but came home every week for two days to help his father. The twenty-four-year-old's face drooped. He knew immediately that something was wrong.

"It's Stanley." said Oswald. The father searched for something in the eyes of his eldest son—help, maybe. Perhaps support. He saw only tears, but behind the tears dwelled a compassion so deep the bond between the two men would never wane.

He gave the form letter to Cyril. Oswald then looked at the second letter that accompanied it. In his initial grief, he hadn't even looked at the second note. Simultaneously the father and son read the letters. The second letter was a hand written one. As Oswald read it, still in shock, he again fought the feeling of being sick to his stomach.

General Hospital No. 18
B.E.F. France
10 April, 1917
222154 Pte. Stanley Boutilier
85th Battalion, NS Highlanders

Dear Sir,

I enclose a note dictated by your son, S.O. Boutilier whom I saw as a patient last night. You will prize it, for it was dictated by him when he was dying. I don't think he knew whether he was or not. His breath was coming short. I repeated the 23rd Psalm and the Lord's Prayer & he said them after me word for word. His abdomen was bleeding and he had no chance. He was a fine boy. His brother carried him from the field to the triage station, and was able to say goodbye.

Let pride then be mingled with your tears.

We laid him to rest in a little military cemetery at Pas de Calais by the side of several of his comrades who have died that England might live. His should be commended to the loving care of Our Heavenly Father, who will keep him until that day when you will find him again and never more be parted.

May God comfort and keep you.

Enclosed also is a note for Miss Lily Durand in your care.

Yours sincerely,

Fr. J.S. Gillis, W.S.A. Chaplain

The next page was addressed to "Oswald Boutilier, Hackett's Cove, NS, and wife."

Dear Mother and Father,

I am sorry to tell you I have been wounded. I am waiting to go to a Base Hospital for surgery. At this point I don't know what it was that wounded me. But I am not in any pain. There is a very fine priest here with me and, Mother, you will be happy to know that we prayed some. I think I will be off to Blighty.

Mother and Dad, you should be happy to know that George carried me from the battlefield. We were still being shot at, and the medics were all busy with other soldiers. George was very brave and he never wavered. Jack Fraser was the first one to find me.

Well don't worry about me, I am comfortable, and God willing, we will see each other soon.

Love to you both and all the sibs. Please tell Belle I loved her card. She is quite an artist.

Your Stanley

And the final page was addressed; "Lily Durand, Hackett's Cove, NS, care of Oswald Boutilier, same." Oswald did not read the short note. He folded it in half and put it in the envelope.

"Cyril," said Oswald. Cyril nodded with tears rolling down his cheeks. He seemed in shock. "You know how much we love all you children." Cyril nodded again.

"My God, your mother is going to take this hard." There was a pause while both men tried to compose themselves. Oswald removed the omnipresent handkerchief from his shirt pocket and handed it to his son. Cyril wiped his face and took some deep breaths as he passed it back to his father, who also used it to dry his eyes.

The men sat in silence for a full ten minutes and tried to adjust as best they could to their new world.

Oswald sat straight up in his chair, took another deep breath and said, "Well, Son, gather the family. I think it should be everybody at once. We will get through this—but if you could stand with me, Cee, I'd appreciate it." Cyril threw his arms around his father. When they finally separated, the men walked out of the post office, through the store, and into the living room at the back of the building. Eleanor still stood by the foot of the stairs, worried about her father. Oswald bent down to her and smiled weakly, and kissed her on the forehead. "Go get Mother and the rest of the family, honey. Tell them to come to the living room." She left at once.

The whole family entered the living room and sat wherever they could. Oswald and Cyril stood side by side next to the fire place. Nothing like this had ever happened before. There had never been "family meetings," or such things. Clara looked very concerned. She had perched herself on the edge of the divan, as all the seats were taken. Oswald whispered something to Cyril who went over and picked up Belle, the youngest, saying, "Let's give Momma a seat." Clara slid onto the divan.

Oswald spoke. "There's no easy way to say this. We all know from the radio and the papers that the Canadians took Vimy Ridge from the Germans. They're saying it will help bring the war to an earlier end." Oswald paused. His voice was shaking slightly. "They're saying the battle might save a million lives." He paused and took the letter from his pocket. Clara gasped and put her hand over her mouth. Her eyes were wide.

Oswald spoke again with a shaky voice. "Our Stanley— Clara shrieked—was killed on Vimy Ridge."

A horrifying sound arose from the room. Gasps, cries and moans so mournful it made Cyril sick to hear it. The crying came from all the sisters deep in their guts, the kind of cry that only comes from profound, painful loss. Clara fell back in her seat, sobbed hard twice, like she was choking, and fainted. The youngest boy, Guy, who was only ten, sat in disbelief; not crying, not making a sound … he just stared straight ahead.

Oswald immediately lifted up his wife and rocked Clara in his arms while Ann, the oldest girl ran sobbing for a cold, wet towel. Amidst the crying, Clara came to. Oswald's piteous, soft pleading for her to awaken may have helped, but when she did, she kept whispering, "My boy, my Stanley."

After twenty minutes, with most of the girls out of breath, someone asked about George. Was there any word from George?

Oswald spoke up, still adjusting the damp towel on Clara's forehead, "There's a note from the priest who was with him—he mentioned that George carried Stan from the field, and got to say his goodbyes." As far as we know, George is alright. Most of the women exhaled, as if to say, *Thank God for that.*

Oswald measured his words. "Now, family; this is news we feared. News we'll always have to deal with...but we must be strong, and be prepared to go on with each day. We must help each other at a time like this. We must each of us pray today. In an hour, we'll get our coats and walk up to the church. Cyril, do you still have the key?"

Cyril nodded. "Yes, sir."

"Okay then," said Oswald, "in an hour we'll meet in the store." Oswald left the living room, went to the big window at the store front and put out a sign: "Closed for the Day." He returned to the little post office attached to the side of the store and finished sorting the mail on the sorting table. He snapped each envelope into the appropriate box, no different than he did every workday, except this time, tears streamed down his cheeks.

The family did meet in the big main part of the store. They did walk the 300 yards up the shore road to St. Peter's Anglican Church, and they did pray together. For Stanley and for George. Little Belle, only eight, did not understand completely what was happening, but she cried just as hard as anyone.

On the way back from the church, a few automobiles

passed the troupe. The neighbours honked their horns and waved as they went by. When Arthur Dauphinee saw their faces, he quickly worked out what must have happened. It was the same look families always had when they had lost their young men to the sea—but which boy?

The rest of the day and the next were spent with the family trying to digest the news and to mourn. Oswald had received the letters on Thursday. On Friday afternoon, he read the letters aloud to the older children who wanted to hear them. By Friday night, Clara was brave enough to talk through her tears about arrangements. The first two things to do, in her mind, were to notify Lily and her parents and the pastor of St. Peter's. The local community would all know before Sunday service anyway.

On Saturday morning, Oswald started the Russell and added a few gallons of fuel. He and Cyril drove along the shore road and up the windy hill to the Durand's farm. Once he got both of Lily's parents together in the old farmhouse kitchen, he told them the news. Neither Oswald nor Cyril cried, but they were sombre. Both the Durands rose from their chairs and gave the Boutilier men hugs—even the fathers hugged. Lily's parents got their coats, and they all left for Halifax. None of the passengers spoke the entire way. All that could be heard for the two hour ride were the rockers of the Russell, the sound of the macadam under the tires, and Mrs. Durand's soft sobs.

☙☞

When Lily floated down the stairs at her boarding house and into the sitting room, all the regular residents who sat there on weekend days were gone from the room. The house mistress was not present either, which Lily thought was odd. She saw her parents first, and said "Mama! Father!" Then she realized her future in-laws were there as well. All four visitors stood up as she reached the bottom step. He parents both tried to smile. Her mother could only bite her lower lip ... just like her daughter often did.

The looks on their faces told her everything. Her legs went out from under her. Her father and Oswald caught her and helped her into a chair. Her mother was sobbing now, and reached out to hold both of Lily's hands. She looked up at her father for reassurance. He could only look at her lovingly and said in a squeaking voice, "He's gone, love."

Lily's cries became disturbingly loud. She buried her face in her father's chest. The cries erupted from somewhere deep down inside her. They were almost unbearable to hear. Cyril stood by to help in any way he could. Lil's mother massaged her young daughter's hands, and her father rubbed her back. The sounds coming from the sitting room were heart-wrenching for everyone in the house.

"When?" asked Lily.

"At Vimy Ridge," whispered Oswald.

'No," Lily shook her head. "When did you find out?"

"Thursday morning," said Oswald.

Lily let go of her mother's hands and put her face in her palms. After a few minutes, her father told his wife to take Lily to her room to get a few things packed. "Come home for a few days, Lily dear. We can bring you back on the train when you're ready." Both women walked slowly up the stairs. When they got to the room, Lily threw her arms around her mother. "Oh, Mama!" she cried. "I love him so, Mama." The women stood embracing in the middle of the tiny boarding room and cried and cried and cried.

The service on Sunday at St. Peter's was as painfully sad. The Boutiliers sat as usual about halfway down the pews on the left hand side. The Durands could not bring themselves to go to service—Lily needed a few days to recover. Clara's sister, Hattie, attended as usual, but this day sat next to her grieving sibling. Hattie Gibbons mourned and cried with her extended family and prayed for them. She couldn't tear her mind away from Hazen, however. As close as he was to Stanley, did he get to say goodbye? Did he see Stan die, God forbid? Was her son alright? Her only son? These were trying times.

The entire congregation knew of the news. All parish members stopped at one point to offer support to Clara and Oswald. Reverend Arnold asked for the congregation to pray not only for the soul of Stanley, but for George and their cousin Hazen, fighting in France, whose fates were still unknown.

On Sunday afternoon, the disconsolate Lily came downstairs, insistent on making her own tea. Her father felt it would be better to wait a few days to tell her about the note from Stanley. He had been overruled by his wife.

"Lily dear," said her mother. "We wanted you to get over the initial shock, but there is a note for you from Stanley that came, care of Oswald." Lily spun around. Her father put up the palm of his hand and said, "Honey, you can have some time first, or have it now, whichever you think is best."

Lily's look of shock faded while she pondered for only a few seconds. "No...I want it now." She sat down at the kitchen table and her father took the note from his pocket. Before handing it to her, he said, "Oswald told me no one has read this." He slid the note to her. "Neither have we."

"We'll give you a moment," said her dad. Both parents started to rise from their chairs, but Lily stopped them.

"No. I want you here. You're all I have. I don't want to be alone. I did before, but not right now." Lily was very brave. She opened the letter. Before she read a word, she noticed it was quite short.

Dear Miss. Durand,

I enclose a note dictated by your fiancé, S.O. Boutilier, whom I tended to last night, as he lay wounded. It was dictated by him when he was dying. I don't think he knew whether he was or not. He was very comfortable, and spoke of you with great affection. I am a Catholic priest, and he received the Extreme Unction.

I hope this helps you cope with your great loss. May God comfort and console you in your time of grief.

Yours sincerely,

Fr. J.S. Gillis, W.S.A. Chaplain

Dearest Lily,

I hope you are doing well. I am sorry to tell you I've been wounded at Vimy Ridge. I don't know if it was some shrapnel or a bullet. I am waiting for my chance to go to a Base Hospital for surgery. I think this will send me to Blighty.

I want you to not worry about me. I'm being well taken care of, and I am not afraid or uncomfortable. Keep studying hard, and if anything bad does happen to me, I want you to remember me, but enjoy a good life. Please do that for both of us.

With much love always,

Your Stanley

It would take weeks for Lily to even start the healing process. It would take months for her to begin to feel herself again, but deep down she knew she would never be whole. She took the last two remaining weeks of school off, but committed to returning to Halifax in the fall. By the end of the summer, she could smile at friends and family again, and she stayed close to the Boutiliers. Oswald and Clara became even more like a second set of parents to her. They visited often and helped her in any way they could. However, Lily found she could not go back to St. Peter's church. She tried once, but the soft, suppressed sobs of Clara's weeping were too much for her. In that church, Lily's cross to bear was made of brass, about fourteen inches high. It had been mounted on the wall in the back alongside another for Robert Arthur Boutilier, a distant relative who had died at the Somme. It seemed no matter where Lily looked during the service, Stanley's name on the little cross burned bright in the church's ambient light. It was too difficult. She attended service in Indian Point instead of Hackett's Cove.

Throughout the summer, the Boutiliers and their neighbours did their best to continue with life. Oswald still worked hard every day to provide for the family. The children did their chores and argued with each other about silly things. Cyril was finishing up a business class in Halifax. Those neighbours who lived close by visited and brought baked goods and told the family how proud they were of the boys overseas. Clara would nod and try to smile in appreciation. Each night, she would cry as she readied herself for bed. Oswald would hold her for as long as she needed.

In July one Wednesday morning, Oswald left the post office with Anne in charge, and walked up the path through the woods with Cyril beside him to Hattie Gibbons' little farmhouse. Oswald sat at the kitchen table in the house Hazen had grown up in as an only child. He gave the little form letter to his sister-in-law. It was the same C-104-82 Form that Oswald had received with the news about Stanley, and although worded differently in the underlined spaces that allowed handwriting, it said the same thing: "Killed in Action."

There was no note from a chaplain. There was no explanation.

In the little communities of Hackett's Cove, Indian Point, and Peggy's Cove, the healing of each new loss overlapped with a previous one. In August, Oswald Boutilier sent a letter to Capt. A. T. Croft, Adjutant in the 85th Battalion, asking for any news of George. The boy had not written home since the month before Vimy.

PART 8

BACK TO BUSINESS

—◇◊◊◇—

When the 85th Battalion of the Nova Scotia Highlanders boarded trains in Surrey, England to fight in the muddy fields of France and Flanders, the battalion strength was seventy-six officers, and 967 other ranks. In March, April and May of 1917, the battalion lost seventy-nine men at the Second Battle of Arras (fifty of those killed in action died during their already famous assault on Vimy Ridge), approximately seventeen percent of their ranks. Five months later at Passchendaele (Third Battle of Ypres), the 85th would go into battle with only 688 men. Of these men, nearly 400 would be killed or wounded.

Passchendaele, for the Canadians, was nothing like the operations on Vimy Ridge. The plans for the battle were not practiced save for a few days before going over the top. There was no massive barrage, at least nothing like on Vimy, and it's worth noting that the battle at Passchendaele was planned by British and French officers. Unlike Vimy, the Canadians were only minimally involved in the development of the plans. Still, after their valour at Vimy, the C.E.F. would figure heavily in any strategic plan.

The offensives along the Western Front had been laid out as far back as December 1916. The Franco-British Nivelle Offensive was an operation designed to force a decisive battle with the Germans. The battle plans and phases of the Nivelle Offensive evolved with each success and failure. Although the battles at Arras (especially Vimy Ridge), Lens, Verdun, and the French attacks at Aisne were all *strategically* successful, they never forced the German army's hand. The Nivelle Plan was suspended by May. Allied attention shifted focus to another plan which had long been in the works, the Third Battle of Ypres. The offensive at Ypres was part of the Franco-British operations which previously had hinged on the Nivelle Plan, to capture the high ground on a series of hills and ridges that ran south, east and then north of the Belgian city of Ypres (Passchendaele being the most northerly of them). From Passchendaele, the lowlands of Flanders stretched out for miles to the east. There was hardly a spot of ground in all this distance not easily visible from that crest. With the hills in British hands, the great advantage long held by the Germans would pass to the Allies. The extreme northern edge of the famous Hindenburg Line might be lost.

This would allow the Allies to control some of the important German-held railways, force the Germans to divert troops from Aisne and quite possibly make the Boche either run or fight. Also, if the Allies could break through to the coast of Belgium, they might be able to destroy the German submarine pens there, which would substantially reduce the loss of merchant ships.

The plan was straightforward enough. The problem was the weather, the time of year when it could be started (late summer into autumn). The French had lost so many men under the Nivelle Plan, Nivelle himself was sacked. There were mutinies in the French Army to deal with. The smart thing to do would be to wait for the Americans to organize in full strength on the continent and get them into the fight. Canadian General Arthur Currie urged this approach in four different dispatches. Other high-ranking Allied officers agreed. It would take some of the burden off the British and her dominions, and let the French troops regroup under new command. Even British Prime Minister Lloyd George was against the offensive. Despite the cautions, Field Marshall Douglas Haig, Commander of the British Expeditionary Force, pushed ahead with it. Though many people were against the offensive at Ypres at the end of July, Haig did have his reasons. He and Foch felt compelled to keep applying pressure on the German armies. To wait for any reason might result in an already stalemated war lasting many more years, perhaps decades. No one knew. The biggest reason to keep the offensives going was Russia. The Germans were already diverting troops by the thousands from the east to the Western Front. If the Allies waited too long, a million men could bolster the German lines.

Although the Second Battle of Arras had effectively ended in a stalemate (even after the triumph on Vimy Ridge), as were most of the offensives on either side for two years, the German armies *were* on their heels. Fortunately, for the Central Powers, the German 4th Army was effectively still at full fighting strength.

❧

As summer arrived, and the fields of Flanders, Belgium, and France filled with flowers and crops, George, Colin and Jack tried their best to get on with the business of soldiering. There were some nice summer "down" days in July and August, with theatre-going, sports, and band music. George still preferred to keep himself to himself. There were never more than five or six days of rest and relaxation behind the lines; the men were still drilled most days. There was always work to be done on the trenches all along the Western Front. Although The 85th Battalion did their share, they were no longer thought of as a "work battalion." Not by a long shot. The unit also had their share of turns "in the lines" throughout the summer. There were many more casualties.

Throughout the summer, it seemed to the men they were moving over every inch of Flanders and Belgium. There were skirmishes here, reconnaissance missions there—and all the while, shelling and sniping. Being kept busy helped George cope with the depression he felt. He spent a couple more evenings with the chaplain, which seemed to help him, though he was no longer going to church service on Sundays.

Finally, in early September, he wrote a reply to the letters he had received from home. He had kept only one—a short note his father had sent in June, over two months earlier. It was the letter informing him they knew about Stan. It read:

2 June 1917
Dear George,

I hope this letter finds you well. We received the news about Stanley four days ago. He was a good boy, and he did what he could and now it is all over. We will have to be reconciled with the will of our Father in Heaven. It is hard on us all but worse I think for your dear mother and Lily.

There was a kind note from the chaplain who helped Stan, and I know you were there. You were the younger one, and I'm sure you are having a tough time. But we are your family, and it is hard not to have word from you. Please send a short note to your dear mother

soon, and try to be safe.
Hoping this gets to you and the war will be over
soon. So God be with you, my boy.
Your affectionate Father,
OGB

George read the letter again and wondered again if he ever could go home. He also wondered how Lily was getting on; *Father telling her... that must have been terrible.* He was fond of Lily, and he thought about how distraught she would be. He would look in on her, he thought, if he ever got home.

Lily was getting on with life as best she could. By the time George finally wrote home in the autumn, she had returned to Halifax and resumed her teaching career. She got herself settled into the boarding house on Robie Street. When she wasn't correcting papers or in school, she would go for walks on the West End where she was less likely to run into the ranks of servicemen like she would see along the docks. They were everywhere, really, but less so in the West End. Each one made her think of Stan and her lost world. She still thought of him every day. She figured she always would. Lily wasn't at the point yet of entertaining thoughts of a future. Not beyond teaching. She poured everything into the children in hopes of making their futures a little brighter. Her anguish was sickening. Little did she know that the only boy left overseas whom she knew well was flailing in a sea of sorrow so deep, he wasn't sure how long he could tread water.

❧

By July the Third Battle of Ypres was underway, although no one called it that at the time. It was just another trench fight on the Western Front. In many sectors, the same old techniques of drum fire by artillery preceded the order to go "over the top." Then the German machine guns would strafe the attackers.

On Monday, October 22nd, the 85th battalion moved by bus from their camp east of Arras due north to the town of Ypres. The bus stopped twelve miles east of Ypres and billeted at the St. Lawrence Camp. This camp was much nicer than Bouvigny Huts. It had been the battalion's main base of operations near Arras. St. Lawrence Camp had a proper base hospital, a theatre, and a commissary. But the men had to prepare right away for battle.

Unlike the battle at Vimy Ridge, the battalion had only five days to prepare for the battle scheme before moving "into the line." While some officers went to the front lines to gain some knowledge of the situation, others went over the plan with the other ranks—using tapes stretched between sticks stuck in the ground. The officers, with the help of some Brits who had been at Ypres since July, tried to show the troops where the most German resistance might come from. Two days training were thought to be enough.

On October 28th, the battalion entrained outside of St. Lawrence Camp and detrained at Ypres Station. From the train station, the men could hear the fighting to the east. It no longer affected them like it had before Vimy. There had been many missions and tours in the trenches since last April. The men were used to it. George simply didn't seem to care. When he picked up his bag near the train tracks, a shell hit the town square about 200 yards away. Some of the men ducked, but George didn't; he strode off like nothing happened. This was odd. Ever since Vimy, George had been skittish with the slightest noise. He would flinch even when someone sneezed—all of his friends had noticed it. Colin saw that George's cheek was twitching again.

"You alright, mate?" Colin asked.

George nodded and kept walking. He went the wrong way. Colin stared at him until he got more than thirty feet away.

"George!" George turned to look back. Colin pointed his thumb over his shoulder. "We're forming up this way."

George threw his head back in acknowledgment, walked back, and joined the line. The men marched the five miles to the front at Potijze, just below Passchendaele Ridge. Before making their way to the front lines, they were given supper, an extra fifty rounds of ammunition, some Mills bombs and rifle grenades.

The men of the 85th could see for themselves this was going to be nothing like Vimy Ridge. Passchendaele Hill was only 160 feet above sea level. The ground was different. In Arras, the city and some of the surrounding villages had been shelled and partially ruined, but some of the infrastructure still stood. The town of Passchendaele was gone. Shattered lumber filled cellar holes. Single, limbless tree trunks remained where forests had once stood. While the land around Arras, including Vimy Ridge itself, was beat-up, barren and muddy, the land around Ypres was nothing but mud. The surrounding farmland had for centuries been drained by small streams and irrigation ditches which needed constant maintenance. The area had been blown to bits for three years. There was no drainage system. So when, in the summer of 1917, there had been the worst rainfall in thirty years, a quagmire resulted. Attacking troops from either side were slowed by the water-filled craters. Some became stuck in the knee-high mud, mired targets for the German machine gunners.

In Flanders, the nature of the ground did not permit another Siegfried Line. Deep dugouts and wood-and-concrete-lined trenches were impossible because of the waterlogged soil. The commander of the German Fourth Army at Ypres had adapted by building hundreds of small concrete forts known as "pillboxes." Sited amongst ruins of what were once farms or houses, they were raised only a yard or two above the ground, and were stocked with several machine guns. There was an entry to the rear. Most pillboxes held between twenty to forty men, and they were easy to construct. The Germans would sneak in wooden frameworks at night and fill them with concrete. The bunker's small size made them difficult to mark for the heavy guns.

The main attack from the 85th Battalion was slated for October 30th, when "A," "C" and "B" Companies would try to take the high ground south of town. If successful, they would control the right flank of the Allied line, and it would change everything for the Boche, who would lose control of the railroad lines beyond the hill. For miles, the German supply lines would be decimated.

But that would be in two days. On this day, "D" Company of the 85th was supposed to relieve the 44th Battalion which had been hit hard and driven back by a large German counterattack. George and Jack were in the lead platoon of "D" Company. As the men made their way along the winding trenches, slipping and sliding in the mud, they could hear the snapping of bullets as they passed overhead. Once past the advance headquarters, they discovered from the screaming N.C.O. that the Boche counterattack had driven through the 44th Battalion, leaving the left flank open; this was the flank facing all of the rest of the Allied offensive. The Germans hadn't filled the opening. They might not have realized the opportunity was there. However, there were a lot of German machine guns set up and firing.

Capt. MacKenzie, the commanding officer of "D" Company, 85th Battalion, integrated his platoons with what was left of the 44th Battalion. He ordered two platoons to launch an attack on the open left flank. He didn't blow a whistle. Every man's eyes were on the captain as they stood in the mud, crouched in the shallow trench. He waved his arm toward the enemy, and over they went. Their boots slid as the men tried to dig their toes into the wet sides of the trench. The machine gun fire intensified. Many of the men slid on their bellies back down into the trench, dead. Those that made it out ran as fast as the mud would allow them toward the Germans. George made it out and so did Jack. Capt. MacKenzie implored his troops to move forward. He saw men falling all along the line. The captain waved his arm again and screamed something to the "boys" when he heard a thud like someone hitting a mattress with a broom. He fell forward with the wind knocked out of him. He could see the men moving forward, loading and shooting on the move. A private stopped and helped him up.

"Are you alright, sir?" asked the private.

Capt. MacKenzie nodded. "Yes, Private. Tell Sergeant Borden to set up the Lewis guns there (pointing at two spots fifty yards apart) and there."

"Yes, sir," said the private. He turned to towards the sergeant.

"And Private..." said Capt. Ross MacKenzie. "You tell Borden to give them Hell."

"Sir!" barked the private, as he slogged off on a run.

The captain looked down at the blood stain on his tunic. He wondered where the machine gun bullet had wound up. *That's an odd thought*, he said to himself. He looked up and could see German troops fleeing from his Canadian fighters. He fired off three shots from his service revolver and then watched as the sergeant set up the Lewis guns in the spots he had ordered. The gunners started firing into the retreating

Germans. Capt. MacKenzie nodded approvingly and then fell over dead.

George just kept running; not firing, not doing anything but running slowly in the thick mud. He wasn't even thinking. He tripped and fell—on what, he couldn't see. He lay there for a moment and realized just how cold the mud was in that October killing field. He rolled over on his side, and pushed himself out of the quagmire. He fell again... and again. He couldn't stand up at all. He wasn't hit. He felt perfectly fine. A man from the 44th stopped next to him and yelled for a medic and ran off. *What the hell?* George tried to get up a fourth time and fell over again.

A medic arrived with two stretcher bearers. They tossed him onto a canvas stretcher.

"Hold this with both hands," said one of the bearers, as he stuck George's helmet back on his head. George did as he was told. As he jostled back to the lines, he asked, "Have I been hit?"

"I told you to hold onto your helmet, boy!"

৩৬

In the Casualty Clearing Station in the centre of Ypres, George was told he had most certainly been shot. The bullet had come from the side and struck right above the knee cap. It had torn through the quadriceps tendon and severed it. That's why he hadn't been able to stand up.

"You'll be fine, son." said the doctor. "You'll need surgery, but you're out of the fighting for a long while—maybe for good."

The moment he heard that, a wave of emotion came over him. He thought immediately about Stanley and Hazen. He remembered vividly saying goodbye to Stan in the dark tunnel, and how his brother had just smiled at him. Suddenly, George felt immense pain in his thigh, and his knee burned. He must have been wincing badly, because a medic stopped and gave him some medicine. It worked instantly, like a wave washing over him and taking his pain away. He glanced around the station littered with carnage. Most of the men there were much worse off than he. He thought about asking if he could help them in some way. He wanted to help. Instead he just laid his head back and waited for instructions. He would do that for the rest of his life.

The Germans knew exactly how important the high ground in Flanders was to their cause. They made the inevitable counterattacks with great fury. The Boche concentrated stronger forces to mount a desperate defence of the Western Front. The Brits, Canadians, and Australians, however, threw them back with heavy losses. The measure of their resolve was extraordinary. The Germans had to hold the ridge from Passchendaele, south to Zonnebeke to save themselves, and they knew it.

German newspapers published pleas for sacrifice at home to support the war effort in Flanders. War correspondent Max Osborne wrote in the Berlin newspaper, *Vossische Zeitung,* about the ferocious fighting at Ypres, *"Nothing more or less was involved than the world-historic decision as to whether England can crush us and break our backbone or not."* He wrote that nobody at the German front concealed *"the colossal gravity of this endless struggle." Osborne said in one of his dispatches to Vossische in early September, "If we are defeated here, we shall be face to face with the certainty that all will be over with the glory of the empire and the splendour of the German name."*

George had to wait two days before being treated other than dressing changes. He didn't care. There were too many boys dying around him every hour. Red Cross volunteers stopped by and gave him food and water and twice a day changed his dressing. When he did get treatment, the doctors discussed the procedure right next to him.

"We should sneak a spinal in him," George heard one of them say, "but we're out of stovain."

"Well then, give him either chloroform or ether. Find one of the nuns and we'll use a drop mask … it'll only take a half hour," said the second doctor.

George was moved into a small room with tanks and electric lights. He remembered the nun and a medic giving him some morphine, but not much else. When he awoke, his leg was in a straight plaster cast, and his thigh muscle had been sewn back to his knee cap. The surgeon had exposed the area where the quadriceps muscles had been ripped off of the patella and sutured it back together. The doctor had to drill some holes along the edge of the kneecap through which he could anchor the heavy sutures.

George had another dose of pain medicine directly after the surgery, and he was amazed at how little pain he felt.

Once he realized he had been wounded, it was if his attention shifted and his deep, malignant sadness waned somewhat. As the novelty of being wounded and the morphine wore off, George started worrying again. He worried about being wounded again (any shell could land anywhere, at any time, he felt). He worried about going home. He fretted about the time months earlier, when he had overheard a couple of his comrades whispering that he might be shell-shocked. He wasn't shell-shocked—he knew he wasn't. He had seen several men like that come through the Casualty Clearing Station in the days before. They were wracked with spasms, convulsing, shaking. They couldn't even walk. Some of them writhed on the floor until several orderlies picked them up. Several of them urinated and defecated where they lay. There seemed to be very little left of them.

George was clear enough in his mind to know that he wasn't shell-shocked. He was not like that. He also knew he was a changed person. He knew he was no longer a boy. Not by a long shot. He just lay there for a day and night, listening to the rumble and roar of the shelling a mile away.

On the second postoperative day, he was to entrain for Boulogne on the coast and then be boated to England. In the morning, he was awakened. "Hello, mate." George removed the towel covering his eyes and looked up at an orderly.

"Do you have your kit ready? I'm supposed to take you to the train." The boy looked about fifteen. George pointed to the duffle against the wall of the tent. The orderly picked it up and read the tag.

"Boo, Bo, Boat..." the orderly struggled.

"Boutilier," said George.

"Boutilier, George Stewart, 1, 2, 6, 0, 6, 2, 6?" asked the orderly.

"That's right," said George.

"Owen Gates. I'm supposed to take you to the train. You ready then?" George nodded.

"'Fraid it's going to be a bumpy ride; all the stretchers are being used for them that can't sit up at all," said Gates. George glanced at the open tent flap. He saw a wheelbarrow, the kind stonemasons and hod carriers use. It had a flat wooden bottom, no sides, and a slightly angled wooden back. At first glance, George thought, that's just great, but after a moment he realized it made sense—in fact, it would be a perfect ride for him with his leg casted straight. Whenever he lay flat, the back of his knee and thigh hurt.

Owen Gates backed the wheelbarrow into the tent and got it alongside George's cot. On the wooden slats were big blood stains—some old, some still damp. The orderly deftly laid down a rubber sheet and plunked George onto it. He then propped up both of his legs, the casted one on top of the other. Gates took the towel George had had over his eyes, folded it, and padded the bottom leg so the cast wouldn't chafe his other shin. Then he placed George's duffle on his lap.

The train depot ramp was about three city blocks away. The orderly got him onto the train and stowed his gear for him, then said, "Good luck," before leaving.

As the train pulled out for Boulogne, George knew in his gut he wasn't coming back to the front. There would be no more artillery. There would be no more blood. He waited for the inevitable wave of relief that was sure to come over him, a wave of relief that he was going to England, and eventually maybe, Canada. He waited a very long time.

The steam engine started to move the train ever so slowly. He was on the starboard side of the train, so as she pulled out of Ypres station, George could see the low rolling hills to the east. Once he cleared the taller buildings, he could make out Passchendaele clear enough. It was late morning, the 1st of November. The 85th had helped other Canadian units take the strategic hill, but the losses were devastating. Sixteen hours later, the rest of the 85th would come off Passchendaele Ridge and board the same train for Brandhoek Siding. Before it was moved from Passchendaele, the 85th Battalion would count twelve officers killed, eleven wounded. One of the mortally wounded officers was the much loved Major Percy Anderson, who had led his men by fighting so bravely at Vimy. In the "other ranks," which included George, there were 371 killed or wounded—out of 662.

The men of the 85th Battalion had fought their way from a "work battalion" into the history books as an elite fighting force amongst a corps of elite soldiers. Still they had not been issued the coveted kilts of the highland combat brigades, though they had been promised a year earlier.

George watched the bloody hills disappear as the train turned west for the coast. He was glad he had seen Stanley's grave, he thought. A tear rolled down his cheek. He could give a shit about kilts now.

PART 9

BLIGHTY AND THE HOME FRONT

———◦◦◦◦◦———

Once in England, George was transferred by train to Addington Park War Hospital in Croydon. George was nervous on the beautiful ambulance train, with its clean white linens, flowers, and tea cups. He had spent so many months in mud and cold, he was afraid he would break or soil things.

Addington Park was a large field hospital that had been set up near Addington Palace Hospital. At the start of the war, Addington Palace had been a typhus asylum. Later the park was turned into an army hospital specializing mostly in abdominal wounds. Because there were beds available, George was taken there along with other upper and lower extremity cases. In the park were rows upon rows of huts and surgeries, with a grid of narrow streets not unlike a tiny city.

George liked it there. Except for the men dying regularly from their wounds or infectious diseases, he felt safe there. There were no explosions. When he had lied about his age and joined the army, he had to declare an occupation for his Attestation Papers. He chose labourer. He was only seventeen years old, and his only jobs had been all the chores around the

Cork & Pickle. Since it was a post office, hardware, general store and café, there was plenty of work to do. George was a very hard worker, and he liked manual labour. He liked the simplicity of it. He liked working for a wage and then going home. He liked the rhythm of a work-a-day job. He especially liked working with horses. It had been different with Stanley. He had wanted to be his own boss. Stan had had high hopes for himself and for Lily. The couple's parents had high hopes for them as well. Everybody knew that. George sometimes wondered if it would be too hard on their parents if he went home to Hackett's Cove now that Stan and Hazen were dead. The community loved both of the fallen men. George knew that he hadn't really made a mark outside of being quiet, getting average grades in school and being a hard worker. He had much to think about.

The doctor who took over George's care at Addington was a very serious fellow.

"Young man," the doctor told George the second time he saw him, "you'll have to be in that cast for weeks. You can get around on crutches well enough. You'll be expected to find some work to do while you heal."

"I've been thinking," said George. The doctor and his followers widened their gaze at the patient. They hadn't expected George to speak. "I'm good at sorting mail. We have a post back in Nova Scotia. There must be a lot of mail here." The doctor almost smiled. Then he took a little circular saw and cut a three-by seven-inch window in George's cast. He cut out the padding beneath with bandage scissors, pulled out the surgical dressing, looked at the wound, sniffed it and said, "Good." Then he walked away.

A nurse standing nearby jumped forward and re-dressed the wound.

The next day, without any warning, George was taken

to the mail hut. He liked sorting mail. He was good at it, and could do it either sitting or standing with his casted leg propped on a stool. If he couldn't work with horses, he would choose to sort mail. Newspapers came almost daily from everywhere, and George gave them to the orderlies to deliver to the appropriate huts. He knew by the postal manifests where to send which papers, be they from Prince Edward Island, British Columbia, or from anyplace else in the Dominion. Each hut was supposed to read the news in one day and then pass the rags along to other huts for anyone who might be interested in them. The odd *London Times* went to the Officer's Mess.

As November passed into December, George was enjoying his job, but each day, as soon as his duties were finished, he would start thinking about his folks, about Stanley, Lily, Hazen and his cousin's mother, Hattie. He would feel the depression descend upon him. He didn't show it. The only positive thing he thought about was that maybe he could go home and get a job sorting mail in Halifax or somewhere. But he doubted he would live in Hackett's Cove.

His cast would come off near Christmas. Then the rehabilitation would start.

❧

On a cold December Thursday morning, Lily walked down the steps of her rooming house on Robie Street and strolled up the hill toward the Richmond School on Roome Street. It wasn't early in the morning; the schools were on the winter schedule, which meant classes started at 9:30. She saw three boys walk to the far side of the street. After less than a week at the school, the boys recognized the student teacher on the sidewalk.

"You boys don't dare cut classes today!" she yelled to them. The boys giggled and ran down the street toward the waterfront. *They're going to play by the piers all day, I know it,* she thought. The piers were a favourite place for delinquents—she had learned that already. It was well known that the harbour these days was one of the busiest ports in the world. The boys would sit and watch the ships coming from and going to Europe, carrying men and supplies to support the war effort. They would dream of being older and being on the ships and seeing the world. The three boys made their way to the water, skipped past the coal yard with all the blackened men, kicking a can all the way to Pier 12. There they watched around corners for the truant officer and darted onto the pier. Their backs were to the Halifax Sugar Refinery. All three boys found a spot to sit on the pier cribwork where they were protected from the eyes of most adults, and from the cold breeze skimming across the salt water. They huddled together for warmth—but not too close. They didn't know about the winter storm that would arrive in seven hours. All they knew was they weren't in school. The boys watched the ships.

Lily made her way up the brick steps to the Richmond School. Herman Knappe, the school custodian, met her as she stepped inside.

"Good morning, miss."

"Good morning, Mr. Knappe. It's lovely this morning," Lily said. She kept walking towards the coat closet.

"'Tis," said Herman, lifting his nose to the sky, "But a storm's comin'. I can smell it,"

"Yes, well, it's pretty now, and I wore my heavy coat."

"Are you likin' Roome?" asked Mr. Knappe. (Herman and many of the neighbourhood people called the Richmond School the "Roome Street School"—after the street where it had been built.)

"Very much," said Lily as she entered the school.

She checked the stove and added more coal. It was Herman's job to start the fire at 4:30 a.m., but the teachers kept it going throughout the day. It was too early to call roll, but Lily noticed the three boys were still not present. In fact, most of the students were not in yet. Lily looked in the direction of the pier. She hoped it was too cold, and the three boys would return up the hill to school. So early in her training, she was already worrying about the children.

The three boys did not go to school. They watched the big ships ply the cold water. One, two at a time the boats chugged slowly up the harbour, guided by the harbour pilots. When one boy mentioned the Mi'kmaq Indian settlement, Turtle's Cove, on the far side of the harbour in Dartmouth, the boys could not make out the tepees. The boy said that his uncle had told him the Mi'kmaq's would stay warmer in their tents during the winter than the white folks in their houses.

"I saw them from my dad's boat last summer," said the oldest boy. "There must have been forty or fifty tepees."

Back at the school, Herman finished chipping the ice off the front steps. Lily sat at a small desk with her instructor, Mrs. Page, who was correcting papers. They said, "Good morning," also and smiled at each of the three children who showed up early for school. Many of the students stayed outside and played in the lot behind the school, or were still on their way.

On the pier the boys began to get cold, but they didn't care; it was better than sitting in a classroom. They were watching a large steamship riding low in the water coming into the harbour, into the Narrows towards the safety of Bedford Basin. It was the French munitions ship, *SS Mont Blanc*, loaded to the gunwales with 250 tons of TNT, 2366.5 tons of highly explosive picric acid, and other volatile wartime materials. The *Mont Blanc* was stopping in Halifax for fuel and to join a convoy on her way to Europe to support the war effort. The boys did not notice the Norwegian vessel, the *SS Imo*, that was loaded with relief supplies destined for Belgium heading out of the harbour, a little too fast through the Narrows.

Amongst the din of the early morning work on the piers along the waterfront, the truants did not notice the sounds of the *Mont Blanc's* horns blowing a single short blast, indicating the vessel's right of way and asking the *Imo* to alter its course and speed. The *Mont Blanc* expected the *Imo* to steer to starboard, allowing her to stay her course and continue up the Narrows towards Bedford Basin. The boys did not hear the *Imo's* two short blasts—her response of denial. The *Mont Blanc* again let out another single blast of the ship's whistle, demanding the *Imo* to alter her course. Again, there was a two-blast denial

The harbour pilot on the *Mont Blanc*, forty-five-year-old Francis Mackey, and her captain, Aimée Le Medec (this was his first command), could not see why the *Imo* was holding her course. The men realized a collision was imminent. The captain shouted orders to reverse all engines. He hoped the current would pull her to port. Once this was done, the *Mont Blanc* was a coasting, sitting duck...at least for a few moments. Unfortunately, the *Imo's* Captain also let out three blasts of his horn, indicating reverse engines. When he did, it swung his ship's bow to starboard. If he had stayed his course, it might have resulted in a near miss.

Sailors on the tugboat, *Stella Maris*, had already noticed the *Imo* driving down the Narrows at a high rate of speed. Her captain, Horatio Brannen, ordered the tug closer to the western shore to avoid a collision. Other vessels in the Narrows had heard the warning blasts and stood to. They watched. Men from the coaling yards by now knew something was up and came running along the piers. They ran past the boys, who were no longer hiding from the truant officer. Everyone on the waterfront clambered to see the imminent collision.

As the two ships met, almost in slow motion, the *Imo's* bow impacted the starboard foreside of the *Mont Blanc*. There was a shudder in both ships. Some of the flammable cargo that had been stowed on the bow of the *Mont Blanc* was upset and spilled. As the two ships separated, the scraping of the metal hulls caused sparks which in turn ignited the *Mont Blanc's* deck. Even such a slow-moving collision produced awesome power. The *Imo's* captain at first thought the damage seemed minimal. There had been small collisions before. Before the fire on the *Mont Blanc* was visible, it appeared that both ships' hull integrity was intact. The collision was only going to be an inconvenience; there would be a minor delay for both ships. Perhaps there would be a short, initial investigation before the ships went on their way, but the inquiry would continue long after the ships had carried on to their destinations.

From the bridge of the *Mont Blanc*, Pilot Mackey and Captain Le Medec could see the fire on deck quickly spreading. No one on the *Mont Blanc* had to mention how volatile their cargo was. Mackey wanted to fight the fire, but the crew quickly abandoned ship. He could not raise the appropriate international flag denoting explosive cargo on board. He didn't know where to find it—it was not his ship. He could not fight the fire alone. He could not scuttle the ship alone. He left with the crew in the ship's boat, and they rowed for their lives toward shore.

The three boys on the pier were joined by a gathering crowd of onlookers and fire crews. One of the boys shimmied up a lamp post to see the spectacle better. The *Mont Blanc*, on fire, had drifted to the Halifax waterfront, and run aground very near Pier 6.

Herman Knappe put down his ice chisel and stepped up onto the school steps to light a cigarette, looking out over the harbour at the billowing smoke. Mrs. Page, after letting the pupils see the smoke, made the children sit back down at their desks. Lily lingered for a moment and stood looking out the window. Only for a second more.

At 9:04 a.m., less than twenty minutes after the collision, the *Mont Blanc* exploded. The vessel was blown to pieces. When detonation occurred, temperatures at the centre of the ship exceeded 5000 degrees centigrade. The shock wave from the blast travelled twenty-three times the speed of sound and was felt in the earth 180 miles away. The blast ripped through Halifax and part of Dartmouth. Every building for a mile and a half was badly damaged. Most were ruined. Melting shards of metal from the *Mont Blanc* rained down on Halifax, igniting scores of fires in the old, clapboard buildings.

Hearing the beginning rumble of the huge explosion, Herman Knappe looked toward the harbour, his cigarette falling from his mouth.

The energy from the blast compressed and accelerated the surrounding air molecules into a supersonic wave. In the wake of the wave was a near-perfect vacuum. The split second after the bodies of the onlookers were compressed, there was an equally massive decompression. The trauma wreaked havoc on the innards of the people within a half-mile radius— onlookers on the pier near the Mont Blanc were torn to shreds, as if they themselves had been detonated. The boy on the lamppost was vaporized. The remaining two boys, along with the other bystanders on the pier, were killed instantly—their clothes ripped off their bodies by the initial shock wave or the blast of vacuum that followed. Body parts were torn away and incinerated by the intense heat of the blast. Most of the people on the waterfront were never found ... those who were could not be identified. Across the Narrows, the Mi'kmaqs at Turtle Cove disappeared completely.

Within a second of the explosion, the shock wave shot up the hill through the streets of Halifax and Dartmouth. Herman Knappe was picked off his feet three yards high and thrown like a rag doll through the thick pine doors of the schoolhouse, breaking the doors off their hinges. At the same moment, all the windows in the school blew inward, creating thousands of shards of glass which almost melted from the heat. Herman was killed before he hit the foyer floor, his lungs, spleen and liver ripped apart from the concussion.

Lily had no time to turn away. She had no time to react. There was a white light, as the shattered glass pushed her backwards and tossed her onto the desks where the children were sitting. The students were shoved by the massive force across the floor and into the opposite wall. Mrs. Page was pinned behind her desk, hard against the blackboard. Seawater came pouring in through the broken windows, a sideways rain. The roof of the school caved in, as did some of the first floor interior walls, but the main structure withstood the blast. In the streets, sheets of water poured from every direction. The city blocks closest to the waterfront were engulfed by a wall of seawater nine feet tall. Survivors later described seeing the damp, exposed ocean floor of the harbour for as long as ten seconds before the sea rushed back in. Of the many children who died while walking to school that day, some drowned.

Lily tried to gather herself. She reached around until she finally grasped a pupil's desk for support. She lifted herself from the floor into a sitting position. Her dress was gone. She wore only her underwear and one shoe. Her hair was burned—she could smell it. She was dazed and confused; everything was black. She could hear moans and crying all about her. All sounds were as if in a distance ... or underwater.

She thought of the children; what of the little ones? And—what had happened?

Lily simply sat upright amongst the pupils, waiting for the blackness to clear. She could feel one of the children touching her lower leg. She could hear the sounds of people moving about amidst the crying. She heard Mrs. Page talking to the class.

"Alright, alright now children, something's happened! Now let's get together. Is anybody badly hurt?" Some of the young ones answered, whimpering, "My leg!" Another, "My arm hurts...both of them." And another, "My body..." One little girl held her abdomen with both arms. Another girl didn't respond—she just sat crying, head down, holding both sides of her head in her hands. Mrs. Page limped over to her and gently lifted her chin and looked into both eyes. The child looked terrified, but acknowledged the kind teacher, who softly rubbed her head reassuringly and smiled at her. As she rubbed her head, she felt for depressions, cuts...anything. Mrs. Page moved to the other children, trying to smile at each one while inspecting them.

"Okay children," said the teacher. She was shaking badly. "Let's all come together now." She repeated, "Something's happened, and I don't know what, but we need to stay together and help each other get somewhere safe."

At that point she looked over at her assistant for the first time. Lily was still on the floor, half-sitting up, propped by her right elbow and forearm on a student's desk. She tried to understand what was wrong with her...what hurt, what didn't, and what had just happened. It looked to Mrs. Page as though Lily was simply waiting, as if she were patiently allowing a child to finish a math problem at the blackboard. Mrs. Page gasped and held her hand to her mouth.

"Lily!" she said. "Lily, darling, you've been hurt, dear."

"I can't see you, Jane. I can't see you … it's black." Lily became more anxious. She held out her left arm. "Jane?"

No sooner had she put out her hand when Jane Page grasped it. "Lily, dear … sit still, honey, sit still." Lily was becoming more anxious. Mrs. Page looked to two of the girls who seemed not to be injured at all. "Girls, she said. "Bring me my chair, quickly now." Some of the children cleared the way as two of the girls stood their teacher's big chair upright and wheeled it over to where Lily sat. They helped the apprentice teacher into the chair. Lily was silent now. Everybody was still in a state of confusion, but she was slowly regaining her senses.

The front of Lily's body was covered in blood; there were many small spots of red, and large blood stains coming through her bra, slip and underwear. But her face… her face was a bloody mess. The shock wave had blown in the windows of all the buildings in town within a mile and a half of the detonation. Her face and neck were cut in dozens of places. Her right cheek was splayed open with shards of glass sticking out of her face at different angles. The worst of the bloody scene was the glass protruding from both of her eyes. Her left eye was closed, swollen and bloody. Her right eye still slightly open—held ajar by a three-inch jagged piece of window glass. The open eyeball was shrunken, and the pupil was stuck in an odd direction, as if looking up and to the left.

Mrs. Page held both of Lily's arms and lifted her into the chair. The two unhurt girls stood by their teacher and tried to help, tears streaming down their cheeks as they looked at their student teacher's face. The other children either simply sat on the floor or stood or stumbled around in shock.

Jane Page looked around the room. She had been thrown under her desk by the explosion, and her clothing was still intact. She pulled her dress up to her knees, reached up under it and pulled down her slip and stepped out of it. She tore it in half, then into long strips about five or six inches wide. She approached Lily.

"Lily dear," she said. Lily turned her head slightly, painfully toward the direction of Jane's voice. "I have some bandages... I'm going to try to dress your face. Honey, there are some pieces of glass in your eyes. We mustn't disturb them... we want a doctor to tend them. It's important. Do you understand?"

"Yes." (She was sobbing gently now.)

"I'm going to wrap your face as softly as I can. I'll try to leave your mouth and nose open, and put the bandages above and below the pieces of glass so they don't move."

The children were now sitting cross-legged on the floor around the two teachers, as though they were listening to a story. One of the girls took Lily's hand in hers.

Jane Page looked at all the children to make sure none had wandered off or passed out. She took a deep breath and wrapped one end of a piece of her slip around Lily's neck, just under her chin. One wrap around and she tucked the end of the slip under itself. She kept wrapping gently. Jane wrapped under Lily's nose, then several layers over the bridge of her nose to build up the dressing to support the shards of glass. She was being as careful as she could, and Lily tried not to flinch from the unbearable pain that was worsening with every passing minute. Jane looped the last few layers around her forehead and tucked the end of the strip of silk under the final wrap.

It was the best she could do for Lily. Blood was already seeping through the silk wraps. Under her left eye there was yellowish fluid coming through.

"You're bleeding other places," Jane told Lily. "I'm just going to look."

"Children, look the other way, now." Jane lifted up Lily's

camisole. There was blood from many small wounds over her breasts and neck. Most were coagulated already. Nothing looked too bad, and there were no shards of broken glass like the ones in her face.

"Okay, honey ... nothing too bad." Lily tried a single nod amidst her light sobs.

The gravity of what was happening became more apparent to Lily. She started thinking of her father and her mother ... of Stanley, God bless him, and of Hazen and George. What could have happened? Was Halifax under attack? Was all of Nova Scotia? Canada? If so, were Germans out on the streets? Would the doctors be able to help her? Thoughts raced through her mind, now. *Will I see again?* She tried to focus on being calm.

Only a few minutes had passed since the explosion, but it felt like hours. The students and the two teachers suddenly realized they were getting very cold. Mrs. Page opened the door to the classroom to gather their coats. The door swung open, but there was nothing there; the part of the building that housed the hall and the stairs down to the first floor had fallen away and lay in a big pile of rubble in the back schoolyard. It was about a sixteen foot jump to the ground. The foyer on the first floor was directly below them, and she yelled to Herman, "Mr. Knappe! Mr. Knappe?! There was no response. In her frustration she thought, how could he have left us here? Since they had all survived, it didn't occur to her he might be injured.

They were all very cold, but Jane was most worried about Lily. She looked around the classroom. The only clothes in the room were what they were wearing; she found Lily's tattered dress snagged on the sill of one of the blown-out windows. She took it and wrapped it around Lily's torso. There were green canvas shades from the windows lying about. Jane gathered these up and placed them like blankets around each of the children. Two pupils had to share one shade. Suddenly there was a voice from the street.

"Oi! Anyone there?!"

Mrs. Page ran to a window. It was a soldier, standing in the sidewalk below. "Yes, we're here! We can't get out."

"Are you hurt?" yelled the man.

"A few of the children are hurt a bit. My assistant is hurt badly."

"Okay," he said. "Hang tight…I'll get help. Won't take a minute!" He turned to leave but stopped, turned back and held his hand to his mouth. "How many of you are there?" he asked.

"Two adults, six students," she called down to him. He hurried off, slipping and sliding down the street. For the first time, she could hear the alarms off in the distance. The fire alarms were all behind her. Everything in front of her—towards the waterfront—was gone. She looked around; there were people walking slowly around the streets. Some were naked, some nearly so, and most of them were limping—some worse than others. They looked half dead. Most of those wandering in the streets were in shock. They did not know what to do or where they were. Amongst the naked, walking wounded, there were others who were fully clothed and seemed to have their wits about them. Those people were draping blankets and overcoats over the naked ones, or pulling at piles of debris and rubble, drawn by the moans and voices below.

The children in the classroom still huddled in the middle of the room under their window shades, sitting in a ring around Lily. Within minutes, the soldier came back with others. They had a large piece of cargo netting from one of the boats left floating in the harbour. There were four soldiers and a few men who looked like regular citizens holding the net taut.

"Come on now, jump!" called the soldier. "Jump now,

we'll catch you!" Some of the children were very slight, and Jane worried that they might fall right through the holes in the netting. She got the children to the window, and had the two uninjured girls jump first.

"You're my brave girls," she told them. "Now jump into the net like you're sitting in a chair ... first you, Barbara ... then you Sarah." She smiled and brushed their hair back with her fingers." And they did, one at a time, just as they were told. A truck had worked its way down Roome Street, and was picking up children and women to take them to Camp Hill Hospital.

Jane wrapped the small children tightly in the canvas window shades to keep them from falling through the netting and tossed them, crying, one by one to the men below. Once all the children were down, she called to the men. "There's a teacher here," and went to get Lily. She had not moved an inch.

"Lily, dear," Jane took both of Lily's hands again. "there are no more stairs ... There are men in the street with a net. We have to jump. You're going to have to trust me." Lily nodded agreement, but started to sob again quietly. She just wanted to be very still.

"Come now, I'll walk you to the window." At the blown-out window, the men below could see the blood-soaked bandage around Lily's entire head. Jane looked down to the men, held both of her hands to her own face and extended her fingers towards her eyes.

"There's glass," she said. The men said something to each other, and two men ran off. The first soldier held up his hand to the women motioning for them to wait. "We're going to find a ramp for her to slide down!" In no time the two men returned with another fellow carrying a very long plank. The men held the bottom steady and leaned it against the building under the window, the lower end into the net. It was a steep angle but it would be better than jumping into the net with glass in her eyes.

Jane explained to Lily what was happening, and placed a piece of window shade on the board. She then helped Lily up onto the sill and guided her feet down the plank.

"Okay, dear, now I'll help you onto the ramp, and you hold your hands behind your neck, keeping your head as still as possible. I'll give you a gentle push to get started. You ready?"

Lily nodded slightly.

"On three then. One ... two ... three," and off down the ramp went Lily.

It couldn't have gone smoother except the canvas became caught on the board and she slid on the rough wood, which ripped her cotton underwear off. She never knew it. In the net, one of the men immediately took off his heavy overcoat and wrapped it around her waist. The slide had not injured her eyes any further, as far as anyone could tell. The men with the net gathered Lily and walked her to the truck where the children waited. Jane jumped next, and was quite matter-of-fact about it. One of the men helped her to her feet. Her first words to the men were, "I think she's blind."

"Aye," said one of the older men, "there's hundreds of them ... the windows." She turned to the first soldier, "What happened?"

"A munitions ship exploded in the Narrows," he said. "There was a collision."

She could see more of her surroundings now. From where she stood, the entire city was in ruins, with fires were burning everywhere. "One ship ... did all this?" Jane asked.

"It's Hell," said the soldier.

Other men were carrying a body down the school's front

steps and laid it next to the sidewalk. For the first time, Jane could see many bodies along both sides of the street. She focused on the disfigured body lying ten feet away. Now, she knew why Mr. Knappe hadn't answered her calls. Jane had focused on her charges in the first few minutes after the explosion. Quickly, she was overcome with sadness. She wondered about her husband overseas. She began to cry.

The men helped Jane Page into the truck. The children were sitting quietly, as was Lily, her bandaged head hanging down, her hands folded in her lap holding the coat closed. She was shaking badly. At that moment, Jane realized the children had no idea where they were. She looked out the back of the truck. The truck smelled putrid. Lily could not see the sign on the truck, *Boutilier's Fish Market*. It was the memory of Stanley Boutilier that helped her through the initial pain, and it was a Boutilier who now drove her to the hospital.

The alarm was sent by telegram within twenty minutes of the disaster to towns and cities surrounding Halifax: "City in Danger. Explosion. Conflagration." Relief expeditions were organized from Toronto, Boston, Montreal, and throughout the province. They did not know the cause of the explosion, or how bad it was. Had the entire city burned? Had the Germans invaded North America? Reports of casualties varied wildly.

Throughout the day, surviving soldiers based in Halifax, firemen, police, and ordinary men and women searched through the debris and rubble trying to rescue those trapped and still alive. They retrieved the dead. Halifax had four public hospitals, one private hospital, and a few military hospitals, each with 200-300 beds. There were thousands of casualties. There were many thousands of homeless. By late afternoon, on December 6th, while the city was trying to collect its dead and find its survivors, it started to snow. That night, with people still trapped in the basements of their collapsed homes and businesses, Halifax had one of the worst blizzards in recent memory.

Jane Page sat with the children and Lily in a hallway at Camp Hill Hospital. The children were tended to first, and all were taken to a dedicated floor in the hospital. Jane stayed with Lily until she was seen. Camp Hill was a hospital with 250 beds. There were 1500 men, women, and children lining the corridors. After a few hours, a nurse took Lily to a room with about thirty other head wound patients. Jane helped the nurse get Lily into some hospital pyjamas. "Lily, you rest now," she told her, "I'm going to check on the children." Lily simply nodded, without a sound. Jane squeezed her hands and left her.

Jane marvelled at how resilient the pupils were; they were scared and sad, but all were well-behaved. She borrowed a coat and went to check on her house—but first she would stop at the Chebucto School to see if she could help with the children there.

The teacher walked along the dark streets and through the swirling snow. She could see fires still smouldering everywhere. The air was heavy from the smoke and smelled metallic from the chemicals burned in the explosion. She could taste the fumes. It was hard to breathe. Dead horses littered the streets. There were "slovens"—flatbed wagons normally used to transport freight from pier to pier, or wharves to ships—filled with frozen corpses on their way to some ghastly place. Some were covered, some not. Jane noticed a difference from the morning. Earlier, people had been milling around the streets immediately after the explosion, showing no apparent reaction to appalling, grotesque, and unusual sights. Now, there was an adroit, workman-like affect to the people on the roads. The people of Halifax were already pulling together in a world beyond comprehension.

Jane found the Chebucto School, and was relieved to

see that it was still intact. It had been constructed of brick, not wood. People were still milling about, rummaging under boards and piles of debris surrounding the school. Standing where the two big front doors had been was a local boy, Tom Raddell. Jane knew him and his younger sisters.

"Are you alright, Thomas?" she asked.

"Yes, ma'am," he said. "I'm just waiting for the men inside…I don't know if I'm supposed to leave or wait for them."

"What men?"

"There's a couple of soldiers," he said. "They needed me to show them where the school is."

Jane went inside to look around. The windows and doors were all missing, and plaster had been ripped from the walls. Jane heard a sound behind her in one of the classrooms.

"Who's there?" she asked. A soldier stepped forward from the dark hallway, followed by another.

"Lieutenant Johns, ma'am. And this is Corporal Mosby. Do you need help?"

"No, thank you, Lieutenant," she said. "I'm a teacher…just making sure…" She wasn't sure what to say—she wasn't even really sure why she was there. "I was just leaving. Are you men looking for something special?"

"In a manner of speaking…I believe we found it in the basement. You should head home, ma'am."

"Yes, Lieutenant, I will—thank you." She turned to leave, but looked back and asked one more question; "Excuse me, Lieutenant…may I ask, what did you find in the school basement?"

The officer looked at the corporal, and then back to Jane. "A morgue, ma'am."

Three weeks earlier, while George was sorting mail and healing his leg in England, the 85th Battalion was moved south from Flanders to the village of Raimbert, between Versailles and Paris. There the billets were excellent. There was good ground for training, and more importantly, they were far from the front where the men could rest. New recruits arrived to replenish the depleted battalion—especially junior officers.

On December 7th, the Division was reviewed by Lieut.-Gen. Sir Arthur Currie, who told the men of the 85th how pleased he was by the work done by the battalion in its battles of 1917. The 85th band played at the Y.M.C.A.

That evening, Jack, Colin MacKenzie and Walter Hoyt were sitting on their cots in their barracks, writing letters, reading, and playing cards when a voice came over the camp loudspeaker.

Attention Camp:
There will be a general assembly in the parade grounds in twenty minutes.
Attendance is required.

The men looked at each other with anticipation and with dread. The Third Battle of Ypres was a God-awful stalemate. *Now what? More marching orders?* The men were beyond getting excited and anxious. Each man buttoned his tunic, picked up his helmet, brushed off his uniform with the palms of his hands, and left the tent. Each platoon assembled along the way and fell in behind their sergeants. All 700 officers, non-commissioned officers, recruits and other ranks fell in and stood at attention. Lieut.-Col. Borden addressed the battalion. Originally, he had planned to set the men at ease, but decided to keep them at attention. That way, the men could not respond until after they were dismissed. Also, he would have their absolute attention.

"Men... I have called you all up to give you some news from the home front. (There was a pause.) I will give you all the information we presently have."

"There has been a disaster at home. The news is just arriving." (Another slight pause.) "In the Narrows at Halifax Harbour, a French munitions ship collided with another ship. The French ship caught fire and exploded. It was a very large explosion." (As yet the men were unfazed.) "As I said, it was a munitions ship, on her way from New York to England; reports read that the explosion has destroyed the entire north end of the city and much of Dartmouth. There are... apparently thousands of casualties." (A barely audible moan went through the ranks.) "There are rescue and relief efforts from all over the Maritimes and from New England."

"Men... I know we are all of us from that part of the world, and though we are now far from the darkness in Halifax, we must keep the light bright in our hearts and pray for our families, our friends and our brethren."

"We have established a direct line with the working communications in Truro, and our information will be constantly updated at the quartermaster's building. There we will post each new communication, except any reports of deaths. Those we will announce privately if they are next of kin. If there are any names of friends or relatives who are not next of kin you wish to inquire about, there will be a short form to fill out starting tomorrow night. We have no other information at this time."

"Now, men, I know this is difficult news... indeed, these are difficult times. I will personally see that you all are guided through this disaster, but I will remind you that we all must first and foremost continue to do our duty."

"There will be a special church service tomorrow at 0900."

(There was another, longer pause.)
"That is all."

The officers about-faced and gave each first sergeant the order to dismiss the troops.

The men fell out slowly and started for their barracks. They were remarkably quiet. Jack slowly looked in the direction of the barracks, far beyond the end of the parade grounds. He saw the men walking slowly away, fading into the darkness.

☙☙

On the second day after the explosion, Jack Frazier filled out the card at the quartermaster's with his entire family's information. For four agonizing days in camp, there was very little to learn about the Halifax disaster. The officers knew it was best to keep with routine, and the men trained and drilled as usual. Each evening, any news from Nova Scotia was posted at the quartermaster's building. The men lined up, orderly and quiet, and read what they could. The mail was censored for several weeks. When it was learned that one or several family members had died in the explosion—or in the weeks afterward from injuries—the man in the battalion was ordered to his company's first lieutenant, who broke the news. The man would be attended to by the battalion's priest, and he would be given some time to collect himself.

Late in the day on December 19th, Jack and Colin were walking back to their billets from shaving. As they climbed the steps into their barracks, the platoon sergeant stood up. He had been sitting on the foot of his bunk, waiting for them.

"Frazier," said the sergeant. "You're to report to Lieutenant Manning straight away."

Jack stood still in the doorway. Nobody in the building spoke. Nobody looked up; they just sat quietly and stared at the floor, or at some book or newspaper. "I'll go with you, Jack," said Colin.

"No," said the Sergeant, "I'll walk with him. You stay put, now."

Colin looked upset. How could he not be there to help his friend? The men in the ranks never got called without there being something wrong. But Colin did what he was told and sat on his bunk. Jack slowly placed his shave kit in his footlocker, stood up tall, dried his face with a towel and picked up his hat. The sergeant walked him out of the barracks. They walked between the long lines of barracks. They walked past men laughing, playing cards or horseshoes or just sitting and talking. At first, the men walked in silence. Finally, the sergeant spoke. "I don't know what this is about exactly. Are you from Halifax, Private?"

"Yes, Sergeant," Jack said.

The sergeant just said, "Ah. It's tough there, right now."

"Yes, Sergeant."

"Do you have family in Halifax or Dartmouth?"

Jack wished he would stop asking questions. He wished he would shut up. His throat was dry. "My family, my wife and three children ... my whole family," said Jack. The sergeant asked no more questions.

They arrived at Lieutenant Manning's office. They stopped in front of the steps. "Frazier," said the sergeant. "Like I said, I don't know what this is ... but if it's bad news, I'll be waiting right here. We'll all get through this together." The sergeant pulled on Jack's tunic pockets and brushed off his shoulders, making sure he was presenting well.

"Thank you, Sergeant." Jack felt very weak. He was trying so hard to be straight and strong. He felt like he was in a dream, an awful dream, so very far from home.

The sergeant leaned toward Jack and whispered,

"Courage, now." Jack nodded slightly and walked through the office door. He knew in his heart this meant someone at home was dead, and he felt like he had no legs under him. First Stan, then Hazen ... and now maybe his lovely wife—*oh, God, not one of the children!* It was all he could do not to fall down.

Another sergeant and some officers were inside. Jack saluted the room and said to Lieutenant Manning, "Private Jack Frazier reporting, sirs."

"Have a seat, son," said the lieutenant. There were three folding chairs along one wall in the front office. Jack sat on the only folding chair in front of the officer's desk. "Well, son," he said, "I have some bad news. It will be difficult to bear, I should think." Jack leaned forward in the chair ever so slightly.

"We wired Truro—and we can wire Halifax now—and one of the responses we received back to our inquiries from the relative cards was about your family. Jack braced himself. *Oh, God,* Jack thought. He felt sick to his stomach.

The lieutenant went on; "You have three children?"

Jack nodded. He started to throw up but held it back.

"The reports are that...," the lieutenant took a drink from a glass on his table. "Your sister-in-law has confirmed that—the officer could hardly speak—the children were killed in the blast in Halifax."

Jack took a deep breath and held his mouth. The sergeant grabbed a waste bucket, and Jack vomited. The sergeant gave Jack a towel and put a hand on the private's shoulder. The lieutenant and the sergeant looked at each other as Jack composed himself. Jack looked down at his lap. In the lieutenant's eyes were all the horror and separation the war had shown him in the past two years. Jack was in shock for only a moment, and then the lieutenant spoke again. "You are wondering about your wife, no doubt."

Jack looked at him with the saddest of eyes.

"Son ... " The lieutenant wanted this conversation to be over very badly. "She's not been found ... and she's presumed gone. It's been some days now. There was a blizzard the night of the explosion ... " The lieutenant decided to stop talking.

Jack oddly seemed to collect himself very quickly. Walking to the lieutenant's office, he had been certain the love of his life—a woman he had loved since childhood, was either injured or dead and gone forever. He was extremely sad that he could not have been there, but the *children*. They would have no life together, any of them.

The lieutenant said, "Reverend Cooke is here in the front office if you would like to talk to him. Also, you can have tomorrow free from training to write letters and to pray." The officer picked up an envelope from his desk. "One other thing; this letter came for you yesterday, but in case it is news of—you understand—we wanted to tell you before reading it from your family. We think it's harder for the men to read it in letters from home sometimes." He handed Jack the letter. It was from his father. Jack couldn't tell from the postage that it had been written before the explosion.

Jack stood up and took the letter. "I'm very sorry, son." said Lieutenant Manning. "We all grieve with you. Is there anything you need?"

"No thank you, sir." Jack saluted the lieutenant, turned, and left the office. Reverend Cooke stood up and shook his hand. Before he would let go, he put his left hand on the private's right shoulder and bowed his head. His eyes were closed, and there was an awkward moment when Jack did not know what to do. Reverend Cooke simply had offered a very short prayer. Then the reverend told him he was always available if Jack ever needed him. He didn't turn left towards his barracks, but rather went right for a very long walk. He didn't want to face his comrades just now. He wanted to spend this time with his Sarah. He wanted all his thoughts and prayers and emotions to be only for his children and his wife. As he stepped down out of the lieutenant's building, he passed another sergeant walking towards the office with another private in tow.

On a hill outside of camp, Jack read the letter twice and started to cry—but only a little. He could see men milling around in the camp below. He had Colin and his mates. He had made other friends since landing in England, but now he felt so alone and such a very long way from home. His throat ached.

Over the next few days, Jack tried to make sense of his new world—one without Sarah and the children. He didn't worry about himself or what it would be like, or how the extended families would respond. He didn't care. He felt unsure of everything now. He had no one else at home now. His one recurrent thought, his pain really, was that he had not been with her, to hold her hand ... to help and comfort her. He was sure that Halifax was still pure chaos, and he wondered about the fate of his parents.

Jack walked and walked. He had no winter coat. He did not feel the December cold stabbing through his tunic.

☙❧

The first eye, ear, nose and throat specialist, Dr. George Cox from New Glasgow, arrived in the wave of relief expeditions to Halifax on the night of the explosion. What was required of him over the next five days seemed impossible. But he tried. Upon arriving in the city, Dr. Cox walked up the hill and into Camp Hill Hospital. There he found the 1500 patients waiting to be seen when Jane and Lily had arrived. Some were sitting on the floor; some were leaning against the walls or lying in the hallways. Some had died and were on the floor, unmoved from the spot where they had expired.

He set to work on a kitchen table, cleaning and suturing wounds and setting bones. It didn't take him long to realize there were a remarkable number of eye injuries that required his expertise. He grabbed an army sergeant and one of the nursing sisters. "Find me an anaesthetist!" he said. They found one already preparing for another case and pressed him into service. Dr. Cox started operating on eyes and facial wounds, and didn't stop for five days.

Sometime after he had returned home to New Glasgow, Dr. Cox recorded for posterity his experience in Halifax. He wrote:

> In many cases, pieces of glass were driven clear through the eyeball, and it was necessary to feel about in the orbital tissue before dressing the case. Eyelids were cut into lateral fringes, and in addition to removal of the eyeball, one often had to hunt for material to reconstruct a set of eyelids.

Cox found pieces of glass as large as a square inch imbedded in the orbit. In many cases, the eyes were completely destroyed. The doctor walked through the hallways, examining eyes and marking those who required surgery. He pinned cloth notes to the patients, listing their name, address, injury, treatment, and future medical needs. Dr. Cox performed 85 enucleations—complete removal of the eyeball—in four days, all under chloroform anaesthesia. He also repaired corneal perforations and extensive facial lacerations. Some injuries were shocking to behold. In addition to many hundreds of pieces of glass, foreign bodies removed from eye sockets included pottery, nails, brick, mortar, wood, and a pencil.

Trains with relief medical supplies and personnel were

delayed in New Brunswick because of the storm. On the fifth day after the disaster, another eye, ear, nose, and throat surgeon, Captain Tooke, arrived. He found Dr. Cox in a tiny back room at Camp Hill Hospital, still operating by the light of a single bulb. He had performed so many operations some of his surgical instruments were ruined.

Over the weeks after the explosion, 322 medical doctors arrived in the city; amongst them were 52 from the Halifax area and 96 from the United States. In total, twelve eye doctors treated 592 people and performed 249 enucleations. Sixteen people had both eyes removed. One person's eyeball had been removed traumatically by the suction of the shock wave. In all, 9,000 people were injured in the explosion, and over 2,000 died.

Lily had her operations on December 8th. She was scheduled for a debridement in one eye, and an enucleation procedure in the other, but when Dr. Cox explored the wounds, he decided neither eye had to be removed. He debrided the eyes and removed all the glass he could see. When she awoke from the anaesthesia, she experienced pain unlike anything she had ever imagined. Oswald Boutilier drove her father to visit with her every third day for several weeks, but on the first visit after the operation, Mr. Durand had stayed in Halifax to be with his daughter. He could not afford a hotel, even if he could have found one. So he snuck into a dark part of the basement of the hospital, curled up in the corner and tried to sleep. There were no bodies there—the big furnaces kept the basement too warm. Almost all the bodies were now at the Chebucto School. His time awake was spent with his girl, holding her hand for hours. He stayed for days, until Lily's pain became manageable.

Thirteen days after the explosion, Oswald, Clara and both of Lil's parents came to visit. Clara delivered a letter from overseas.

"Lily..." Clara said. "Lily, I've brought you a letter. It's from George."

Lily turned her completely bandaged head, as if she could see. She held out her shaking hand for the letter. "Do you want me to read it? Or would you rather one of the nurses read it to you?"

"Please..." she reached out further. Clara placed the letter in her hand. Lily felt it carefully with both hands and with both hands clutched it to her breast. She started to cry. Clearly, it was Stanley she was longing for, but it was nice of George to write to her. Lily knew he didn't often write letters. The parents visited for another hour, but Lily was distracted. They sadly said their goodbyes after Lil's father told her he had spoken to one of her nurses.

"Honey, he said. "In a day or two, you'll probably be moved to one of the temporary hospitals that have been set up in some of the schools and sporting clubs. The nurses are going to wire the post office at Oswald's and tell us the details." Lily reached out for her father's hand, the other still clutching the letter to her chest. She patted her father's forearm to reassure him. They all hugged the pretty patient. It was hard for the Boutiliers to see the tears in her father's eyes. And they left, each man holding his wife. Leaving Lily at the end of visits was not getting any easier.

Lily thought it odd that she had not recently been consumed with thoughts of Stan's loss. Perhaps she was being pragmatic—she was going to need a lot of help, and Stan could not be here for her.

On the same day Lily was operated on, over fifty people gathered at the City Club in downtown Halifax, including Prime Minister Sir Robert Borden. They worked together to coordinate relief work and formed twelve committees. The

Medical Relief Committee became responsible for setting up medical stations, assessing needs, allocating medical supplies, and coordinating medical efforts. They were the ones, along with the Red Cross, who were setting up the temporary hospitals. At that place and time, Sir Fredrick Fraser became a very important man. Sir Fredrick was the superintendent of the Halifax School for the Blind, and he set about organizing a series of clinics for patients with eye injuries. He also helped organize the Blind Relief Fund through the Halifax Relief Committee (H.R.C.). A year after the explosion, he placed a full-page notice in the *Evening Mail* asking for information from those with eye injuries. Hundreds of patients wrote and described their injuries, the treatments received, the costs incurred, and their outcomes. Several indicated that they had had to have an eye removed to save the sight in the other eye. The H.R.C. covered all medical bills, expenditures for eye glasses for those who still had sight, and artificial eyes.

The Massachusetts Halifax Relief Committee did much to help with the redevelopment of public health services throughout the city, and gave $25,000 to the blind relief, which was used to supply special equipment for blind households, including kitchen cabinets, bread mixers, washing machines and sewing machines.

After Lil's mother and father and the Boutilier's left her hospital room, Lily felt her way over to the corner of the small ward and sat in one of the empty wooden chairs by the window. Only her eyes were bandaged now, and there were exposed sutures on one of her cheeks. The swelling was starting to go down, and during the daily dressing changes, the nurses had told her, "Things are looking very good." Lily's sleep was odd now ... she never knew if it was day or night, or what time it was. She would ask for coffee at two o'clock in the morning. Lily's internal clock was calculated by mealtimes and dressing changes.

She liked to sit in the chair in the corner by the window. In the floor beneath the chair was a vent, and heat wafted up from the giant coal furnaces in the basement. If it was sunny outside, the warmth from the window felt good on her sutures. *I will never see the trees again,* she thought. Since the blast, sitting in that spot, feeling the warmth from below and on her face from the sunlit window was the only time when Lily nearly felt comfortable. She sat with letter in hand, unopened ... words from her dead fiancé's brother. A lovely, well-meaning boy and a childhood friend. And she knew she held in her hands, no matter the words inside, more pain.

One of the nurses stopped and whispered Lil's name, and placed her hand gently on her shoulder. "Can I get you anything?"

Lily was crying softly—again. "No, thank you."

"Okay, dear."

As the nurse started to walk away, Lil said, "Actually, there is one thing."

"Yes, dear?"

She pulled the letter from her lap. She was speaking straight ahead, even though the nurse was almost behind her, "I have a letter. It's from a friend in France." And she held it outstretched. The nurse took the letter and looked at it. It was stamped from France and from England. She could see "85th Battalion, 4th Division, C.E.F." Her eyes went from the envelope to Lily's bandaged, sutured face. "Dear, why don't we find someplace quiet ... there are people nearby," she whispered. (They were alone in the ward.)

The young nurse helped Lily up and guided her through the double glass doors. They walked slowly along a corridor and into a small room, and sat down on what felt to Lily like a bench. She obviously could not see the big crucifix on the room's door, or the small altar.

The nurse was nervous that there would be sad news and she would be the bearer of that news. This could be heartbreaking for a woman who has already lost so much. She knew nothing of Lily's personal life, certainly not that she had lost her fiancé at Vimy Ridge. "I'll open it now," said the nurse.

Suddenly there was a voice from outside the room, "Clair... are you here?" It was the nurse's supervisor.

"Yes, ma'am," she replied. An older nurse came to the chapel door.

"Clair, there's a visitor for Miss Durand." Jane Page stepped into the doorway.

"Hello, Lily." Lily immediately recognized her friend's voice—after everything they had been though, she definitely counted her as a friend.

"Jane!" Lil held out both of her hands. She seemed very excited. The nurses stood by as the two hugged.

"Excuse me, ma'am," said the young nurse to Jane. Jane turned to her. "I was about to read this letter... perhaps you would like to read it instead."

And to Lily, "Would that be alright, Miss Durand?"

"Yes... please," said Lily

"I'd be happy to," said Jane.

The younger nurse touched Lily's shoulder again. "Excuse us for just a moment." The nurse motioned for Jane to follow her into the hallway. The older nurse stayed with Lily.

"This letter," she said, "it's from a boy overseas. I'm worried what it will say. I just thought you should know." Jane nodded and took the letter. They went back into the chapel. While Jane did know her student's fiancé had died at Vimy Ridge, she did not know a great deal about Lily's life. She couldn't anticipate what news the letter might bring. The two nurses left Jane and Lily alone in the room. Lily could hear most of what the nurse had said.

Jane said, "It's so good to see you, Lily … to see you doing well."

"Is that what I'm doing? Actually, I'm alright," Lily said. "Jane, are the children alright?"

"Yes, they are fine, thank God. There were a lot of children lost. It's a horrible thing … but none from the Richmond School."

"Jane, could you read the letter now, please. I'm a bit nervous, I must say." Lily looked down as if she could see her hands folded in her lap. *Was George now dead as well?* Jane opened the envelope and unfolded the pages. It was George's third letter to her since Vimy.

Dear Lily,

I just wanted to send you a letter to let you know that I'm alright, and to ask you how you are getting along? The battalion is taking a beating in Flanders, but I am now in England, living on Easy Street. I was wounded in Passchendaele, but many had it worse. I may end up with a hitch in my git-along, but I'll be alright.

I do hope you're doing well, and enjoying the teaching game again. We all miss Stan and Haze in the unit, but they wouldn't want us to dwell too much—we guys who fought with them all know that.

I don't know if I'm going back to the front after I heal up or if I'll be invalided out. When I do come home, I would like to visit. Our families are close, and I have always loved you as more than family. It's as if our families in Hackett's Cove are more like one family.

Sorry I'm not a good writer like Stan was. You

*should know I haven't written home about being
wounded yet, I want to wait and find out my fate first.
So mum's the word.*

Please let me know if you would like to see me.
Yours,
George

Jane was touched by the letter. It wasn't silly or filled with
cuteness and amorous adjectives like some eighteen-year-olds
might write, but rather it was heartfelt, simple, and supportive.
Jane started to fold the letter. Lily heard that. "Wait," she said.
"Could you ... would you read it again, please?"

"Of course, Lily." Jane read it again, slowly and in a nice
rhythm, as if she was reading Keats for her classroom. Again
she folded the letter, placing it in Lily's palm. A tear rolled
from under the yellow-stained bandage and down the scar on
Lily's cheek. She thought only of Stan.

Lily sat back in her chair, clutched the letter against her
abdomen and turned as if she could gaze out the window.
"What a life I have now," she said. Jane had to avert her eyes.
Not that Lily would know.

There was a little pause, with Lil's head still turned
towards the window. Then she turned straight ahead again.
"I've known him since I was five years old, but it was his
brother I loved." She held the letter to her face. "It doesn't
smell like anything." Lily took a big breath before she went
on. Jane couldn't help but notice Lily's affect was different
than it had been only thirty minutes ago.

"Am I reading too much into this?" Lily asked, and held
up the short letter.

"Maybe he just wants to know there are still childhood
friends like you around."

"I am around," Lily said, "but now I'm blind. His brother

and I were engaged. I'll have to write him. I hope he visits me, and that we can be close." Jane nodded in agreement, but of course, no one saw her.

"It's funny," said Lily, "His brother had a bit of a jokester side to him, but only with me. He was always daring me to do things. I don't know if it was only to test me or just his way of teasing me."

"If you don't mind me saying so, dear, this boy has probably always been enamoured of you, as pretty as you are," said Jane. Lily smiled and wiped another tear from the sutures in her cheek. She had very pretty lips beneath the bandages that covered her eyes, and Jane notice the small dimple at the corner of Lily's mouth when she smiled. *She will still be pretty*, Jane thought. *I hope she can still find much in life to smile about.*

"Well, I'll let you rest, dear," said Jane. "I'll come by again in a few days."

"The doctor told me I'll be transferred again in a couple of days. If you can leave your address with the nurses, we'll let you know where. He also told me there is a man in town, Fraser—I think an OBE—who is in charge of the Halifax School for the Blind. He is setting up clinics in the city for those of us with eye injuries. My doctor said I can either be discharged to home or to one of the clinics."

"That's great news," said Jane. "Which would you prefer?"

"I definitely want to go home for some time, but given the chance, I'll go first to one of the clinics. I don't want Mother to have to change my dressings twice a day. Dad will want to do it ... but that's a lot to ask of them. Plus, I need to get used to all this. Besides ... maybe I can start my Braille lessons."

"Lily ... I know you'll do fine; better than most. I have faith in you. I'll leave my address on the way out. If there's anything you need, I'll try to help."

"I miss my books. But I imagine many of them are

available in Braille." She paused. "Jane?"

"Yes, dear?"

"Thank you so much for everything. You were so strong and calm. I can hear everything now, and I've overheard so many people talking. They say right after the blast, people were walking around naked and bleeding as if nothing was wrong, strolling amongst dead people and stunned horses that were lying about. But Jane, you were wonderful. It couldn't have been easy."

"Well, dear, it wasn't easy, but we're a tough people, aren't we?" Jane rubbed Lily's hand. "We're getting through this."

Lily smiled slightly. "Yes, I suppose we are. I look forward to your visits. Goodnight, my friend. You're probably getting tired"

As Jane left she thought, *It's 10:30 in the morning.*

☙

On December 8th, forty hours after the *Mont Blanc* exploded, George took his place at the sorting table in the post hut at Addington Park. His leg was feeling better every day. He was getting much better on the crutches now that someone had taken the time to show him how to use them correctly. He was standing over the piles of letters and newspapers when he suddenly saw the special edition of the *Illustrated London News*:

Halifax Rocked by Explosion

French Munitions Ship Blows;

Over 2000 Dead, 9000 Injured

The crutches hit the floor. Two workers ran from the front of the hut to see what the crash was. George was leaning on the table, staring at the headlines. All the papers said the same thing. *What of Lily?* He thought.

Addington Park erupted with talk of the disaster. Had the Germans taken the fight to North America? That's what many voiced aloud. But anyone who had relatives living or working in Halifax needed to know only one thing—were they alive? George stood still for quite some time, still staring straight ahead. He could not move. Lily was the only person he knew living in Halifax. He frantically read the article. His mind was racing: *What school was she working in? Where was she living? Was she in the North End? Dartmouth? Oh, God … is she okay?*

There was much discussion about the Halifax Explosion in the hospital "village" for the next two weeks. George didn't notice that the news of Halifax and his worrying about Lily and her parents had temporarily cured him of his depression. He now had little time to worry about himself or about his future place at home.

It wasn't until two days before Christmas that George received an unexpected letter from home. He had not sent word to his family yet informing them of where he was, so the letter had traveled to France before finding its way to Addington Park. George had had his cast removed early in the morning, so he had a day off from the post office when the letter was delivered to him.

Still on crutches, he carried the letter, swinging his very stiff, undersized leg, to the tiny garden behind the Addington Palace and found an empty granite bench.

He looked at the letter. For the first time, it was his mother's handwriting. She had always been too busy to write an entire letter, so his father had written news from both of them, for the whole family. His mom and usually Belle or one of the other sisters would write a line or two at the end. A few times, Belle had included a drawing. He opened it with trepidation.

9 December 1916
My Dear Son,

By now I'm sure you have news of the terrible explosion. I will tell you about the disaster, but first and foremost I must give you the bad news that Lily was injured in the blast. She was looking out a window in her classroom, and struck in both eyes by the flying glass. George, I'm sad to tell you that your boyhood friend is now blind in both eyes. The doctor told your father that she will never see. You see, Father took the car over to the Durand's and took Lily's father to Halifax the day after the explosion. The wire asked for only rescue people go to the city, but your father wouldn't wait. They found Lil in Camp Hill Hospital waiting to be operated on. She was in some pain and quite nervous, but Father said her faith was carrying her through. Her faith in God, and in all of us that know her, Son.

The doctor told your father that there were several hundred people blinded by the shattered glass that day, and there are eye doctors coming from as far as Boston to help with all the patients.

We all know that Lily will not be deterred by this turn of events. Lil's father told us that you and she have been writing, and we want you to know we are fine with that. You should know as you write her letters that she is not over Stan and she may never be. We know you care for her, as we all do. She is part of our family. Your father has been very good, George … he loves Lily as if she were his own daughter.

We will be visiting her regularly in the city, so if you want to send letters here, I will take them to the hospital. I will have a nurse read them to her when we're not there so there will be some sort of privacy and you can feel free to write what you want.

It will be alright. Just thank God she's alive ... so many in Halifax are not. Pray for her, George, and we will pray for you.

We will keep you informed of how she does.

Please write and tell us how you are.

Love, Mom

George put away the letter. He looked up at the windows of the palace and wondered briefly how many men had died of fever in those rooms.

George walked with his crutches until he reached the rock wall on the far side of the camp from his own barracks. He sat on the wall and looked over the fields and hills beyond. He could only think of the pain and suffering that Lil must be going through. He looked up to the grey, cold sky and thanked God aloud. Lily was alive.

PART 10

CLEANED UP AND KILTED

———◇◇◇◇◇———

By late December 1917, the 85th Battalion was rested, fed, showered and reinforced to some degree and back on Vimy Ridge, taking a turn manning the lines there. George was still at Addington, sorting mail. He thought of Colin and Jack and the rest of the boys occasionally but mostly he tried to forget. The therapy on his leg was progressing. He must have displayed some traits of "stress" as he was examined several times by doctors specializing in shell shock. At least once, George interrupted a line of questions from the doctor and said, "Doc... I'm not shell-shocked. I've seen those guys before, and it's not me."

The doctor was kind and patient. When he was done interviewing George for the last time, he assured the patient that his status in the medical chart would say "Aged by Service," and not "Shell Shock." George had no idea what that meant, but he was fine with it. In one session with the "shell shock doc," George told him that he had never fired his rifle—not at Vimy or Passchendaele. The doctor didn't write that down. He just nodded.

George continued to write Lily, but seldom wrote home. He did write a short note to his mother to try to assuage her fears, asking her not to worry about him. In the letter he told the family that he had been "slightly injured," and he was careful not to tell his mother he had been wounded in battle.

Christmas 1917 for the Battalion came and went with only a few men singing carols in the trenches and dugouts. One man was shot through the chest Christmas night while on a wiring party. He died the next day. It was very sad. Typically, men only had to worry about getting tangled in the barbed wire and getting cut, but that night, he made too much noise.

On New Year's Day, the battalion moved off the line, and there was a belated church service followed by investiture at which two dozen men were decorated by Division Commander Major General D. Watson, KCB. CMG. There was a Christmas dinner for the other ranks, followed by a pantomime theatre presentation.

George got a belated Christmas gift himself on January 2nd; he was given an appointment to see a special doctor—a lieutenant who evaluated his rehabilitation. The officer watched George walk, rise from a chair and from a cot, stand on one leg at a time, climb and descend stairs, and run short distances. George could do most with no problem, but he clearly was inhibited by the leg when he tried to run. He also had a slight limp as soon as he got tired.

That evening, the head doctor for the Park Hospital came to George's hut to talk to him.

"Have a seat, Private. How are you feeling?" he asked George.

"Fine, sir. No complaints." said George.

"We're afraid we can't send you back across the channel," said the doctor. "You probably aren't quick enough. We don't want to give Fritz any easy targets." The doctor smiled slightly when he said that. He had a very proper English accent.

George looked at the physician with a look that could only be described as confused.

"We're going to invalid you out, son. You'll be sent home. We had hoped to keep you from the "Unfit for Service" category, but we just can't, you see."

George's world was changing again. Two weeks later, still using a cane, he was bound for Halifax on a troop transport.

❧

The 85th spent the first three months of 1918 with tours in the line around Lens and the St. Emile Sector of the Western Front in France. There were raiding parties, nighttime wiring parties, and work parties. In March of that year, there was no planned attack or offensive involving the 85th, but while holding the line in the outskirts of Lens, there were 63 casualties.

On April 9th, 1918, the first anniversary of Vimy Ridge, there was a dinner party to commemorate it for the officers. For the other ranks, there was a work party sent out. April saw 41 casualties.

The 85th Battalion, like all the battalions of the Canadian Expeditionary Force, had their downtime for at least a week each month—unless they were in the heart of a major offensive. Downtime consisted of more training, rest, and sporting events. Occasionally, a dignitary or an officer of high rank or stature would be scheduled to review the troops. By the end of June 1918, the 85th had become a renowned battalion for their exploits at Vimy and Passchendaele and for holding the line at Lens. Their expertise in raiding enemy trenches and intelligence gathering added to their reputation, along with their prowess in the inter-unit sporting competitions.

On July 8th, near the village of Lozinghem, France, there

was a mix-up with supply trains and the men ate very late in the evening. It is unlikely there was much complaining but if there was, it would have subsided quickly. When the train with the chow finally did arrive, along with it came the 85th's long-awaited, hard-earned Argyle and Sutherland kilts. (The kilts had been promised nearly three years earlier.) While a few kilts had arrived in mid-May (the officers and first sergeants got those), now the battalion was fully kilted. For the men, it was at once exciting and bittersweet; so many who had originally made up the battalion never saw the kilts. They had died fighting, not only for the cause but also to prove that the unit was more than simply a "work battalion."

The 85th were no longer "*Highlanders without kilts.*" Ten days after being kilted, Canadian Prime Minister Sir Robert Borden inspected the battalion. They looked splendid in their new kilts with their box pleats and cleaned tunics. Prime Minister Borden looked dapper in his medium-brimmed derby hat, starched white collar and grey tweed suit. The men stood at attention in a courtyard in front of a massive chestnut tree, with shouldered rifles and fixed bayonets. They had come far in the two years since the Prime Minister's wife presented the colours to the battalion in the common at Aldershot, Nova Scotia. For all the men, it felt very far. Colin could see the rows of men in front of him. He saw how proud some of the men were of the kilts. He thought of Stanley and Hazen who never got to wear one. And George, who was gone now. And Jack—a shell of his former self since losing his family. Jack was distraught for so many months that he was asked if he would like to be transferred home or discharged to take care of his affairs. He had no home, he told the officers. He wanted to stay and fight. In his mind, he blamed the Germans entirely. The commanding officers were afraid Jack would commit suicide while seeking vengeance, and he was not detailed on any raids all summer.

Yes, Colin thought. *We've come a long way.*

❧

George had left Southampton, England, in Januaury, on the *Olympic*, the same ship that had brought them overseas, and arrived at Pier 4 in Halifax Harbour at 6:00 p.m., to no cheers and with no one waiting. Why would they? He had written to his family and to Lily that he was being invalided home, but gave them no idea when. It could have been in six more months as far as they knew. George tied the cane to the handles of his duffle bag. He only needed it now if he was very tired or on uneven ground. It took him two hours to get off the ship.

George was unsure how to feel about being back in Nova Scotia. He felt odd as he walked up Upper Water Street to Cogswell Street and then to the Y.M.C.A. He was devastated by the extent of the city's damage. The boys in the battalion had no idea of the destruction in Halifax. George thought briefly about getting a cheap room on Water Street amongst the pimps, drunkards and prostitutes. He didn't really know why. Maybe because they were all just floating through life without any responsibilities, and that sounded good to him.

He was to wait for discharge papers from Ottawa. He had no idea how long that would be. He had plenty of money. He had been in such a dark place since Vimy that he had spent hardly a cent overseas. He brought with him a French amulet for Lily, but nothing for the family. He figured they would all rather forget France and England. He would get a pension from the government of twenty-four dollars a month. That would be plenty. He would work somewhere, and rent a room as cheap as he could find it—the smaller the better. A closet would be perfect, if anyone would let him stay in one. The Y.M.C.A. maintained Red Triangle Huts for returning servicemen in all the principal centres—that is to say, cities of disembarkation. Once he got his discharge, the "Y" gave veterans a six month membership, free of charge. The beds were cheap anyway; some places were only thirty cents per night. Meals at the "Y" were reasonably priced, with writing materials provided for free.

George made his way to the "Y" Hostel on Barrington Street and plunked the thirty-five cents on the counter. His room was tiny, but more spacious that he needed. He was hungry, but decided to wait until morning and have breakfast.

At 9:00 the next morning, fed and showered, George asked directions for the School for the Blind, which was on Morris Street, near Dalhousie. He walked there, carrying the red and silver amulet. All along the way, the city buzzed with construction. He stood outside, staring at the building for almost an hour. It was January and he finally got cold. He went into the foyer. There was a kindly, older lady at the reception desk who smiled at George.

"May I help you?" she asked.

"Ma'am," said George, "do you have a Miss Lily Durand here?" There were glass French doors leading to big rooms on each side of the foyer. The kind lady leaned forward and looked through the doors to her right.

"Who may I ask is calling?"

George looked to his left, and there was Lily, practicing setting a table. She was beautiful. She looked just like she always had; fit, strong, pretty brown hair pulled back with barrettes and her little dimples at the corners of her lips.

"Sir?" asked the lady.

George just stood and stared at Lily. She was carefully, softly caressing the silverware and napkins. The way she moved her hands, it was so lovely. Suddenly, for that amazing moment, there was none of the ugliness of war. In the past two years, George had carried his dying brother from a battlefield as the life ebbed from his eyes. He had lost his first cousin, and watched men writhing from a shell-shocked agony of Hell. He had seen men fall to the ground when they were shot, as though they were nothing but sacks of flour—instantly dead. George had undergone surgery. All this he had experienced, still months short of his twentieth birthday. A tear rolled down his cheek. At the very moment he saw Lily, he saw no more killing. He didn't hear any artillery in the back of his mind, though he had heard plenty in his sleepless nights on the way over on the *Olympic*, and in his room at the "Y" the night before.

At the same moment he saw his childhood, not so very long ago. He saw Lily adoringly watching Stanley doing something athletic or brave. He saw himself watching Lily discreetly from a distance, always understanding his place, always being supportive. And always being quietly happy for them both.

"Sir?" said the receptionist again. George just breathed heavily and leaned on his cane, and put up a finger indicating he needed a minute. He couldn't speak. The lady finally noticed the tears. She wasn't unwise to the world. She didn't know much about the lives of the resident students, but she knew a powerful moment when she saw it. Here was a soldier, very young, wounded, weeping at the sight of a girl he obviously knew well, who had been blinded not long ago.

"Excuse me," she said as if to leave, but then almost in a whisper, "but if you want me to get her, I'll have to announce you. You'll have to tell me your name." George nodded as if to thank her. The lady got up and stood by the opposite side of the foyer. That seemed to give him a little room.

George relaxed for the first time in a long time. He felt good there, standing in the entryway, almost in Lily's presence.

He was so glad she was safe. She did not look at all unhappy. She looked … contented. With that thought, he turned to the lady.

"Could you give her these after I've left, please?" George placed the amulet and a card on the receptionist's desk.

"Certainly," she said, reclaiming her seat. As George turned to leave, relying heavily on his cane now, the woman said, "Thank you for your service … "

George looked toward her and nodded again. Before he went out the door he said, barely loud enough for her to hear, "I didn't do anything."

☙

George stayed at the Y.M.C.A. for three days. He wasn't sure what to do. Each day he walked around Halifax, observing the busy rebuilding of the city. Those streets and buildings still in shambles were all too familiar. As he walked, he thought about asking some of the construction workers for a job, but he knew deep down he would have to go home first. There were signs posted everywhere detailing instructions from the Halifax Relief Committee. He would call on them, he thought, once he heard from the army what he was to do.

George purposely walked by Lily's school each day. He missed his friend. Although she and Stan had always been together, she had been an important part of his life also. Before any of them knew what a boyfriend or a girlfriend was, they were all just a group of youngsters, playing, laughing, teasing, and dreaming. Seeing her at the school days earlier was the first time his heart had been warmed since the 9th of April, ten months ago. He had no idea what that meant, other than it felt good to see her. He sat down on a sidewalk bench across the street from The School for the Blind.

God, Lily's blind… maybe he should leave her be. Maybe she would not want him to visit her. He was so confused. *I'll go home tomorrow*, he thought.

The train to Upper Tantallon near the head of St. Margaret's Bay usually ran every other day, but because of the disaster it was running daily now, ferrying building supplies into the city for its reconstruction, and ferrying wounded soldiers to outlying hospitals. George packed his things and showed up at the train station on Water Street at 5:00 a.m. He hadn't checked the schedule. He sat and waited six hours to board his train. By train it was only an hour ride, if the old steam locomotive got up to speed quickly enough. Soon George was leaving the city houses behind, and through the spruce and fir trees he sped. *Too fast*, he thought. He needed to have more time to prepare. *I've had months.*

He loved his family above all else. He was torn between just wanting to be home where it would be safe, and the dread of seeing his mother and father for the first time—without Stanley. Knowing they would never have Stan in their lives ever again was eating away at him. How would they respond to him? Would they even want him?

The train whistle blew. Upper Tantallon. *I'm not ready for this.*

The people everywhere in Canada were proud of their boys overseas; before George, in his brown uniform, could step off the loading platform with his duffle bag, three different men asked him, "Need a lift anywhere son?"

George thanked them, but wanted to walk the ten-and-a-half miles to Hackett's Cove. The doctors had told him to walk a lot, anyways. *It will do me good*, he thought.

The sea air wafting off St. Margaret's Bay smelled sweeter that it had on Water Street or on the *Olympic*. It was cold, and George had to walk in the slush beside the road. *Still drier than the trenches*, he said to himself. His mind raced. As he trudged along, he felt increasingly conflicted; his heart was leaping in his chest with the thought of being in the old homestead, feeling his mother's arms around him one more time. Yet he knew it was going to be difficult to explain away Stanley. Would he have to? He felt he had done nothing in his life—Stanley was the one. Stan was the boy with the highest goals. Stan was the one who made his mother laugh.

Whenever a car passed by, George flinched. He tried to focus on things—like the old saltwater farmhouses, the leafless rosa rugose bushes, the boats pulled up high and dry, but his mind kept falling back to France and Flanders. Not the battles so much, but just the drudgery and the anguish of day-to-day living. He tried to put one foot in front of the other.

At last he walked over the hill above Hackett's Cove. He had made it more than ten miles. It was a good test for his leg, though now he was limping slightly. *Should've caught a ride, he thought.*

As he moved down the hill, he stopped by the side of the road in front of St. Peter's Church. There was no snow on the ground around the church, and the whitewashed clapboards looked clean and bright in the soft afternoon light. He looked to his left. The back of the Cork & Pickle was there, a couple hundred yards away. He could see the back door where the photographer had positioned the family in better light for their portrait two years ago. It seemed like ten years ago. George stared back at the church and choked back a tear.

He composed himself and walked down the hill. He strode slowly onto Boutilier's Cove Road and took the quick right into the driveway and up onto the broad open porch. His throat hurt. His heart was pounding, but he remained calm on the outside. He slipped the strap of the duffle off his shoulder and opened the door.

To the left, the post office was empty, as it should've been that late in the day. The great room was empty also. George set the duffle down on the red and black braided rug and breathed in deeply. His father's lovely pipe smoke from earlier in the day lingered still. It mixed subtly with cinnamon coming from the kitchen in the back. It was unmistakably the smell of his mother's cooking—cinnamon sticks and pinwheels. He was home.

The kitchen door swinging open awoke him from his dreamlike state. It was little sister Laura carrying a tea cup, holding it fast to a little white saucer. She took two steps before she realized someone was standing by the front door. Laura looked up with a start and almost dropped the tea cup. She sucked in air deeply and stood frozen. Shocked, she wasn't even smiling when she yelled, "Mama!" She still didn't move. Thinking Laura had dropped the cup and cut herself, Clara burst through the door. She stopped quickly and looked at her middle child—who looked as though she'd seen a ghost. Slowly she turned towards George. He was still standing next to his duffle, arms hanging down, unsure what to do. Clara's face told the tale: the anguish, love, happiness, sadness—all could be seen at once in her eyes. She stepped in George's direction, but had to grab the arm of an overstuffed chair. The tears rolled down her cheeks. She held her hand over her mouth. "Georgie!" she said, reaching for him with her free hand. She was crying hard now. All the younger siblings were running from the kitchen. The youngest, little Belle, bolted across the room and threw her arms around George. Like Stanley, he had always doted on Belle. George had always given her his time and attention, even during the adolescent years, when young boys typically would rather not be bothered by younger sisters. Belle was crying also—they all were.

All the girls hugged him now. Clara pulled a tissue from

her apron pocket and wiped her nose. George gently broke free of the girls, touching each one on the back or shoulder, and limped across the room. He threw his arms around his mother, and they both started sobbing. George hadn't cried— not like this. Not yet. The girls all gathered around the mother and son, patting George on the back. There might have been thoughts about Stan, but they were overshadowed by the joy of having George home. They just let go in that moment. Belle held on to George's uniform belt.

It was some time before they all composed themselves. It felt good for George to let down his barriers. For those few minutes, he didn't think about his difficulties in France, or his perceived shortcomings, or his worries about the future, or his past. He just stood there, surrounded by love. Almost a full minute passed, but it seemed longer. Clara let go of her son, wiping away George's tears with her thumbs and smiled. That made George smile. They both took a huge breath and Clara said, "You'll be hungry. Come on, we'll fix you something. I'm baking cinnamon rolls." They started for the kitchen.

"Where's Papa—and Guy?" asked George.

"They went to the city to pick up Cyril," snapped Belle.

"Yes, big brother is on the Halifax Relief Committee," said Laura.

"I don't know exactly what his job is but he's helping with the planning of building new buildings made out of cement," said Clara. "You know your brother ... he's always trying to get into more and more businesses. He'll probably make a million dollars someday." George smiled at that. Cyril was definitely the business man in the family.

"They should be back soon," mother said, "Oh Lord—I hope your father's heart can take it."

"Take what? Me being home?" asked George.

"Why, yes. He's been worried sick about you." George

hadn't considered that. He assumed his father would be too overcome with grief about Stanley to worry much further.

"What would you like?" asked Clara. "Supper will be in an hour. Did you eat lunch today? George shook his head.

"Then something to tide you over."

☙

George heard the Russell pull around to the back of the house. He was seated in the rocking chair by the wood stove in the kitchen, with the girls all still huddled around asking questions—too many questions. George had answered most of them, usually with one or two syllables. They all heard the car door shut and excitedly took their places around the room. They were giddy. They knew it would shock their father and their two brothers. "Shhh!" they all said to one another.

"Should I stand up or stay seated and see how long they go before noticing me?" whispered George. "Oh, yes, stay in the chair," the girls giggled. Clara stood at the sink as though everything was normal. Unlike her six daughters, she was a bit worried about her husband's reaction. He could be a stickler for decorum.

The door from the back yard swung open, and twelve-year-old Guy came running through the room and out the other side, on his way to the front room where he played with his lead army men and tin trucks. He never noticed a thing. The girls all covered their mouths, trying not to laugh. Next came Cyril, followed closely by their father. Cyril immediately went to his mother and kissed her cheek. "Hi Mom," he said. He reached for one of the cinnamon buns, their smell so thick in the air.

Clara gently slapped his hand away. "Supper in ten minutes." Cyril smiled. Oswald stepped toward Clara to hand her a bag of things he had picked up in Halifax. His back

219

was to the wood stove. The girls were being awfully quiet, he thought. He started to hand the bag to Clara and then froze. He stiffened. He stared into Clara's eyes, which were smiling at him. She looked so incredibly... happy.

Oswald took a deep breath, placed the bag on the sink counter, and turned around.

There was Cyril, grinning from ear to ear, standing next to his other son, George, who stood up. His knee was swollen now from the long walk, and he got up gingerly. You could hear a pin drop. Oswald's short but very thick frame slumped a little. He just nodded his head slightly as he stepped forward to shake George's hand. He was smiling under his very thick moustache.

"I'm very glad you're home, Son," said Oswald, lifting his left hand and clasping George's wrist. *A two-handed handshake,* thought George. He hadn't expected that from his dad.

The door to the great room opened. "Mom, when is..." Guy finally saw his brother. "George!" The youngest boy dove in between George and his father and grabbed his brother hard around the waist. It jostled the two men and they smiled at that. Guy was a very precocious child, and they often joked about that. Before the boys had left for overseas, on the day they had taken the family portrait, Oswald had said, "You boys don't need to go... just send Guy over there for a week. That'd soften the Germans up."

Finally, the girls all started talking at once. They were still very excited to have George home.

Belle tugged on Oswald's shirt sleeve, and her father looked down at her.

"Daddy... now you can go back to sorting the mail again."

☙

George loved being home. Cyril had come home just for the day and had returned to Halifax. The girls were happy beyond belief to have their soldier-brother home, though they pestered him about his leg wound, which he tried to ignore. For two days, George helped his father harvest ice from the pond across the road and stack it in the icehouse near the end of the driveway. Clara could not stop feeding her appreciative son while she doted on him. Guy kept badgering him about the war, but Oswald stopped that right away. Their father took the twelve-year-old to a separate room, and they had a conversation. He explained that it was too early to ask his brother about such things. The boy was smart as a whip. He asked George no more questions.

Within three days, George knew he could not live at home, not for now, at least. He would catch his mother looking at him, and she would smile, but he could tell she was weeping inside. His father seemed genuinely happy he was home but he could tell that he was a constant reminder of Stanley. George had gotten out of his uniform as soon as possible, hoping that would make a difference. But it didn't. His stay at home taught him he would always be welcome there and that he needn't have worried. But George felt it was just too soon. Time would heal the wounds. For now, he would go back to Halifax and await his discharge from the army.

In the morning of his fourth day home, George went to see his father. He had not yet opened the post office.

"Father?"

"Yes, George?" Oswald said with a smile.

"What can I help you with today?"

"Why don't you just relax today, George? You've done a lot already. You should take a day to rest."

"Do you have a moment?" asked George.

Oswald half-laughed, "Well, considering nobody except old Eleanor McGinn will be in for their mail for two hours, I guess so." Oswald winked at George. "She hasn't received any mail for over a year. She keeps right on coming every other day, even though I've told her a hundred times I'll deliver it to her if something comes in. I think she likes the walk."

"Father, I think I'll be going back to Halifax tomorrow. Just for a time." Oswald stiffened, looked out the window towards the sea, his back turned towards his son.

"You're welcome to stay here, of course... as long as you want. There's always lots of work. I thought you might like to take over the place someday."

"It's just for a while—I'm awaiting my discharge. They want me to see a doctor at the army hospital in Halifax anyway. And I thought I could help with the rebuilding there, I'm sure there's something I could do even with my bum leg."

"Still trying to do your bit, eh?" said Oswald.

"Father?" asked George. Oswald looked pensively at his son and motioned for him to sit. "Father—I think when mother looks at me, she thinks of Stan." There were tiny tears welling in George's eyes. Not because of what he had just said but because of everything. Oswald leaned forward, put his elbows on his knees and clasped his hands together.

"Son," he said, "we are simply pleased to have you back. There's no more to it than that. As far as Stanley goes, there's got to be more time, is all. Though I don't believe your Mother will ever be fully over it. But don't you make that about you in any way. You did what you could. We all know that. Okay?"

George whispered, "Yes sir. I'll be alright. It was not good, Dad... it was not good."

Oswald reached out to put his arms around George and patted his back. He took a deep breath, and then he squeezed his son hard, like never before. "We're very proud of you,

Son," his father said.

When Oswald sat back in his chair, he said, "There are two things I'd like to talk to you about." He looked out through the glass doors into the great room as though to be sure no one else was around. "Number one, we know you've written to Lily." George looked at his father. He was surprised by this and taken off guard.

"It's good you've written her." Oswald could see George was nervous, so he tried to calm him by holding up his hands and said jokingly, "God knows, you're not the best soldier at writing letters." George tried to smile.

"I've been around Lil recently, said Oswald. "She's doing very well. Adapting. Have you already seen her?"

George winced, "Seen her, but haven't spoken to her. She didn't know."

"Well George, is it just as friends—like when you kids were young?"

"Yes, Father. But when I saw her, it was the first time I'd felt fine since Vimy. Maybe it's because she was the first person I'd seen from this life, and it felt so good to be back in the province. Maybe more... I wouldn't know."

"What do you mean you wouldn't know?" asked Oswald.

"I don't know. I've never had a girlfriend, and if we're being honest, for the past year, I haven't understood anything going on in my head. When I'm doing manual labour—some kind of task—I'm better. But after, when I'm not focused, my world goes crazy. It goes bad." His father looked worried. George tried to reassure him. "I suppose I just need more time too, to readjust."

"Well, Son, if you want to see her, it's alright with us. But I don't want you to get hurt. Please be careful. Everybody knew that what she and Stanley had together was powerful. Sometimes, George, *sometimes* people can't let go of a love like that."

George nodded and staring at the floor said, "She is just a childhood friend, father."

"What was the other thing?" asked George.

"Oh, well, it's a family matter you need to know about. We were going to write you boys about it, but decided you had too much going on over there to worry, so we decided to tell you when you got back. You're here so I'll tell you now." Oswald sat back in his chair.

"When you boys shipped out, Cyril and Ella were going to have a baby." George's eyebrows lifted.

"They didn't know it at the time. They had a little boy last June. It was after Vimy, obviously." George looked at his father inquisitively. "We wrote you about it, but we couldn't tell if you'd received the letter." George shook his head. He had not.

"They named the baby after you boys, 'Stanley George Boutilier.'" George looked confused. "Sadly, Son, the baby died last month. Just found him in his crib. He might've caught a cold or took a fever." Oswald looked as though he might cry. In that moment, George noticed his father looked a lot older than he had only two years ago.

"I'm telling you this now, because if you found out later on, I wouldn't want you to think that we failed to keep you abreast of what was going on."

George was appreciative. He felt bad for Cyril and his young bride. *What a hard year for Mother,* he thought.

"If you're sure about going, I'll give you a ride to the city in the morning," said Oswald.

"That's okay—but I'll take a ride to the train station, if you don't mind."

"George," said Oswald, squeezing his son's shoulder, "I am so glad you're home." George smiled at that.

৩৩

For the 85th Battalion, the campaigns of 1918 went on like most others: frequent, filthy, and dangerous. Within the unit, Colin and Jack became increasingly distant. Jack, morose most of the time, could not get his devastating losses out of his head for a minute. He was sinking low. Colin tried to help but didn't know how. Jack was courteous but standoffish. It was similar to George's behaviour after Vimy, except much more intense. Everybody knew Jack was struggling—even the officers—but he was doing his job and causing no trouble. When he was on guard duty, he would stiffen against the edge of the trench, staring into the darkness in the direction of the enemy, looking as though he wanted to pounce. His hatred for all things German was palpable. He was still blaming them directly, and the blame grew daily. Some of the men were certain he was going to break for the Boche trenches without orders and take out as many defenders as he could before they could kill him. Some of the British troops stationed next to the 85th were making bets on when he would do it. Then again, the Brits would bet on anything, even who would get rat bit in the night.

In spite of the mental and physical ravages of trench warfare, the battalion performed extremely well. They kept on fighting, and they kept on dying until the war's end. In early September, 1918, at the Battle of the Scarpe, ten miles south of Arras where the battalion had whet their appetite for fighting, 62 men died in only minutes. The men from Nova Scotia are buried all over France and Flanders, in old battlefields long remembered by some, in places like the Scarpe, Canal du Nord, Valenciennes and Drocourt-Quéant.

The German soldiers and the citizens back home were

getting worn down as early as July. In his war diary, Lieut.-Col. J. L. Ralston wrote, "The enemy is lacking an offensive spirit...his morale has apparently suffered."

But the war raged on. Men on both sides made the "supreme sacrifice," not only throughout Europe, but along the Mediterranean and in the Middle East. All summer long, American soldiers were pouring onto the continent. Byng's Boys were attacking along an eighteen-mile front south of Arras, while General Foch coordinated French and British efforts southward from the northern flank on the Belgian coast and northerly from the Swiss border. Foch's policy was pressure and more pressure on both flanks and on the centre of the German line from the North Sea to Switzerland. He wanted to push to the limit his growing numerical superiority. By the time the Armistice was drafted, the Americans had landed two million men in Europe. Still, nearly half of the Americans who had already been fighting with the Canadians chose to stay with their units rather than transfer to the U. S. Army. In letters home, it is obvious that they experienced no lack of devotion to their own country, but rather they chose not to leave their comrades with whom they had lived and fought. Those who lived through it together had unique relationships, unbreakable friendships that can be forged only in combat and through surviving great peril.

Foch's relentless pressure worked. The British, Canadian, American, New Zealand, Australian and Moroccan efforts prevailed. Russia had taken its toll with remarkable brutality. Greece, Romania and Serbia fought hard for four years. Indians had died for the cause. The Newfoundland regiments showed their toughness, time and again, asserting pressure on the German 4th and 6th Armies when it appeared the day had been lost for the Allies. Soldiers from Brazil, Montenegro and Portugal came to fight the Germans. It was more than the

Germans and the Austrians could bear.

In late September, the Battle of Canal du Nord at the Scarpe, a British and Canadian offensive, and the Battle of St. Quentin Canal by the Australians and the Americans pushed a hole in the Hindenburg Line and finally broke the Western Front. At St. Quentin Canal, near the commune of Bellenglise, Allied airmen reported seeing "masses of men running haphazardly in retreat." The French and British smelled blood. The Americans were relatively new on the scene but fought well with the Australians. The two had a demoralizing breakthrough of the German lines on the 29th at Bellenglise. Four months later, Field Marshall Haig wrote about the long-awaited breakthrough:

"North of Bellenglise, the 13th American Division... having broken through the deep defensive of the Hindenburg Line, stormed Bullecourt and seized Nauroy. On their left, the 27th American Division met with very heavy enfilading machine gun fire, but pressed on with great gallantry as far as Jouy, where a bitter struggle took place for the possession of the village. The fighting on the whole front was severe, and in Bullincourt, Nauroy, Guillemont Farm, and amidst a number of other points, amidst the intricacies of the Hindenburg Line, strong bodies of the enemy held out with great obstinacy for many hours. These points of resistance were gladly overcome, either by the support troops of the American divisions or by the 5th and 3rd Australian Divisions."

In the German Reichstag on September 28th, the chiefs of the six political parties were summoned to meet with Vice-Chancellor von Payer, which was about a week after the

Americans had captured the St. Mihiel salient, 180 miles east of Paris, and the day after the Hindenburg line was breeched at Bellenglise. Payer probably knew also that Bulgaria at that time was about to surrender (which she did the next day). Things were falling apart. He said to the six party chiefs, "Gentlemen, I have an extremely painful announcement to make to you. The High Command telephoned yesterday to the Government that it was convinced of the impossibility of winning the war, and that it was necessary, as soon as possible, to ask for an armistice."

The assembled deputies were later described as "thunderstruck" at the statement, having had no information of an impending disaster at the front. One flummoxed statesman from Bavaria asked, "Then the Alsace-Lorraine is lost?"

"Yes... it is lost," replied the Vice Chancellor.

By early October, all signs pointed to a massive German retreat in the north of France. At point after point, there were significant breakthroughs in the Hindenburg Line. German fortress positions had been either taken or cut off. General Foch vigorously maintained pressure on the flanks. The Germans fought stubbornly in Flanders and the Argonne, in order to create some breathing room for a withdrawal of their main forces. By the autumn of 1918, the Central Powers were collapsing. After Bulgaria had asked the Allies for terms, Turkey, quite isolated now that her neighbour was out of the fight, fell to pieces with no discernable government for some weeks. The Austro-Hungarian monarchy was collapsing. The threat of dissolution of the empire had been a large contributing factor of the cause of the war. The Hapsburgs could no longer keep the minorities under their dynastic thumbs. Germany was the last to give in.

By November 8th, Germany as a country—never mind

empire—was in tatters. Revolution engulfed the streets. Mobs were crowding all major cities. Government buildings were stormed and documents were being destroyed. Soldiers were deserting by the thousands. On that day, Kaiser Wilhelm met with the Crown Prince, Marshall von Hindenburg, and the Quartermaster General, Wihelm Gröner. The Kaiser was indignant, ferociously defending his title and rights. He declared that he wanted to personally lead the army in one last grand attack and die in some grand, theatrical way. Hindenburg convinced him the great loss of German soldiers' lives would be for nothing. Next, Wilhelm demanded to be the one to lead the army back into Germany from the Western Front. Hindenburg told him the soldiers would probably kill him. At that, the Kaiser became less indignant and more attentive. The Marshall pressed him to abdicate and would not yield. At the end of a very long day for the Kaiser, Hindenburg argued that he could best serve the country by leaving it and saving Germany further loss of life and incalculable misery. With the Marshall's help, the Kaiser fled to Holland and there wrote his abdication in his own hand. By all accounts, he was visibly shaking. The abdication would be finally published in Berlin on November 28th.

After numerous extraordinary notes, demands, threats, and concessions amongst all the governments involved, a German armistice commission met with Marshall Foch on November 8th. The Germans blanched when they read the terms, yet very early on the morning of the 11th, they sat down in Foch's railway carriage and quietly signed the papers. At no time was Foch polite. The cease fire would go into effect at 11:00 that morning.

The news of the Armistice circled the globe in a welcome rush. People flooded the streets of major cities and small town; they ran from their homes and sang to the heavens. Cars drove up and down country roads, honking their horns. Bells rang out in Sussex, Arras, Roujan, New York, Ottawa and Humpty Doo—and in St. Margaret's Bay. The world over, people danced in the streets.

In the trenches, the soldiers who had been doing the fighting and dying showed mixed reactions. All along the Western Front, every man knew the cease fire was coming. They kept a close eye on their watches. In some places, it was eerily quiet in the hours before 11:00 a.m. In most areas, the artillery fire was typical, like any other day in the months and years before. Still other sectors saw enormous barrages from both sides, as though neither side wanted to carry the shells home with them. Certainly, nobody on the front lines knew what to expect.

In Halifax, when the news hit the papers, the streets filled with revellers. Upper and Lower Water Street, Barrington, Gottingen, Market and Grafton Streets were crowded. Men and women hugged, danced and filed into pubs and clubs all over downtown. Parties were extemporaneously thrown together. It was the same everywhere. Families knew their soldiers and nurses would be coming home. If the Armistice held, men and boys would no longer be dying by the tens of thousands.

When the news reached the Halifax School for the Blind, Lily was at once elated and profoundly sad. She walked resolutely into the music room and plunked down onto the piano bench. She ran her fingers lightly along the keys. So lightly she could feel them, but just barely. They made no sound. There was the "C," the "D" ... they felt so uniform and smooth under her soft, knowing hand. There was a clambering. "Lily! Did you hear? The war's over!" snapped one of the young volunteers. Lily smiled and turned her head slightly in the girl's direction.

"Yes, Aideen, it's wonderful news," said Lily. She heard the young lass scamper off to tell anyone else she could find. Lily could hear the commotion in the street. She thought of how it might have been, if Stanley could've been one of the boys that would soon be coming home. He would not care in the least about her scars, and he would love a blind girl. She was doing better these days, staying busy, but she still missed him terribly. She missed him now. Lily's index finger dropped onto a white key, and then another. Too many measures went by, as she thought of Stan, and then she pressed another key. The notes became music and the music became a song. She played softly and a bit too slowly, "*Let the Rest of the World Go By*," and the tear which fell from her lovely, scarred cheek landed on the keys.

PART 11

THE STREET SOUNDS TO
THE SOLDIERS' TREAD

———◇◇◇◇◇———

On the 9th of June, 1919, the streets were abuzz again. Many battalions had made it home since the official end of the war to end all wars, but *this* day was special. At noon in downtown Halifax, there was to be another parade. *This* one was for the 85th Battalion of the Canadian Expeditionary Force. Today's parade was for a group of men who had been personally sent off by thousands of Haligonians, three years earlier. Though the ranks were comprised of men from all over Nova Scotia and beyond, many of the boys were from Halifax.

Though the battalion had arrived in harbour on the 8th of June, the 85th assembled after disembarking along the waterfront. The Pipe Band led the battalion, and the Silver Band took up the rear. The working people along Lower Water Street—the coalers and shipwrights, the longshoremen, the businessmen, the policemen, and the prostitutes—all cheered and applauded the soldiers as they assembled. Downtown knew the parade was coming. Downtown knew what the 85th had accomplished. All of Nova Scotia did. All of Canada knew. All of Canada knew also what they had lost. Along the parade route, a huge banner had been strung across Gottingen Street. The men would have to march underneath it.

At eleven o'clock in the morning, with twenty-nine of the officers mounted, the pipes were ready and the command was given. All the pipers struck in at the same time, and they made a loud, mournful groan, as if warning that something was coming. It was a slow march, and the men were drinking it in. The crowds swelled along the route.

The route went up Barrington Street, then left onto Cornwallis, then right on Gottingen Street. Barrington, in the business district, was choked with spectators. As they passed underneath, the men looked up at the banner: "You Won, Boys—We Knew You Would." Young boys climbed up the ivy-covered streetlamps that held up the sign. Hanging below the banner was a smaller sign with the 85th battalion cap badge on it. Tied to the ivy on either side of the street were white signs that listed Passchendaele, Vimy Ridge, Cambrai, Bourlon Wood, Mornelle River and Lens.

The men in the ranks couldn't help feeling overwhelmed by the reception. Colin, marching in Company "D," was in the final section of the battalion. He could almost feel the wind from the players of the Silver Band marching behind him. All the band members of the 85th had seen action. Colin looked up at the banners as the crowd cheered them home. He couldn't help but feel deep, gut-wrenching sorrow. Stan was gone, Hazen was gone—even Captain Anderson was gone. George wasn't the same, he knew that. He wondered what had become of him. He knew George wasn't much for writing letters ... Stan was always getting on him to write his folks. No one had heard where George ended up. Maybe he was at a hospital in Blighty still. The friends in his company were still convinced he was shell-shocked.

The battalion made their way down Gottingen Street, took a left and then worked their way back up the hill to the Citadel. There was a reception there, with some last minute citations, and then they were dismissed. It had been quite a show. Lest anyone wonder at the notoriety the unit was receiving, 60,000 people crowded the Halifax streets to welcome the boys home. (The entire population of Halifax was only 65,000.) They were proud of their boys. No one in Halifax or Cape Breton had heard the nicknames, "work battalion" or "highlanders without kilts." The 85th had kilts now, and they wore them with pride. They had earned them.

As George watched the parade, he was very proud. He was moved beyond words, yet he felt very disconnected from the battalion. He was quiet. He wished Stan and Hazen could've been marching with them. Stan probably would have been in the Pipe Band by now, having to replace one of the six members lost at Passchendaele. *He was a really good piper*, George thought. Women and children stood cheering by as the last of the battalion and the Silver Band marched past. He stooped in the shadows of the crowd, picking his way through the cheering mob from his flat on Hollis Street, up Sackville to the Citadel and beyond to the common.

George saw the unit march onto the common and get dismissed with great fanfare. He found a grassy knoll to sit on where he could watch from a distance. George's discharge orders had come long ago. He had worked very hard, though unsuccessfully, to forget the war. Still, he undeniably felt great pride that he had been a part of the 85th. He remained conflicted by the war forever.

George watched as some medals were given out to a few of the officers. Two of the unit's favourite officers, Lieut.-Cols. Borden and Ralston, gave short speeches but George couldn't hear them. The men liked all of their officers, it seemed.

Colonels Borden and Ralston seemed to be the favourites of the enlisted men.

When the parade was over, the soldiers milled around, shaking hands, slapping one another's backs and mock punching one other. George lay back in the grass with the warm June sun on his face. He started to daydream. He wished Lily could've seen the parade. Perhaps he could go to her and tell her about it. No... others at the school would tell her. Besides, the school was putting out a Braille biweekly newspaper now. It would all be in there.

George still hadn't talked to Lily, though he had left her several notes, and he had wrapped another small brooch he had purchased for her from a street vendor in Belgium and left it at the school for her with one of the notes. She had replied to all of his notes and expressed happiness that he had returned safely.

As he daydreamt, a voice spoke to him: "You should have joined us in the parade... " It was Colin.

"Oh!" George jumped to his feet. He shook Colin's hand, but the soldier put George in a bear hug. "How are you? How's your leg?" asked Colin.

George patted his knee. "Good as new," he lied as he smiled. Colin looked splendid in his kilt and feathered balmoral. He seemed to George to be much, much older than the kid he'd met two years earlier.

"We didn't know what happened to you." said Colin. "You remember how it was, they never told us anything."

George nodded. "I had surgery in France and again in England. I was in a cast for two months. It itched." George leaned to the side and looked past Colin. "Where's Jack?"

"Oh—you don't know. When the unit made it back to England, Jack asked to be discharged. They gave it to him and he just left that night. Didn't tell anybody where he was going. I don't think *he* knew where he was off to. Don't think he cared. He just left. He didn't say goodbye to the lads or anything."

"God," said George, "I wonder where he ended up."

"Probably north, in one of the slate mines," said Colin. "He just couldn't get it out of his head, losing his whole family like that. They never did find his wife's body. Right before we crossed back over the Channel, one of the guys in "C" Company said he heard Jack mention that he couldn't go back to Nova Scotia." Colin and George squinted at each other in the midday sun. Colin offered, "I suppose he figured everything would remind him of them."

Trying to change the subject, Colin slapped George's arm. "But you're okay, mate. Glad for that." George smiled and nodded. "What are you doing now?" asked Colin.

"I'm in the cotton mill down near the corner of Kempt and Robie. Waiting to get in at the post office."

"Good—that's great," said Colin.

"And you?" asked George. "What are you going to do now?"

"Well, as you can imagine, I've given that some thought." They both chuckled at that. "I think I'm going to go out west to the lumberyards. See a little of the country while I'm young. All the guys from B. C. kept going on about how beautiful it is; I thought I'd check it out and see if they were lying." "Hey!" added Colin. "You want to throw in and go with me?"

George shook his head. "Naw, thanks. It's damned beautiful right here, I think."

"Well come on, get something to eat. There's a buffet in a tent," said Colin. George was tentative and then gave in to Colin's persistence. They walked through the crowds of soldiers inside the roped area where the men were holding plates of food and chatting before joining their families and well-wishers. They mostly laughed and shook hands, and talked about finally going home. More than one conversation George overheard as they walked along was about "what a fucking mess Passchendaele was."

After he said goodbye to Colin, George caught the eye of the chaplain who had spent time with him after Stanley and Hazen died. He remembered George—and their conversations—which shocked the young soldier, as there had been thousands of deaths in the battles. They shook hands. The captain asked how he was getting on. Together they thanked God it was over. As they separated, the chaplain told him, "Now, son, it's time to live life, and to cherish what those we've lost died for." George nodded obediently and walked away from the common.

He walked across Sackville Street and into the Public Gardens. He loved the gardens. He sat on a park bench along the west side walkway. He always sat on the same bench, at least four times a week. From that bench, in the spring, he could smell the lilacs blooming, and behind where he sat were some clove bushes that smelled so sweet just after the lilacs. The cloves were his favourite. He knew Lily was partial to them. The strong pungent smell reminded him of the clove flavoured chewing gum that he and the other kids in Hackett's Cove used to chew. Stanley hadn't liked it, but Lily loved it, so George always made sure he had extra pieces for her. There was a walkway fifty feet from the bench. In the warm afternoons of spring, summer and fall, the students and faculty of the Halifax School for the Blind would walk there. George accepted shifts at the cotton mill that allowed him to be in the park at that time of day, hoping to see Lily from his bench. It warmed him to know she was doing well. Sometimes when it rained, the students and faculty from the school did not go to the park, but George did. He would sit in the rain and wait. At suppertime he would go home to his ten-by-twelve apartment on Hollis Street, dry off, and take his meal at the Y.M.C.A.

On the days the students did go to the Public Gardens, George's heart would leap when he saw Lily. He would often feel the same way he had when he first visited the school and watched her setting the table in the dining room. Seeing her made him feel that not all was lost; that somewhere in each person who had endured that horrible war there was a remnant of their youth, or some decent part of what they had been before. Where there were no whispers of what they had become.

Several times, while watching Lily and the other blind students, George thought for a moment—just for a second—that Lily was looking right at him. It unnerved him at first. He had to remind himself that she was blind. Once, while staring in his direction, she appeared to smile. *She must smell the cloves*, he thought.

George had become a simple man. He liked it that way. He tried to hold down jobs of menial labour. His existence through the years became one of a gentle man—an uncle to many—he was always jovial and very happy to be around his family. He lived a solitary life, otherwise. He worked when he could and ate and slept. He did not participate in any battalion reunions or activities. He kept to himself. His family was his deepest joy. He was well looked after through the years. Over time his traumatic experiences and profound losses became too much for him. "Shell-shocked," was what people said when he wasn't around. His generation called him and his brethren "the walking wounded."

His older brother, Cyril, became an established Halifax businessman who owned racehorses. At every opportunity, Cyril would pick him up and take him to the stables where he could curry the horses. George still loved the horses.

Lily did respond to his note with the brooch. She wrote that she had loved it very much, and would "cherish it forever." She took the initiative to write him in July 1919. Though George had never actually proposed any sort of relationship with her, she decided to offer her thoughts about the future, in case he was inclined in that direction. *"Though I am blind,"* she wrote, *"I'm afraid I would see your brother's face in yours at all times. Indeed... I see it now."* George was happy that she loved the brooch. It and the amulet were the only things he would ever purchase for a woman. Lily ended the letter with, *"You are my brother, George—my only brother. I am so happy you're here in Halifax. I do hope you will see me sometime."*

George saw Lily every week for many years, although she never knew it. Lily became a teacher in the school where she learned how to read Braille and to manage life as a blind person. Later in life, she became a sought-after piano tuner in Halifax. George never stopped caring for her from a distance.

Lily died from breast cancer in the spring of 1968. She was very specific in her affairs. She was buried in her English shawl, and pinned to it was a Belgian brooch. Her hands were crossed against her chest, holding a linen envelope. Inside were every one of both Stanley and George's letters. She had transcribed them all into Braille as well. Not one to make assumptions, she wrote to her solicitor, "I would hope in Heaven my sight will be restored... but just in case, I'll take both copies with me."

George wasn't at the funeral or the wake. Cyril had stopped to pick him up, but he feigned illness. He didn't want to see Lily that way. He would instead go off and be with her in his own way. As soon as his brother left for the funeral service, George got out of bed and walked up Spring Garden Road to the Public Gardens. He walked to the west side of the park and sat down on his old, familiar bench. He closed his eyes, and he pictured Lily strolling purposefully along the walkway, her cotton dress dancing in the sunlight. She was never his, he knew that. But she was his friend, and he knew that as well. Throughout their adult lives, she had remained a connection to his innocent past, to a time when he was young, when Stan and Hazen were helping him with chores. Before he had ever watched someone die. Before the incessant barrages of artillery, exploding day and night, landing all around him. Before any of it.

George was overcome with grief. He slouched on the seat and spread his arms out along the back of the bench. His hand felt something draped off the back of the bench. He picked it up, and stared at it for a very long time. It was the red and silver amulet he had purchased in France. He couldn't read it, but engraved by hand on the back, in Braille, were the words, "*George, With Love, Lily.*"

He tilted his head back to face the sun, and with his eyes still closed, he smiled. He breathed in deeply and smelled the clean, spring air. *The cloves are early*, he thought.

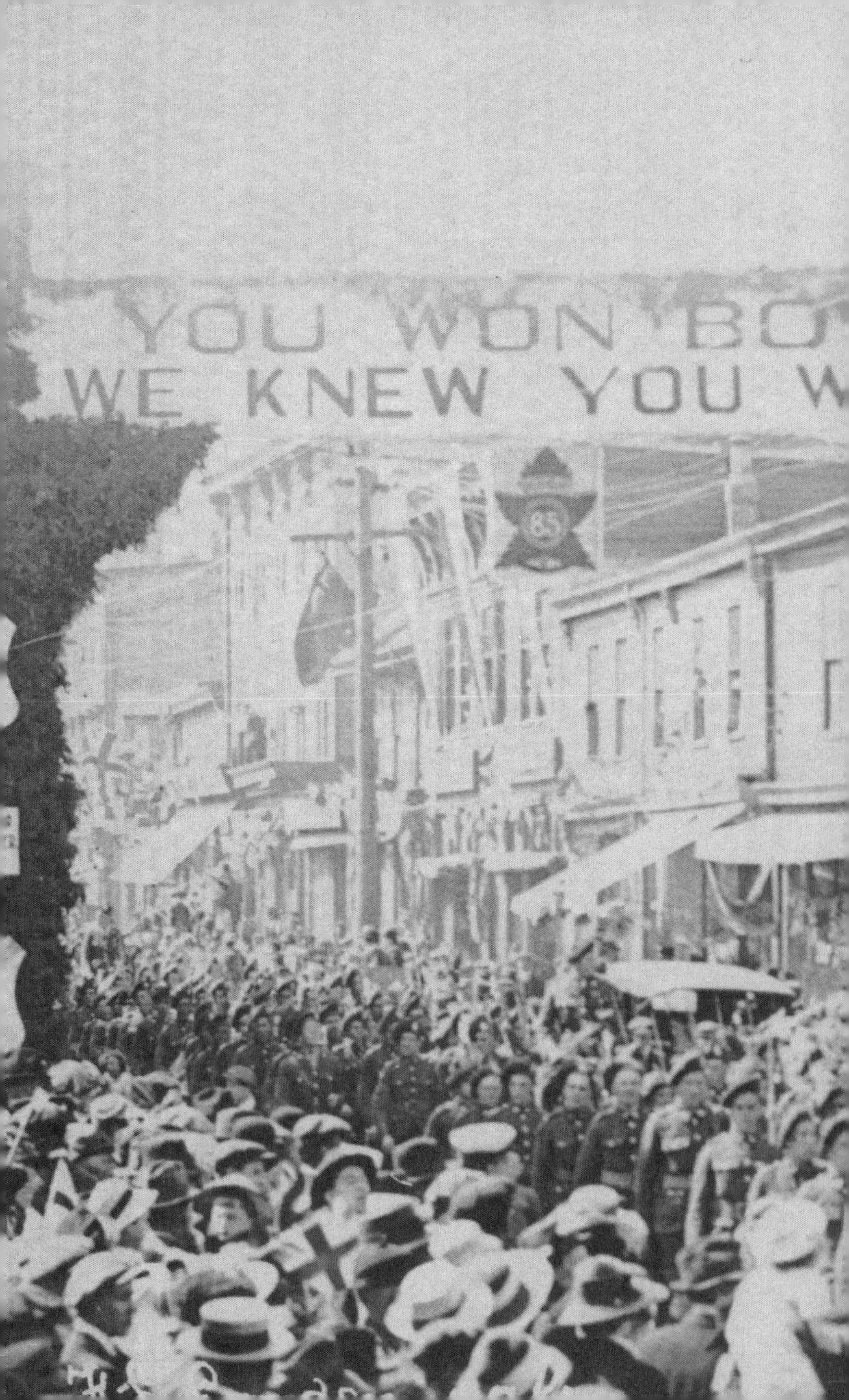
YOU WON
WE KNEW YOU
85

WELCOME HOME
PARADE GOTTINGEN
HALIFAX N.S.
JUNE 9th 1919

The 85th Battalion welcome home parade in Halifax

AFTERWORD I

After two years of researching the Great War, I must say I became absolutely astonished at the level of hubris on both continents, and just how stupid and senseless the conflict was. It was about putting a check on the monastic European empires, settling old scores from the Franco-Prussian War that had ended 43 years before and ushering in the modern, industrialized world. Millions upon millions of boys dying to do so was an inauspicious start.

Historians for the last seventy years have argued that the Treaty of Versailles was the cornerstone of the rise of fascism in Germany in the late 1920s-1930s. I have read and re-read the treaty in its entirety, and it does include some remarkable clauses meant to harm the German people—the everyday citizens who quite possibly never wanted Germany to fight in the first place. Article 231, which has become known as the "Guilt Clause," stated that Germany was responsible for starting the Great War. The German people were furious. Most Germans felt no more responsible than her enemies.

One thing that came out of World War I that cannot be argued or disputed is the tragedy of the incalculable trauma so many returning soldiers endured—especially those who had spent any time in the trenches at the front. The affliction P.T.S.D. was just as real in 1919 as it is now, lacking only the name. The "walking wounded" who returned shell-shocked from the Western Front could only hope for some semblance of normal life. Many never realized it.

George Stewart Dauphinee, Regimental No. 1260626, C.E.F., died in February 1969 in a group home in Halifax. He never married. He finally did go home to Hackett's Cove, when he was buried next to his parents. Sharing the headstone with him is Belle, the youngest sibling, who lived to be ninety-nine years old and died in 2007. The base of Oswald and Clara's headstone reads: *Stanley O. (Dauphinee) Killed In Action At Vimy Ridge... At Rest.* Alas, Stanley, Regimental No. 222154, C.E.F., is still in France, in the Pas de Calais cemetery. The other eight siblings are buried in their own family plots throughout the country.

John Hazen Perry Gibbons (Stanley and George Dauphinee's first cousin went by Hazen), Regimental No. 624801, died on the 9th of April, 1917, at Vimy Ridge. His body was one of thousands in World War I that was never found or identified.

The Second World War killed twice as many people as the first, its destruction reaching even farther across the globe. Again Canada fought the good fight, and again the Allies prevailed.

Still, in the wake of the World Wars, the hearty people of Nova Scotia and the rest of Canada carried on with grace and fortitude.

How important was Vimy Ridge? Plenty.

While Canadians did take Vimy Ridge by themselves during the Second Battle of Arras, there was help from the British in planning, supplies, medical facilities, etc. One simple fact should be explored by any young future Canadian scholars of the war. The Canadian Expeditionary Force never actually engaged in a major operation in the war without British involvement. We should give the British Expeditionary Force their due. Canadians have always been fair in assessing world events, and the allowance of that fact will give a more accurate view of the war overall. That being said, there are references galore in both World Wars of Canadian units pulling more than their share of close combat.

General Sir Arthur Currie himself (who after Vimy assumed command of the entire Canadian Corps) questioned in 1920 whether Vimy Ridge was in fact Canada's most important military campaign. He felt that there were other battles fought by his corps that were perhaps more significant to the war effort—especially toward the end of 1918. Gen. Currie was one of Canada's finest generals of all time (I say *one* of the best, because in my research I have come to realize there were several unsung high-ranking heroes of that war), but if the readers will forgive me, I will, in making my own assessment of the importance of Vimy Ridge, refer to the enemy. I thought the best evaluation of the battle might come from German opinion at the time.

There are many pieces of literature available from German archives that verify the supreme importance of Vimy Ridge in the *Germans'* minds—of the elevated tactical advantage Vimy offered, and of how demoralizing it was to the German high command *and* to the other ranks when the summit was lost to the Canadians.

If the Canadian troops had not been successful in taking the ridge, and rather had been repulsed back from the high ground to their original trench positions, one can assume the stalemated war would have extended over a longer period of time—perhaps long enough for German troops and supplies to be diverted from the Eastern Front to the Western Front (which was already in progress). One can also argue that, had that occurred, there might have been a renewed sense of success for the Germans in France and Flanders, and perhaps there would not have been rioting in the streets of Berlin.

The capture of Vimy Ridge—regardless of the mythical manifestation of the place in popular culture—did set into motion a chain of events that led the war to end when it did.

Therefore, based not on the cultural importance in the world's history, but rather on the German assessment of the battle at the time, I believe yes, Vimy Ridge should be considered Canada's greatest military achievement. The danger of making a statement like that—if one feels compelled to make it—is what I believe General Currie was concerned about. In studying the Great War, we mustn't place any less value, be it in lives lost or tactics, on all the other magnificent battles fought and won by the Canadian Expeditionary Force and the Allies. Not if we are to truly understand the conflict. Not if we strive to never fight another world war.

Did the battle of Vimy Ridge contribute to Canada's independence in the world view? Absolutely, though not in one glorious, cathartic moment. When at Vimy Ridge all the Canadian units worked together and reached that unattainable goal, all the Allied powers were forced to give the act its due acclaim. So were the Germans.

The following year of fighting throughout the Western Front would not have proceeded the way it did, had Vimy not been taken during that week in April 1917.

The truth is, before the war, Canada was well on her way to gaining true independence in the international theatre. When Britain passed the Colonial Laws Validity Act in 1865, Canada was already evolving and maturing as a nation. Many Canadians weren't comfortable with the idea that they could not make their own way and negotiate their own treaties. But evolution takes its own course, despite the actions of monarchs. Forty years after the Act, British officials did not intervene when Canada negotiated a treaty with the United States. In addition to geopolitical changes, Canada was holding her head high in many fields. The completion of the Canadian Pacific Railway in 1885 was a remarkable feat which enabled settlement and expansion of the west. In 1899, the first Canadian troops sent overseas had fought brilliantly in the Boer War.

At the turn of the century, the winds of change throughout

the world were strong. A socioeconomic storm was brewing in Europe. When that storm hit in 1914, Canada was ready to test her mettle and all the prideful pieces were in place for her to prove herself. And she did. Few historians writing about the conflict have ever omitted or glossed over the tremendous tenacity and sacrifices of the Canadian Expeditionary Force in the Great War. They cannot.

Considering all the achievements made by Canada in the half-century before World War I, it is difficult to definitively say that her independence was born on the fields of France and Flanders. In the midst of evolving into a strong, independent state, Canada found her legs on the muddy, slippery, blood-soaked slopes of Vimy Ridge. Now they are the sunny slopes of long ago, but damned worth remembering.

It has been interesting in my research (as a non-Canadian looking inward) to find in thousands of pages of literature, not *one* Canadian veteran, citizen or documenter seeking any accolades whatsoever. Their only hope and request is that the soldiers are not forgotten. It is little enough.

AFTERWORD II

(SETTING THE RECORD STRAIGHT)

The surname of the family in the book was, in reality, *Dauphinee* (see photographs). I chose to use the name *Boutilier*. Since my own name is Dauphinee, I wanted the protagonists to have a different one. My options were to keep their real name and use a pseudonym, or to change their name in the story. Boutilier was an easy choice, as it is a surname intermingled with the many Dauphinee's along Nova Scotia's South Shore for over 200 years. I had reservations about changing the family's name—I didn't want to offend any of them. In my research I nervously mentioned to one of Stanley and George's relatives about the name change in the book, and she waved her hand and said, "Oh, Boutilier...Dauphinee, it's all the same anyway." I felt fine with it after that.

The families of the Boutiliers and the Dauphinees still live in Hackett's Cove, but many are more spread out now. They are a warm, giving people in a harsh, cold world. They remember where they come from. They remember their sacrifices. They remember Stanley and George and the family from the Cork & Pickle. The older family members still speak of Clara who, for many years after the war, cried in St. Peter's Church during Sunday services. She cried for the loss of her sons—the one who did not come back, and the other who came back lost and shattered. In 1919, the Dauphinee's of Hackett's Cove pressed on and mourned. George didn't give up, but he lived a diminished adult life because of the war and did the best he could. His trauma was a familiar story across Canada and the United States—and in Germany. It was familiar worldwide. The same traumatic stressors George

Dauphinee dealt with were treated and dealt with by countless Englishmen and Frenchmen, by boys and men in every other country touched by that horrible conflict.

I chose to write *Highlanders* as historical fiction rather late in the process. There were several reasons. While I could have written a historical account of the 85th Battalion and easily filled a book, I very much wanted to touch on the home front experiences, the profound worry and losses of the people at home. In researching a single Canadian family, stories piled onto stories. I could have written forever about many battalions in the C.E.F., all of which have a tale of heroism to tell, or about Arthur Currie and his postwar years. I could have written an entire book about the Halifax Explosion, but there are some fine books already, and I wanted to report it from a personal viewpoint. I didn't want to write an enormous book. I wanted people to read this story. In addition, since many of the men from the 85th who were fighting overseas in 1917 were from the Halifax area, I felt it was important to include the December 6th Halifax Explosion. A great many men in France, Flanders, Belgium and England lost friends and family members in the disaster. It must have been difficult for them to be so remote in a time of such need back home.

The only important fictitious character in the book is Lily Durand (though Jane Page is also made up). The other main characters were real, but I did have to give them personalities—which I developed from interviews and letters, and consideration of the times. I wanted to include Lily in the story because I needed to find a person who would be able to represent the incredible fortitude of the people from Halifax in 1917. Truly it is an amalgam of Lily and her teaching instructor, Jane Page, to whom that role falls. I say I *needed* to develop Lily's character, and that is true because I, over time, came to admire the pluck of the Haligonians.

The rest of the people in the story who lived and died and persevered through those trying times represent for me all of Canada and her sacrifices.

Readers who are students of the Battle of Vimy Ridge may find a few small details in the book that are inconsistent with other writings. That is because in my research (I have friends in academia in the U.K., France and Germany who helped me by unearthing non-digitized documents), I have found some common errors. None were important. There are several, but I'll offer two examples. First, the number of Allied artillery pieces typically listed at Vimy is just under 1000. There were actually an additional 223 artillery pieces—some captured German guns and some French howitzers—which I found, listed in a single, obscure British dispatch. Also, it is commonly held that the German defenders at Vimy Ridge believed the ridge was impregnable, but that could not be further from the truth; one has only to read the defending German officer's war diaries, personal journals and battalion dispatches.

Another historical discrepancy (and some may consider this blasphemy), is the total number of Canadian casualties in taking Vimy Ridge. The usual number listed is 10,000: 7,000 wounded and another 3,598 dead. Researching thousands of pages of literature, I kept coming up with a number close to 19,000. I offer this only as food for thought for anyone seeking a more accurate number.

In the book, I wrote the heading for the newspaper after the Halifax Explosion as indicating over 2000 dead—higher than the official number. I did that because many newspapers around the world did so in the days after the disaster. Personally, after the extensive research of the past several years, I put the number over 2000. Unofficially, of course.

I chose to use the measurements of yards instead of metres

in the book because that is what was used by the soldiers at the time in the dispatches.

In reality, there was no account of George Dauphinee carrying his dying brother from the battlefield. (But it did happen to others.) George was at Vimy, in an ammunition column in the 4th Division. He did see his brother and their cousin Hazen in the 85th Battalion periodically. And, in fact, Stanley did die as in the story, from a gunshot wound to the abdomen, just below the summit of Hill 145 at Vimy. One report states simply, "Shot in the stomach. Died sometime later."

The Cork & Pickle general store and post office where Oswald and Clara Dauphinee raised their large family is still standing in Hackett's Cove, at the head of Boutilier's Cove. The little pond across Peggy's Cove Road, where in December the boys harvested ice for the hot summer months is still there, and in it grows frogs and pretty lilies, and the ice house across from the diner's parking lot is still standing, though it's used for something else now.

The building is now The Finer Diner, run by the husband and wife team of Peter MacPherson and artist Sarah Irwin. Peter was gracious and great fun to talk to about the book project, and was incredibly well informed and helpful.

A few doors down the road from The Finer Diner, my son and I were invited to a Dauphinee family reunion. It was a sixtieth annual reunion, and many of the family members were descendants of Oswald and Clara. True to form of Canadian people everywhere, the families took us in and made us feel welcome and appreciated. They fed us, beat us royally in every sporting event there was and filled us with laughter and information about the family's history. At the end of the reunion, almost the whole tribe, young and old, made their way to the cove and swam across it and back. I don't know exactly how far across Boutilier's Cove is, but I do know it was way too far for me to swim. Or walk.

There is a short story that I would like to share with readers regarding a portion of the book. Stanley's fiancée, I felt was very important to the story. Even well into the writing, I was struggling to give her a name. I tried many "older" names—Margaret, Emma, Emily, Annie, Hannah—but nothing seemed to fit. At least not in my mind.

In July 2014, my son and I were sitting on the porch of The Finer Diner (the current name of The Cork & Pickle, remember) to have lunch and to speak with the owner, Peter MacPherson, about the building and the book project. While we waited for Peter to be free, I told my son I would be right back. I snatched up my fly rod (we both are addicted to fly fishing) and skipped across the road to Oswald's old freshwater pond to see if I could catch anything while we waited. I couldn't. Not even a rise. But for a moment I stood at the edge of the tiny pond and imagined Oswald and the boys cutting out big blocks of ice, a hundred years ago and before the war broke out. *What a wonderful place to grow up,* I thought.

I couldn't help notice the wonderful smell of the pink lilies poking up from their pads in the pond, and how pretty they looked.

That's it! I thought. It felt perfect from that moment on; I would name the girl *Lily.* I broke down my fly rod and stuck in its tube, ran back across the street to the Finer Diner and wrote it down in my journal. A great name, inspired by some flowers in Oswald and Clara Dauphinee's pond. I was pleased by the connection.

I finished the book, but before the final edit, I received in the mail the delightful book, *St. Margaret's Bay, a History,* by my genealogy mentor, Alfreda Withrow. I read the chapter about Hackett's Cove and the Dauphinee family, whom I had gotten to know so well. I was quite moved when I read the last paragraph. Apparently, lily pads were not originally in the little pond across from the Finer Diner that I fished that July day in 2014. Alfreda wrote her book in 1985:

> *There is a story attached to the lily pond across from the Cork & Pickle. Oswald Dauphinee, who travelled to Halifax frequently, bought lily roots from an American at one of the hotels on Bay Road. They were put into a potato sack along with stones and were dropped into the still, dark waters of the pond. Only one pad appeared the first year. But later, the pond was filled with pink lilies giving a lovely fragrance and beauty. The... lilies are still blooming, just as they did in 1920.*

The year after the war ended, Oswald planted the lilies in the pond where he and his sons had harvested ice. No doubt he was still grieving for Stanley. Almost 100 years later, his lilies gave me a name. The perfect name.

As for the photograph used for the front cover, it is not of the 85th Battalion of the Nova Scotia Highlanders, or even of Canadian troops. There were no photographers attached to the 85th Battalion or any Canadian unit that I could find. There were only a few "embedded" with any Allied forces, which was very different from modern war correspondents; they were allowed to wander.

For the book cover image, I looked carefully at thousands of photographs, trying to find one that would be compelling without being sensational. As a former photographer myself (Peru, Middle East, Columbia, Nicaragua, Honduras, etc.), during the search I became interested in two photographers: Frank Hurley, an Australian who had attained some fame as a member of several polar expeditions, including Sir Ernest Shackleton's Imperial Trans-Antarctic Expedition in 1914—which was marooned for nearly two years—and Englishman Ernest Brooks, who was the first official photographer to be appointed by the British military. Both were, shall we say, colourful characters.

I chose the image for the front cover, *Troops Moving up at Eventide,* by Ernest Brooks, for several reasons; to me it conveys the commitment and diversity of the everyday troops. The men look very young and some older, some tall and one short and slight, and they are moving to the line with a deliberate, courageous resolve. This photograph is of a Yorkshire regiment and was snapped during the Third Battle of Ypres, specifically, the Battle of Broodseinde—a one day battle (part of the Battle of Passchendaele) which would become the most successful Allied attack there. One of the compelling reasons I chose this image was because, without the success of the battle that these men were going to fight, and the success of the Canadians very near to them at Passchendaele three weeks later, the Third battle of Ypres may have had a very different outcome.

I studied the attack maps of the Battle of Broodseinde and of the 85th's position at Passchendaele on October 30, and although the scales are different, I believe the 85th fought less than 1000 yards from where Brooks snapped the image. No matter; the tactical importance of both fights is indisputable. It is worth noting—as I mention in the book—that the 85th Battalion went into the fight at Passchendaele with only 600 men left of the 1000 who had enlisted. Of those 600, there were *428* casualties. Of those who died, 85 bodies were not recovered.

Many battalions from throughout Canada and Newfoundland experienced similar or higher casualty numbers. At Beaumont-Hamel, in the Battle of the Somme, the Royal Newfoundland Regiment went into action with 753 men. There were 710 casualties, including 324 killed. It didn't take long to call roll the next morning.

The bravery of all those boys, in that time, is staggering.

AFTERWORD III

There are—thankfully—many people out there still passionate about doing what they can to commemorate the memories and the deeds of the 85th Battalion, along with the rest of the C.E.F. Amongst them are Harrison Irvine of Dartmouth, NS, who, though young, is a bona fide expert of the C.E.F. in WWI, along with Allison Bell of Middleton, NS, and Chip Buerger of Oak Park, Illinois. (Chip was helped immensely by Donald Pugsley of Halifax, NS, whose father, Carlyle "Lyle" Pugsley, fought with the 85th.)

I would like to thank Colonel (Ret'd) John B. Boileau, CD, BA, RCDS of Nova Scotia, and Colonel William D. Bushnell, U.S.M.C. (Ret'd) of Maine for their advice and encouragement.

This book—any of my books—would likely not be worth reading if it weren't for my "First Readers," Monica Coffey, Greer Kaiser (whose Grandfather fought with the 85th Battalion), Ian Harmon and Richard Hill, and especially for my editor, Jennifer Caven, who did such a remarkable job on this project. They make my writing easier on the eyes and the ears, and in many cases they make it correct. I would also like to thank Karl Richter, of Mannheim, Germany, and Jean Herron of Paris, France.

Many thanks to my wife and daughter who help me spell the words. (I was graphlexic as a child, so it matters little if I spell-check a word—it will often still look wrong to me.) I often will shout words from my office, to be spelled back to me verbally from other rooms in the house, frequently accompanied by an exclamation mark.

I'd also like to thank those friends who invariably offer support: Drs. S. Craige Williamson (my Ed Ricketts), Paul Denoncourt, Molly Collins, John Frankland and Col. Lloyd

Harmon, U.S.A.F. (Ret'd), and life-long friends Alan Comeau and Doug Oldham.

I have a passel of sisters who, thank God, still feel the need to mother me (their instincts are correct), and their support is unconditional. I want to thank them, because it helps a great deal.

At every turn during the research process, the people of Canada were helpful and respectful. There were many who went out of their way to engage us and guide us. Lynn-Marie Richard, Assistant Curator and Registrar at the Maritime Museum of the Atlantic, was a great help, and went out of her way for us. Captain Colin MacKenzie of the Nova Scotia Highlanders (North), John Clarke, CD (Ret'd) of the Cape Breton Highlanders Museum in Sydney, NS, C.W.O. Ray Coulson, CD (Ret'd), curator of the Nova Scotia Highlanders Regimental Museum, and Philip Hartling, archivist at the Nova Scotia Archives. I would also like to thank Gary and Marilyn (Dauphinee) Meade, Head of St. Margaret's Bay, Nova Scotia, for the images of the Dauphinee family and of Stanley and George. Thanks to Allison Bell, a Facebook friend who helps through his social media platform to perpetuate the memory of the C.E.F.

Allan Cameron of Sydney, NS, deserves great recognition (though he will surely turn it towards the veterans). Al is the Founding Executive/Producer of Veterans Voices of Canada, whose work digitally preserving the veterans' stories has touched so many people. Al is a member of that class of people who are giving constantly of their time and resources to make sure Canada's veterans—and their stories—are not forgotten.

There are two people in Nova Scotia who have helped more that they know: Nancy Boutilier, from Hackett's Cove, whose father was Guy, the youngest son of Oswald and Clara

Dauphinee, and Barbara Mackenzie from Dartmouth, whose mother was Laura, one of the "middle girls" in the Dauphinee family. Nancy and Barbara are two giving, lovely ladies whom I shall not forget.

The one person without whom I likely would not have finished this book is Alfreda Withrow, an author from Halifax, who helped me at every turn.

I would like to thank my son, Hazen, for his help with the research, and for accompanying me to Halifax.

This book was a labour of love, which is good, because it turned out to be extremely laborious. Wondering what happened to a couple of boys from the far side of my ancestral tree became an endeavour I wouldn't trade for the world. The real story wasn't about how they lived or died but rather what difference they made. How did their sacrifices—and tens of thousands like them—make a difference? Every story is a journey, and in the end, this journey became about the family, and how the boys' lives helped shape their country and the world.

Oswald & Clara Dauphinee family portrait at the Cork & Pickle:
Back row: Ann, Vera, Eleanor, Mabel, Clara, Cyril, Hazel, Stanley. Front row: Laura, George, Guy, Oswald, and Belle.

HIGHLANDERS READING RECOMMENDATIONS

Whereas *Highlanders* is a work of fiction and therefore it is unnecessary to list a full bibliography, I will list my recommendations for those readers who want to understand more about The Great War, and what lead up to it.

Although I spent countless hours poring over army dispatches, diaries, letters, reports and books, there were several works that were invaluable in the research, which I will list here.

Probably the best condensation book about the war, is *A Short History of World War I,* by James L. Stokesbury, a former Professor of History and Chairman of the History Department at Acadia University in Nova Scotia. (I found that interesting because *Highlanders* is based in Nova Scotia.) Professor Stokesbury wrote dangerously. Instead of writing a book about a single battle or battalion or event, he stuffed the entire conflict into a 336 page paperback—and was successful. It is very well written. Books like this one are extremely easy to criticize, and extremely difficult to write. I would like to have taken a course taught by him. Unfortunately, I found the book in a used bookstore in Boston quite late in the two-year research process, but I put it here at the top of the list on readability.

For students of history and international affairs leading up to World War I, I recommend most of the works by David Jayne Hill. Dr. Hill was a diplomat, a scholar and a publicist from 1874 to 1930. He was the youngest college president in America captaining Bucknell University and the University of Rochester through difficult times. He was First Assistant Secretary of State, and the U.S. Ambassador to Germany in the years leading up to the war. After an interesting relationship with Kaiser Wilhelm, he resigned his post as Ambassador during President Taft's term.

Dr. Hill wrote extensively about world affairs, often with an insight which only firsthand knowledge of international politics could allow. He saw the storm on the horizon, and tried to tell the world. He wrote such works as; *The Contemporary Development of Diplomacy*, 1904, *World Organization as Affected by the Nature of the Modern State*, 1911, *Diplomacy in the Age of Absolutism*, 1914, *Impressions of the Kaiser*, 1918, and *The Establishment of Territorial Sovereignty*, 1906, and *The Rebuilding of Europe: A Survey of Forces and Conditions*, 1917, to name only a few.

Dr. Hill's beautifully written works are worth reading. His command of the written word prompted me to learn more about the professor, and interestingly, I found that in 1878 he had written *The Elements of Rhetoric and Composition* while at Bucknell, years before Professor Strunk had written The Elements of Style at Cornell University. It was evident in all of the papers I read by Dr. Hill, that he was clearly ahead of his time.

Other books I recommend are:

The Eighty-Fifth in France and Flanders 1919, by Lt. Col. Joseph
    Hayes, D.S.O., C.A.M.C.
The Battle for Vimy Ridge-1917 Jack Seldon & Nigel Cave, Pen and
    Sword Books 2007
Vimy Pierre Burton, McClelland and Stewart 1986
History of the World War, Francis A. March, Ph.D., University
    Press of the Pacific, 1919 and 2004
The German Army at Vimy Ridge 1914-1917 Jack Sheldon, Pen
    and Sword Books 2008

The Real War 1914-1918 Captain B.H. Liddell Hart, Little, Brown and Company 1930

War Letters 2001 Edited by Andrew Carroll, Scribner 2001

Ordeal by Fire 1961 Ralph Allen, Doubleday 1961

A Soldier's Diary of the Great War 1929 Douglas Herbert Bell, Faber and Gwyer 1929

St. Margaret's Bay—A History 1985 Alfreda Withrow, Four East Publications, Ltd. 1985

Reading Hands—The Halifax School for the Blind 2003 Shirley J. Trites, Vision Press 2003

Faithfully. My war Diaries (First, Second and Third Tapes) Munich, 1929 Crown Prince Rupprecht of Bavaria

Les Armees Francaises dans la Grande Guerre (Tome Premier & Tome II) Ministere de la Guerre 1930-1934

Canada's Sons and Great Britain in the World War 1919. Col. George G. Nasmith

Robert Laird Borden: His Memoirs 1969 vol. 1 Toronto: McClelland & Stewart

Up the Stream of Time 1945 Byng, Viscountess, MacMillan of Canada 1946

Haig's Command—a Reassessment 1991 Denis Winter, Viking 1991, Penguin 1992

Although I did not use the following book for reference (I obtained it just before publishing *Highlanders*), I also recommend *Valiant Hearts-Atlantic Canada and the Victoria Cross* by John Boileau, Nimbus Publishing Ltd. 2005

<u>I have selected several of the unpublished papers and manuscripts from my research:</u>

Robert Borden Papers (Public Archives of Canada)

A. W. Currie Papers (Public Archives of Canada)

Harvey Crowell Papers (Provincial Archives, Nova Scotia)

A.M. Taylor War Diaries (Provincial Archives, Nova Scotia)

Das kgl. bayr. 2. Infantrerie-regiment 'Kronprinz' am 28. Januar 1916 bei Vimy :

(The Royal Bavarian 2nd Infantry Regiment ' Crown Prince ' on 28 January 1916 at Vimy)

Heeresgruppe Kronprinze Rupprecht Oberkommando Ia/No. 2857 geh. H. Qu., den 21

(Crown Prince Rupprecht high command Army Group Ia / No . 2857 go . H. Qu . , 21)

Aussage von 82 Gefangenen vom I.R. 226 70 Div. N. O. No. 4202 A.H. Qu. 1917

(Statement of 82 prisoners from I.R. 226 70 Div. N. O. No. 4202 A. H. Qu . 1917)

Kommandeur der Flieger 6 Nr. 25500 Wochentlicher Taetigksbericht vom 31.3. mit 7.4.1917

(Commander of the airmen 6 no. 25500 Wochentlicher Taetigksbericht from 31.3 . with 07.04.1917)

Vater Wills Kriegstagebuch 1931 Karl Meier-Gesees (Father Wills War Diary)

ABOUT DENIS DAUPHINEE

Called "Dee" by most, is an American author who has worked as a farmer, a photographer, a fishing & mountaineering guide, a semi-pro wide receiver, and many other things—some of which ended-up being nothing more than "experiences".

Born with a wanderlust in Bangor, Maine, his writing and photography has taken him to places like El Salvador, Peru, the Arctic, Europe, Nicaragua, Venezuela, Iraq, Israel, Egypt, Ecuador, Jordan, the UK, Panama, and many places in between. No matter where he was, he was always in the company of a book, a journal, and a fly rod.

Dee has had two books published; *Stoneflies & Turtleheads*, a collection of fly fishing essays from Maine and around the world, and *The River Home*, a novel, both published by North Country Press.

Dee lives in Bradley, Maine, with his wife and two children, who all fish.

www.ddauphinee.com

Facebook; Denis "Dee" Dauphinee – Maine Author

OTHER BOOKS BY
D. DAUPHINEE

Stoneflies & Turtleheads

The River Home

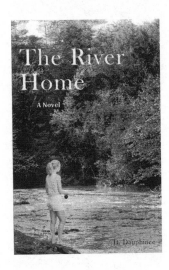

Made in the USA
Middletown, DE
30 October 2015